Not so Far Away

LL MEYER

Not so Far Away

Other Books

For my beloved daughter, Mariana, who lives her life with one foot in English and the other in Spanish.
Te amo muchísimo, Chulis.

Many thanks to my wonderful beta readers Leila, Monika, Ursa, and Akiko for all their input and hard work.
I couldn't have done this without you.

Prologue

For a long moment, the warmth between sleep and wakefulness cradles me in its lazy embrace. I do my best to sink further into it, but the pleasure evaporates with my next breath as my body's complaints pull into painfully sharp focus – thirst, headache, nausea, and, most urgently, a screaming bladder.

What the hell?

Confusion swamps my barely functioning brain cells until the obvious slowly comes to me. I'm hungover – in a very bad way.

I groan.

Wasn't I going to cut down?

My arm snakes out to test the space beside me on the bed, but it's empty. Cracking my eyelids by a sliver, I'm greeted by an unfamiliar bedroom. God, even frowning hurts.

Figuring out where I am will have to wait though. There's a more pressing matter. I need to find a bathroom. Clumsily, I throw off the covers and my muscles rebel. Every part of me aches, and not just the usual hangover victims, but my legs, my shoulders . . . between my thighs . . . even the back of my throat. *What did I do last night?* I make an attempt to comb my memory for an explanation, and come up with . . . nothing.

Ignoring a twinge of unease, I swing my legs over the edge of the bed and get hit with the mother of all head rushes. When my world settles, I realize that I'm lopsided. Looking down, I find only one black stiletto. And my mini dress is bunched up around my waist like some kind of retro tube top, leaving my bottom and top halves exposed. Reflexively, I pull it up and shove my arms through the straps, but one side of the dress flops back down, the strap broken.

I tamp down on the rising panic as I scan my surroundings. In the corner of the dimly lit room, I spy my missing shoe, and then, my cell phone on the bedside table. Relief courses through me until I reach for it and freeze at the sight of a red ring around my wrist. *Is that rope burn?*

Snatching my phone off the table, I grunt in dismay when it stays dark. The battery's dead.

"Stay calm, Piper," I whisper. "You're fine."

Standing on wobbly legs, I pull down the dress. The fact that I'm not wearing any underwear would bother me if I didn't know myself so well. I first hobble my way to the corner to collect my shoe and then head to the door. My hand shakes disconcertingly as it closes around the knob before I pull the door open and stick my head into a hallway that's even dimmer than the bedroom. I'm not sure which unnerves me more, the utter silence or that I have no recollection of this place.

Cautiously, I nudge the door across the hall open and find the bathroom. The sound of the door closing behind me makes me jump, and then thunderbolts of pain shoot to the center of my head when I hit the light switch.

Since I'm leaning forward on the counter, the first thing I

see when my eyes have adjusted to the sudden brightness are the bright red rope burns around both my wrists. Swallowing hard at the mounting evidence, I stumble to the toilet to relieve myself. I hate that I have no clue what I did last night.

My now tear-blurred gaze catches on the trash can beside me. It's littered with used condoms . . . way more condoms than one man would need in a night – or even two.

Oh my god. What did I do?

Keeping my eyes averted, I strap my bare foot back into my shoe with trembling fingers, pausing only briefly when I see more rope burns around my ankles. I make more of an effort to think back and images of getting ready for a night out with my best friend, Candy, come to me, but it's hazy. I'm not sure if they're actually from last night or just generic stand-ins for the millions of times we've gone out together.

Frustrated, I go back to the sink where there's nothing reassuring waiting for me in the mirror, just blood-shot raccoon eyes and tangled blond hair. After I wash my hands, I make a brief attempt to clean myself up while trying to cajole my memory into giving up its secrets.

Slowly, it starts to trickle in . . . getting ready with Candy. Gunnar and Cody picking us up, the club, shots, dancing, more and more shots . . . sitting on some guy's lap . . . some guy who's not Gunnar. The memories become even murkier at this point, but I'm definitely getting the impression that I made out with this guy who's not my boyfriend.

Where was Gunnar? Another deep breath brings more information, and I'm suddenly wishing it hadn't. Gunnar *was* there. And we agreed to . . . *Swap? With strangers?* Damnit, Gunnar . . . except maybe it was my idea.

After that, even though my mind tries to shut down the

memories, I get flashes of ropes and sex, lots and lots of sex . . . with strangers.

With my hand covering my mouth, I watch my head give a tiny shake of denial in the mirror. *Did I want that? Why did I want that?* While I'm the furthest thing from a prude, it doesn't make sense. I promised myself I wouldn't do things like this anymore. The nagging ugliness of regret will stay with me for days and knowing it wasn't me who made such potentially unsafe choices, but the alcohol, makes it even worse. Gin doesn't just lower my inhibitions, it obliterates them . . . and Gunnar knows that.

"That's not important right now, Piper," I whisper to myself.

I slink into the super-quiet hall and teeter my way toward the light coming from the living area. I'm in an apartment and it's bright. Floor to ceiling windows flood a combined kitchen and living space with light, but I get not a hint of recognition. My already jittery heart takes off at a gallop when I spot a guy sitting in an armchair in the corner with his head bent over his cellphone.

Fight or flight?

"Who are you?" I demand.

Fight it is then.

The guy's head jerks up. This is *not* the guy from last night, and worse, I don't like the disdain he paints me with from head to toe. I step closer to the kitchen island to shield my lower half as his disgust morphs into annoyance. "Finally. You got your shit together?" he says. "I've got things to do today."

"Like tie a completely wasted woman to a bed?"

He blanches slightly under the dark brown of his well-trimmed beard. His eyes linger on the ripped strap of my dress that hangs low enough to show a bruise forming on the slope of my breast.

"Don't pretend you weren't into it."

He gets to his feet and *fight* immediately becomes *flight*. With fear rushing me like a linebacker, I turn on my heel to dart for the door.

I hear, "Hey!" just as the door closes behind me. Unsure of which way to go, I feel panic begin to well up in me until the elevator dings about twenty feet down the hall. Scurrying in my heels, I slip past a mom with a stroller who's getting off. Another, "Hey!" echoes down the hall, making me punch frantically at the lobby button until the door finally slides closed.

For all eight floors of the descent, I stare at the number panel in a daze while my heart pounds in my chest. *Why would I put myself in that situation?* The swooping sensation of coming to a stop forces me to brace my unsteady legs. The door opens and I squint against the bright, natural light as I stumble out onto marble tiles. I don't make it very far. Propping myself against the wall, I haul deep breaths into my lungs in an effort to think clearly.

I need to get home. *Uber. I'll just order a ride.* That, combined with the thought of my emergency cash being tucked into the case of my cellphone, loosens the vise around my chest. That is until I hear the sound of the elevator being summoned. *That creep wouldn't follow me down here, would he?*

Out on the quiet sidewalk, I turn a desperate circle, searching for something to tell me where I am. But nothing stands out among the parked cars or the few trees; it could be any street in any city in California. *What if I'm up in San*

Francisco or something? Or Sacramento?

I feel my heel twist over.

"Whoa. Careful."

A hand catches my elbow to steady me and then just as quickly lets it go. I turn to find a guy whose expression can only be described as appalled, or maybe stricken. "You okay?" he asks with such intensity that I flinch. He doesn't give me a chance to answer before he's unzipping his hoodie and pulling it off. "Here. Put this on."

I stare stupidly at the gray sweater.

"Should I call an ambulance?" he asks gently when I don't take it. "Or the cops?"

What? No! I shake my head jerkily.

His gaze locks on my shoulder where my dress is ripped, causing shame to burn across my skin and set my heart on fire. The mixture of alarm and horror on his face reduces me to what he must see; a pathetic and broken woman.

I reach for the sweater and he doesn't hesitate to help me into it. I jam my cellphone, that's still clutched tightly in my hand, through the sleeve.

"Thanks," I whisper, looking him straight in the . . . chin? As I raise my eyes, I frown. I don't look up to many men when I wear heels.

"Let's sit over there," he suggests, indicating a bench down the street. I go willingly, surprised my instinct to run isn't being triggered like it was upstairs.

Once we're seated, I try to wake my phone again, but the screen remains stubbornly dark. I pry the case away from my phone. "No!" I hiss. My ID is there, but my emergency cash is missing.

"Don't worry," he says from beside me, stretching out his long frame so he can dig his cellphone out of his jeans pocket.

Offering it to me after he punches in his code, he seems to be focusing on anything but my face.

Cautiously, I take it and then we both watch my thumbs hover over the numeric keypad until a choked sound erupts from my throat and my shaky hands fall to my lap. "I don't know any of the numbers. They're all in my phone." Feeling completely defeated, I backtrack in his phone and punch the location button. The incredible relief I feel almost brings me to tears. I'm just in Mountain View, not far from my apartment in East Palo Alto at all. Now I just need a way to get there.

"Listen," the guy says. "I'm not going to offer you a ride because that would be creepy, but I'll order you an Uber, okay?"

I look into his concern-filled brown eyes. "I'll pay you back," I whisper.

"That's not necessary. I've got three sisters and a daughter," he says darkly, pushing his long blond bangs off his forehead. "If any of them," he takes in my appearance again, "were in a similar situation, I'd want someone to help."

I hand back the phone, gratitude and mortification warring inside of me. As he pulls up the app to call a ride, I suddenly wish that I was worthy of his concern, that I could reassure him that this has never happened before, that I was just a good girl caught in a bad situation. But I don't want to add *liar* to the growing list of negative words that could be used to describe me, a list that already includes *fool* and *binge drinker*.

The few minutes it takes for the ride to arrive are mostly filled with my worried glances being thrown in the direction of the apartment building's main door, and my stranger's concerted effort to keep his attention averted.

"Thank you," I murmur when he opens the car door for me.

He barely nods, probably eager to be rid of me, like the sight of me is too awful for him to contemplate. It gives me a second to get a better look at him though. He seems younger than I first thought. With his sun-kissed skin and sandy blond hair, I feel like he should be headed to the beach with a surfboard under his arm. But I'll never know because the car pulls away from the curb and I leave him behind forever.

During that quick, ten-minute car ride, I resolve to change my life.

This isn't who I want to be.

Chapter One

Scott

On my way out the door, the convenience-store smell of greasy hotdogs and stale coffee gives way to the almost warm, evening air of late March in Northern California.

University Avenue outside Stanford is busy with people looking to unwind on a Friday night and I'm definitely one of them. I hope the caffeine in this soda gives me enough of a boost to keep me awake after a long week of busting my ass at work. I almost wish I'd gone home to get some shut-eye instead, but twenty-two is much too young to be acting like a middle-aged stiff. Friday is the one night of the week that I allow myself to forget my million responsibilities. I may not party like my friends from high school, but it feels good to keep in touch with them.

The sidewalk becomes more crowded the closer I get to the campus. I know my best friend, Jorgie, is around here somewhere. He always is on a Friday night.

In the growing twilight, I spot him another block down, sitting on a low wall on a corner. A couple of girls are standing in front of him, one blonde and one brunette. I'm not close enough to tell if they're rich princesses of the Palo Alto variety or just Stanford Ivy League girls. Either way, they're looking to score something to make their night more interesting.

The brunette is saying, "I bet you do," in a sly voice when I sit next to my life-long best friend. Jorgie's response of, "You know it, *bonita*," has me rolling my eyes. Jorgie likes to think he's God's gift to women.

Without taking his attention off the girls, he acknowledges me with the handshake we've used since we were seven, interlocking each of our fingers together.

"Who's your friend?" the blonde asks, eyeing me up and down like I'm on Jorgie's pharmaceutical menu.

"This, ladies, is Prescott McCarthy the Second."

"*No seas cabrón*," I tell him, backhanding him lightly across the chest. *Don't be an ass.* That may be my full name, but I can't stand that it makes me sound like I should be this rich chick's cousin or something. Nothing could be further from the truth. Not for the first time, I wish I was more like Jorgie, whose Spanish name and obvious Latin roots never cause confusion. With my pale skin and blond hair, people do a double take whenever Spanish comes out of my mouth, something that stopped being entertaining years ago.

Both girls giggle before the brunette asks, "You guys wanna party with us tonight?" She twirls her hair like she's trying to be sexy and my dick twitches at the thought of getting laid. My brain quickly overrides the inclination though. I need to be sticking my dick into a girl with a possible drug problem like I need a hole in the head. Plus, she's just so . . . Caucasian. Not my type at all.

"Sorry, baby girl," Jorgie croons at her. "We've got other things going on, but maybe there's something *else* I can do for you?"

"You know there is," she shoots back.

I take a pull of my soda and casually give the girls another once over, wanting to make sure Jorgie's not about to deal to undercover cops. My instincts have saved him a couple times over the years. But he doesn't even check with me for confirmation on this one. We're both 99% sure these two are what they seem.

He gets to his feet and wraps an arm around each girl's waist, leading them around the corner so they can complete their transaction.

I briefly hope that Jorgie's not ruining those girls' lives. But I recognize that the choice is theirs to make. It's a free country after all. No one's forcing them to buy whatever he's selling . . . something I know nothing about. Jorgie and I never talk about the specifics of his extra-curriculars. For my daughter's sake, I need to keep my nose so clean that it shines. It would only take one little run-in with the cops to have Child Protective Services all over my ass. The mere possibility of Rosa being taken away from me and placed into foster care makes me sick. At least I know Jorgie's not carrying anything on him; he'll text someone, probably Mike, to meet the girls a few blocks away to hand over the product.

I sigh. I haven't been able to convince either of my best friends to get on the straight and narrow. Unfortunately there's not much incentive for them. Working a regular job doesn't generally involve easy money, working whenever you feel like it, or offers to party with college girls. Besides, Jorgie likes the buzz of his semi-celebrity status too much, and since he's dealing under the protective wing of his uncle, Alejandro, who's known as *El Jefe* on the streets, there's not much to worry about.

Alejandro is as deep into organized crime as one can get, whereas Jorgie just 'dabbles.' Jorgie's mother, Alejandro's sister, has made it very clear that her son is not to be involved with *Los Santos del Diablo* in any real way. Nevertheless, I worry that Jorgie has a false sense of invincibility. And no one's invincible, just ask *my* uncle. All his association with *El Jefe* and *Los Santos del Diablo* got him was four bullets to the chest in a drive-by eight years ago.

"What's with the face?" Jorgie demands as he re-takes his seat next to me a few minutes later.

"Nothing," I tell him, brushing my depressing thoughts aside. "How's it going?"

He flashes me a smug smile. "You know me, man. I'm always good."

It's hard to be a cranky bastard when I'm hanging out with Jorgie. He's the world's biggest optimist. The guy is never in a bad mood.

"You?" he tags on.

I shrug. "Meh."

"Well, I've got something that'll cheer you up." His smirk deepens. "It involves Juanita."

"What about her?" I ask warily. Juanita and I have a long-standing 'friends with bennies' thing going on. Whenever she's single, she calls me up.

"I heard she ditched that guy she was seeing."

"Oh yeah?" I can't stop the corner of my mouth from tugging up and he sees it right away.

"You lucky dog."

"Not lucky yet. She hasn't called me."

"Yeah. Like you say, *yet*."

I frown a bit. "She didn't say anything, did she?"

He tsks. "You know she's not like that. She's an actual woman who can keep shit private."

That's true. Juanita is a few years older than I am . . . like ten years. But that's what I like about her. She's not looking for a ring. At least not from me. It's a perfect situation for both of us.

"Anyway," Jorgie keeps talking, "I immediately thought of you when Cindy mentioned it."

"Cindy? You guys back together again?"

"Yeah. You know I can't give her up."

I laugh. "Even if your *abuela* doesn't approve?"

"Fuck, the only women my grandmother approves of are the ones who spend all their free time at church. The only man I want my woman getting on her knees for is me."

Snorting, I can't help but shoot back, "Then I don't know what you're doing with Cindy."

He makes like he's going to punch me, but he knows I'm only kidding around. I've known Cindy almost as long as I've known Jorgie.

He catches me up on all the latest gossip about our neighborhood, our high school friends, and *Los Santos* – and in between he makes his deals. People seem to materialize out of the woodwork every five to ten minutes.

We're heading north to change corners when he hits me with a topic I could do without.

"You seen Lolita lately?"

I chuck my empty soda can in the trash sullenly. "Not in a couple weeks. What'd she do this time?" Lolita may be the mother of my daughter, but she's not my favorite person. She has the right to see Rosa every Wednesday evening and every other weekend, but she doesn't always show.

"I've seen her out at the clubs a lot lately."

Before I can remind him that that's not a crime, he goes on. "She's been hanging out with Richie."

"Richie?" I draw a blank for a second, but then, "Vasquez?"

He nods, and my stomach plunges.

"Are you serious?"

"Yeah, man. Last Saturday, they were going at it hot and heavy at Insignia."

Richie Vasquez grew up in our neighborhood. He was a few years ahead of us in school, so I've never dealt with him personally, but he has a serious reputation for being a mean, lazy bastard.

"What's she doing with him?"

"Don't know. But it's possible she was on more than just a booze-high last weekend."

"Dammit, Jorgie." I lower my voice to a hiss. "Did you sell to her?"

"No! Of course not," he says indignantly. "I'm not stupid and I'm not the only game in town, not even close."

I huff out a breath. "Yeah, I know. Sorry." If Lolita is back to getting high, it will kill my sweet Rosa. Her mother just got her visitation rights back three months ago. "Keep an eye on her, would you?" Though I'm not sure if I mean to keep my ex safe or if I just want an informant.

"That's what brothers are for, right?" he says as we both make note of a big dude coming toward us on the sidewalk. He lifts his chin at Jorgie, a sure sign he wants to do business, and I choke back a scoff at the way he's wearing mirrored aviators at night. What a douche.

Our steps slow as we all casually move out of the flow of foot traffic. "I know you?" Jorgie asks.

"Nah, man. I know you."

"That right?"

My radar pings. First time buyer. I study him more closely. This guy's almost as tall as I am. He's got crew cut dark hair and he's wearing a light blue polo and khakis, but then my eyes hit the ground. He should be wearing some kind of loafers to go with this preppy get up, but instead there are scuffed black boots on his feet that are much too . . . utilitarian. My radar pings again. I don't like it.

They're casually shooting the shit about people they may or may not have in common, feeling each other out when I interrupt with, "What's with the shades?"

Jorgie shoots me a quick, calculating look, reading my comment for the warning it is.

The guy hesitates before he pushes the glasses up onto his head, revealing some seriously bright blue eyes.

Jorgie starts to crack up. "Jesus, I think I'm blind. Put the baby blues away and let's step into my office."

No way. I clear my throat to repeat the warning, but Jorgie shakes his head, telling me it's fine. The asshole smirks like he's giving me the finger and follows Jorgie around the corner. *I really don't like this.*

Standing there, alone on the busy sidewalk, I feel tentacles of unease start to slither up my spine. Then I see it. Movement. Down the block, two guys with similar crew cuts emerge from a doorway.

Shit! My instincts are never wrong so I do the only sensible thing. I run.

Cutting directly into the traffic, I take off across the street, narrowly missing getting smoked by a blue Toyota whose tires bark against the pavement when the driver slams on the brakes.

"Stop! Police!"

Holy fuck!! They *are* cops.

My heart pounds against my ribs as I take the first street to get off the main drag. I fly down the block, arms and legs pumping hard, my mind almost frozen with all the adrenaline.

"Stop!"

Faster! This block is a long one. There are a couple cafés, but the crowds are definitely thinning out. *Is that a good thing or a bad thing?* I can't think. At the next corner, I dive onto a busier street, and then boot it kitty-corner across a bank parking lot.

"Stop! I'm serious!"

I can barely hear the pounding footsteps over my own, but I don't dare look back. All that rolls through my head is an image of my little girl being hauled away to foster care. *Rosa, I'm so, so sorry.*

Chapter Two

Ellie

If I've learned anything over the past year, it's that sometimes friends just don't understand.

"Come on, Piper, please," Vanessa whines. "We'll have so much fun. Come with us."

I wipe at the espresso machine with a bit more elbow grease, keeping my head down because Vanessa is right. It would be fun. But if she notices that my resolve is faltering, she really won't take no for an answer.

"Oh, yeah," I respond, my tone sprinkled with sarcasm to throw her off. "Spending the night as a fifth wheel is every girl's dream." Then, belatedly, I register what she called me. "And I've told you to stop calling me Piper. My name is back to plain-old Ellie now."

Piper ceased to exist that Saturday morning all those months ago.

"Well, *Ellie*, as your boss, I'd like to remind you that just because you're on an nine month sobriety streak –"

"Ten."

"Sorry, a ten month sobriety streak, that doesn't mean you *never* get to have fun. And I'm not planning to drink much tonight. I have to work tomorrow, remember? My favorite employee asked to trade shifts."

She means me. I'm her favorite employee. Vanessa is the manager here at *1001 Beans* and she went above and beyond to get me this job. I'm still incredibly grateful to her so when I glance up, I wish I hadn't. Now she's not only begging with words, but she's using her eyes as well. "Pleeease, Ellie."

Indecision assaults me. *A couple hours wouldn't hurt, right?* Maybe I could look at it like a pick-me-up, like I'd be re-charging my batteries with a quick shot of the socializing that I miss so much. It's not like I'd be drinking. I'd be home and in bed by midnight, one at the latest.

"Besides," Vanessa goes on, interrupting my internal negotiations. "Since when are you worried about being a fifth wheel? If it makes you feel better, bring your boyfriend along."

I throw her a scathing look. She knows I've sworn off men as well as alcohol.

"You've got the model every girl dreams of," she continues. "Huh?"

"He may be battery operated, but he's never needy or argumentative. You can keep him tucked in your purse, give him a reassuring pat every now and then. And best of all, he'll be ready to go when you are, in more ways than one."

I snort out a laugh. "You're insane."

"I'm not. I miss hanging out with you. Come with us."

I shake my head, still chuckling. I don't tell her that the laughter has put an end to the wavering. I have to stay strong, and I can't do that if I go to a *bar*, where everyone around me will be drinking. Restaurants are hard enough.

I've made a promise to myself and I'm going to keep it. Too much of my life has involved taking the easy road. I'm done with coasting downhill. Nothing but slow-moving, up-hill battles from now on. I've come too far to sabotage myself now.

"I appreciate the invitation," I say, "but not only is my 'boyfriend' waiting for me at home, but I've got that thing tomorrow for my mom's birthday."

She sighs sadly. "Fine. Will you at least finish closing up, so I can get out of here a few minutes early?"

"Sure."

"Thanks, Pipes! You're the best!" she calls over her shoulder as she heads out the back way, chucking her dirty apron onto a table as she goes.

"It's Ellie," I mutter, going back to cleaning the equipment. Working here at *1001 Beans* has been a godsend. The customers are generally nice, the hours are flexible enough to fit around my class schedule, and Vanessa is the manager. It may not pay much, but who else but a friend would hire an ex-party girl with no practical work experience whatsoever?

The bell over the front door jingles and I curse. *Didn't Vanessa lock that?*

"Sorry," I say as I turn. "We're clo—"

I jerk back in surprise as a guy sails over the counter and lands not ten feet from me in a crouch. *Holy hell!* He huddles into the corner of the counter near the register, still on the balls of his feet. My heartrate spikes in fear. He doesn't make a move toward me, but our gazes collide. The dread and anguish rolling off of him steal my breath away. But that's nothing compared to the recognition that plows into me like a wrecking ball seconds later.

It's him.

A few more long seconds tick by with us staring at each other, the only sound his chest heaving with exertion.

Oh my god. It's him.

Blond hair, longer on top, and dark, expressive eyes set in a handsome face. Even the gray hoodie he's wearing is almost an exact replica of the one I still have at home.

It's really him.

The bell jingles again and my gaze snaps up.

"Police! Which way did he go?"

Without thinking, I look toward the back hall. The cop takes that one small gesture and runs with it – literally – dashing through the small café, past the bathrooms, past our cubicle of a staffroom, and out into the alley. The backdoor thuds shut.

I turn back. The emotions on the guy's face have multiplied to include confusion and shock. Clutching my hands to my chest, I whisper, "You should go."

He stays frozen for a moment longer before he gets to his feet on shaky legs. Glancing at the counter, he dismisses the idea of leaping back over it and walks toward me. I press myself up against the back counter so he can get by, my eyes tracking him as he makes his way around the display case and then back toward the entrance. When his hand lands on the handle, he hesitates. Throwing me one last confused look, he pulls the door open and disappears.

The breath I was holding comes rushing out. *Did that really just happen?* I press a trembling hand to my mouth while my mind trips through the last sixty seconds. What are the chances of *him* jumping over *my* counter? One in a million? One in ten million? But why was he running from –? *The cops.* I should go before they come back and start asking me questions that I don't want to answer.

Grabbing my purse from under the counter, I dig out my keys and hurry to lock the front door. Making sure everything is mostly as it should be, I hit the lights, set the alarm, and leave through the back door.

The two-block walk to my car is nerve racking. I'm half-expecting the cops to jump out and arrest me for aiding and abetting, or more likely, to find them shoving him, handcuffed, into a police car.

When my old Jetta rumbles to life, I scowl briefly at the illuminated check engine light before my mind goes back to wrestling with the night's crazy turn of events. *What did he do?* The short drive home is filled with speculation, though I can't seem to come up with any crime that could fit with what little I know of him.

It's not till I'm inserting the key in the lock of the main door of my low-rise apartment complex that I realize it doesn't matter what he's done. Nothing could change my opinion of him. Over the last ten months, I've thought about my stranger more times than I can possibly count. In fact, sometimes when I feel myself getting really overwhelmed with the urge to return to my old ways, I conjure up his appalled expression to shore up my defenses.

"Stupid door," I mutter when the usual jiggling of the key refuses to convince the lock to turn. Through the glass, I see Mrs. Stanfield, my elderly neighbor from across the hall, shuffling closer, so I wait patiently for her to let me in.

"Piper," she says sharply, suspiciously. "What are you doing out here?"

Not even bothering to correct my name, I give her a tight smile and hope for the best. Mrs. Stanfield and I have a rocky history. "It's the lock again. Didn't they just come to fix it yesterday?"

She takes the bait, thankfully. If there's one thing she dislikes more than all the noise I used to make, it's our landlord, Mr. Bostwick, and his lack of timely repairs around the building. Despite her small stature and advanced age, Mrs. Stanfield is no lamb. Two minutes into any conversation with her and her wolf status becomes clear. "It's not working?" she demands as she turns to lodge another complaint.

"No, it's not," I lament, though really, I'm brimming with satisfaction. Mr. Bostwick is a grade-A creep, one who constantly hounds me when my rent is short. You'd think it was his job to collect the rent or something. Thank goodness, I'm paid up . . . at least for the next few days until the first of the month comes around again.

Heading down the hall in the opposite direction from Mrs. Stanfield, I curse Stephanie Lo. She, and her revoked student visa, left me without a roommate mid-semester and I haven't been able to find anyone willing to replace her yet. With a sigh, I unlock the door to my small, one bedroom apartment.

Slumping momentarily against the door, I reach behind me to twist the deadbolt, but don't bother to turn on the lights. A short hallway leads me into the kitchen and living area where I eye my bedding that's still out on the sofa. I should probably move back into the bedroom now that my roommate is gone, but lately, my energy for anything more than the bare minimum is at an all-time low.

Tiredly, I throw my keys onto the island and let my purse slip down my shoulder to the floor before I kick off my sneakers and flop down onto the couch. Stretched out in the quiet, my mind picks up where it left off in the car.

It was really him.

Irrationally, I feel a twinge of regret that he obviously didn't recognize me. But why would he? I look a lot different with my hair back to its natural brown, very little makeup on . . . and wearing proper clothes.

And of course, the context was wrong. He hadn't exactly been in a state of mind to allow for casual reflection. *You look familiar. Have we met?* My lips twitch at the thought.

I wonder if he'd be proud of how I've gotten myself together.

I huff out a short laugh. *God, I'm delusional.* But having something other than my usual problems to think about is a reprieve I'm more than willing to indulge in. Instead of worrying about how I'm going to pay the rent or how much of a disaster my mother's birthday brunch is going to be tomorrow, I drift off to sleep with fantasies of my stranger's approval filling my head.

The next day, my heels tap out a staccato rhythm on the peony lined walkway that follows the circle drive to my parents' front door. With so many guests arriving, valets scrambling to accommodate their cars, and vendors making last minute deliveries, the scene is chaotic. The decision to park down the block was definitely the right one. My Jetta may have fit in when I got it brand new for my sixteenth birthday ten years ago, but according to my mother, it's an eyesore now, especially here in this very upscale Palo Alto neighborhood.

I grew up in this house . . . well, mansion, really. If the fountain in the center of the drive didn't give it away, the size of the columns would. It's never really felt like home though, not even when I lived here. Except when I see my father just inside the open double doors, greeting guests and directing traffic, I feel a surge of affection. He's a good man who's always done his best, not only for me, but for all of his children.

"Ellie," he says, greeting me with a warm smile that crinkles the fine skin around his eyes behind his glasses.

"Hi, Dad."

He pulls me in for a hug and then holds me at arm's length to study me. "*Ellie* looks so good on you, sweetheart. You're doing well?"

At sixty-five, my father is still a tall, imposing figure but I'm sure he's grateful that I've finally out-grown my wild, unruly ways. While my sister and three brothers have contributed to some of his gray hair, I know I'm responsible for most of it. "I'm good. How about you and Mom?" My gaze skitters to my mother who stands a few feet away, talking brightly with one of her charity friends.

He leans in as if letting me in on an amusing secret. "She's a bit . . . disconcerted with turning fifty."

"I bet," I whisper, my lips twitching with a knowing grin. My mom is a firm believer in looking one's best. Beauty may only be skin deep, but she claims it's the root of all success. To say she's not a fan of the aging process would be an understatement.

She approaches wearing a perfectly tailored Chanel suit and a polite smile that my dad interprets for what it really is, thinly veiled contempt. "Doesn't our daughter look wonderful, Janine?" he says quickly, hoping to head off whatever cutting comment is about to come out of her mouth.

"Piper," my mother coos condescendingly, setting my teeth on edge. "Yes, you look . . . wonderful. But darling, must you stick with this dreary brown color?" she asks, taking a lock of my hair between her thumb and forefinger like it disgusts her.

"We can't all be natural blondes like you, Mom."

She purses her lips. "You're right of course, but that doesn't mean we have to settle for what we're given."

"I suppose it's my fault," Dad says, trying to diffuse the situation. "She got her coloring from me."

"That still doesn't explain why she settles for it." Over my shoulder, her eyes catch on someone. "Well, anyway, thank you for coming, Piper."

"It's your *fiftieth* birthday, Mom. I wouldn't miss it."

Childishly, the way her body stiffens at the gibe makes me feel better. At least until I see my father's disapproval. He hates it when we bait each other. *Sorry*, I mouth as I slip away so they can greet their next guests.

Sometimes I wish my relationship with my mother could be more amicable. But what began as normal mother/daughter teenage angst has never let up. I know I should make more of an effort to understand her points of view. She grew up the daughter of strictly religious Polish immigrants who, I've been told, fought constantly – mostly about money, or the lack thereof. The fact that my mother didn't *settle* is something she's proud of. She scratched and clawed her way out of poverty to where she is today and I respect her for that. But not only are we separated by a generation gap, but also by every gap you can imagine. My leftist leanings cause endless friction with her conservative views. We simply don't have anything in common.

I make my way through the house, which is teeming with guests who mill about making small talk and sipping mimosas. A few of them I know and acknowledge, but mostly I'm able to slip by unnoticed, thank goodness. If I have very little in common with my parents, I have nothing in common with their friends.

The kitchen is hectic with the caterer's last minute preparations for the sit-down champagne brunch, but I spot Amelia in the center of it all, keeping an eye on what's going on in her domain. She waves me over. *"Mi amor!"* Her enthusiasm is my homecoming. Amelia has worked for my dad for longer than he's been married to my mother and she's loved and cared for all five of his children. While I was growing up, she was my safe haven.

"Look at you," she gushes. "You're positively radiant."

I laugh, absorbing the warmth of her greeting. "It's a side-effect of being here with you."

"You always were a charmer," she says wryly. "Come, come, let's sit over here." I follow her diminutive frame over to the breakfast nook. The years have been kind to Amelia, but every time I see her, I notice more signs of her advancing age; the liberally gray-streaked hair that she refuses to dye, the deepening lines on her face, the swollen knuckles of her slightly arthritic hands.

"Have a seat, *mi niña*. Tell me everything. How is school?"

My smile is huge as I tell her, "I'm so close to being finished." I hold up a single finger. "Only one more class to complete."

"I'm so proud of you. Going back to get your degree was the right decision. And you're staying sober?"

"Yes," I assure her. "And I'm still keeping good company." I don't tell her *good company* basically means *no company*. Like my father, Amelia has worried about me enough to last three lifetimes. She deserves better and I want to give it to her. "How about you, how are things?"

She sighs, though with the din of voices and clanking dishes around us, it's barely audible. "With Sophie gone, there's not much keeping me here anymore."

Sophie is the youngest of us kids. She moved to San Diego last September to start her master's degree at UCSD and I know Amelia has felt at loose ends with her gone. She's not the only one who misses Sophie; my sister is my best friend.

Reaching out, I cover her hand. "Are you finally going to retire?"

"Soon, *mi amor,* soon."

A crash on the other side of the kitchen brings her to her feet. "Go," I say, waving her off when she appears torn. "I'm fine."

I pull out my phone but my attention is back to where it's been all morning; the pros and cons of asking my dad for the money I'm short for my rent this month. After everything, I'm not sure I can go through with it. The look of disappointment that's going to show up on his face as soon as the words leave my mouth will be excruciating.

My shoulders sag. I'm going to have to find another way . . . which means selling something online. There's not much left though. I've sold off most of the designer handbags and jewellery that my ex, Gunnar, gave me during our two-year relationship. Really, the only things of value that are left are the Wii and the PS4, which don't technically belong to me. But my apartment is not a storage facility and I've asked him to come get his stuff many times over the months.

A text comes in from my sister.

Sophie: How's the party?

Ellie: You'd know if you were here. Traitor.

Sophie: Please. After all the events you've missed?

She may have a point. For years, I didn't come to a single one.

Ellie: It's the usual. Current score: me 1, mom 1.

Sophie: You're so ridiculous. Did Matt show?

Matthew is our older brother. Well, all three of our brothers are older, but Matt is the only one of them who would come to an event like this since he's our mother's biological son. Christopher and Evan are dad's sons from his first marriage. There's a bit of an age gap between the two sets of kids. When I started kindergarten, Christopher was starting college.

Ellie: Haven't seen him. I'd say chances are low.

Sophie: Poor mom.

I roll my eyes. *Poor mom?* But that's my sister for you, she's all heart. Thinking of others before herself is her thing, along with *forgive and forget.* I think it was Amelia who insisted that Sophie go away to San Diego to continue her schooling. If Sophie had her way, she would live at home forever so she could take care of the entire family from a central location.

The noise level rises and I realize brunch is about to be served.

Ellie: I gotta go, sis.

Sophie: Ok, give mom a hug and kiss from me. Try to have a good time!

The back patio has been set up with one long expansive table, and I'm dismayed to see there are little name cards at each place setting. I know immediately that my mother and her friends are playing matchmaker. I come to a stop when I finally find my name.

"May I pull out your chair for you?"

I turn to find a fairly good-looking guy. Mid-30's maybe, dark hair, my height with me in kitten heels, so he's about 6 feet. *Who knows, maybe this won't be a waste of time after all.*

"Thanks," I say with a genuine smile as I lower myself into the chair and sneak a peek at his name card. "Peter, is it?"

"That's right." His tone is pleasant enough, though I'm not thrilled with the way his eyes linger on my chest as he sits beside me. But hey, I was just checking *him* out. It's human nature, right? "I believe you're John's daughter."

My gaze steadies on his. *John?* Nobody who's at least thirty years his junior calls my father John.

"He thought we might hit it off," he goes on.

"He did?"

Peter completely misses my sarcasm and launches into what sounds like a rehearsed run down of who he is. Peter Denton, 33, master's in Finance, investment manager, 1 brother, 1 sister. He even manages to hint at his family's substantial net worth without being gauche. On paper, I suppose he's a real catch.

"How about you, Elsa?" he asks when he realizes I haven't said a word.

"It's Ellie, and I'm finishing up my undergrad at Stanford."

"I went to Princeton myself. What's your major?"

"I'm a poli-sci/Spanish double major."

His face briefly contorts before it smooths back into its polite façade. "How interesting," he says like I've announced I have a contagious skin condition.

A waiter at my elbow saves me from having to respond. "Miss, some champagne?"

"Oh, no thanks. But I'll take some orange juice, please."

"Yes, of co–"

"Hey, *amigo*, I'll take some of that," Peter interrupts as he leans forward to pull out his wallet from his back pocket. Extracting a twenty dollar bill, he waves it at the server and adds, "And keep it coming, would you?"

The server's jaw clenches slightly, but nods as he slips the money into his pocket before he fills Peter's glass.

"Too early for you?" Peter asks, taking his first sip. It's a long one.

"I don't drink," I inform him tightly.

"What, like ever?"

"Nope."

"Can't hack it, huh? Must get so boring at parties."

I finger the butter knife and consider stabbing this idiot. If only these parties weren't always filled with the same kinds of people. Absently, I wonder what my stranger in the gray hoodie would make of all this.

Chapter Three

Scott

"**M***ijo.*"

A hand nudges my shoulder gently.

"*Mijo, despiértate. Ya son las seis.*"

Las seis? Six? O'clock? Shit, it's Monday. "*Cinco minutos más,*" I mumble.

"Okay, but that means no shower for you this morning," my *abuela* warns, continuing on in Spanish.

I groan. My grandmother's right. If I wait the five minutes, there's a real possibility of being stampeded by my sisters before I make it to the only bathroom in the house.

Peeling my eyes open gives me a view of the dust ruffle that runs around our dated and well-worn sofa. A foam mattress may not be the most comfortable bed in the world, but at least down here on the floor I can stretch out. It's so much better than the actual sofa.

By the time I'm on my feet, my grandmother is already rattling around in the kitchen, something for which I'm very grateful. It's no small task taking care of our family, considering there are four generations of us living in this small, three-bedroom house. I have no idea what any of us would do without her. She's our heart and soul.

After folding my bedding into neat piles, I take the bare mattress to the girls' room. I push the door open quietly and ease the mattress in against the wall for storage. The sun is just starting to rise so I can make out my daughter, Rosa's form, huddled next to her cousin, Daniela, on the bottom bunk while the top bunk is occupied by my youngest sister, Carmen. With them being so close in age, Daniela and Carmen are more like sisters to Rosa than cousin and aunt. Rosa is the baby at six, then Daniela at seven, and Carmen at eight. The three of them are always together.

I carefully take the work clothes I laid out last night from the dresser and then hit the shower. I make it quick because the contents of one hot water tank can only be stretched so far, and listening to my sisters whine about cold water will ruin my morning.

"*Buenos días, Abuela,*" I tell my grandmother in the kitchen, trying to hold back my amusement at the mug of coffee sitting on the countertop next to the assembly line of lunches she's got going. It took forever, but I think I've finally convinced her to give up her wretched instant coffee and drink the freshly brewed stuff.

"*Buenos días.*" She gives me a warm smile as she adds an apple to each lunch box, mine included. "So, *mijo,* I need to talk to you about taking Daniela to the optometrist," she announces in Spanish. "Her teacher sent a note home again."

The stress on the word *again* makes me flinch, and I almost spill the coffee I'm pouring. "It's still on my list." I pause. "You're sure we can't take her to the community clinic?"

"I told you, they lost funding for that."

"Yeah," I grumble. "You told me. I'll take care of it."

Flopping myself down at the old kitchen table, I push out a sigh.

"*Gracias, mijo.*" I feel her hand ruffle my hair. "That girl needs you. You're a good uncle. And . . . ," she pauses for effect, smiling sweetly, "the best grandson."

I chuckle. "Are you sweet talking me, Abuela? Should I be worried?"

I catch a glimpse of her grimace as she sits in the chair next to me. "Perhaps. Yesterday, after Mass, I had an interesting conversation with Señora Alvarez."

My brain flips through all the señoras at church yesterday. "Jorgie's grandmother?" As I say the words, it all falls into place. *Oh, shit. Here we go.*

She nods. "It seems he got *arrested* on Friday." I watch her shake her head with disapproval. "That family, I tell you."

I grit my teeth. "You can't blame them for Tío Javier's death, Abuela. He made his own choices."

Her lips compress into a straight edge, deepening the lines around her mouth. I know she's holding back on starting an argument, one we've had a million times in the past. Her only son, my Tío Javier, came up in *Los Santos del Diablo* with Alejandro, Jorgie's uncle. They were best friends until my uncle was killed eight years ago. I was fourteen at the time and his murder left a huge crater in our lives. He was the only thing close to a father that I'd ever known – and in an instant, he and his long-time girlfriend were gone, shot dead outside their house that's not four blocks from here. They left behind their three month old daughter, Daniela, and now *I'm* the only thing close to a father that she's ever known. The world is a messed-up place, but my grandmother's need to place the blame on Jorgie's family's doorstep isn't right.

"Well, I don't see you getting arrested, now do I?"

My stomach clenches but I manage to keep my face neutral. She doesn't need to know how close I came to landing my ass in jail right alongside Jorgie's.

"I talked to Jorgie last night," I say. "They didn't file charges, so what's his grandmother worried about?"

Her expression sours even more. "She seems to think that I'd be willing to ask you about getting Jorge a job at your company." My grandmother never calls Jorgie by his nickname, it's always the proper Jorge.

I laugh. "Jorgie? With a nine-to-five job? That'll be the day."

"That's what I said. But then Father Martín added his support for the idea."

My heart falls. "Father Martín wants me to get Jorgie a job?" This morning is going downhill fast. I can't say no to Father Martín. I owe him. He was the one who got me my first construction job when I was seventeen. Without him vouching for me, I'd still be working for minimum wage at Walmart or something.

"Unfortunately, yes. He thinks that some structure will keep Jorge out of trouble."

Like a harbinger of doom, the house phone that's mounted on the wall by the fridge rings.

"That will be Father Martín now."

Glancing at the clock, I sigh. It's 6:25 a.m. "He wanted to catch you before you went to work, mijo."

Before it can ring a third time and wake the whole house, I grab the receiver and proceed to very politely agree to Father Martín's request – against every single one of my instincts. Jorgie with a job, especially one that I have to put my neck out for, is the worst idea I've ever heard. At least there are a few possible ways that this will fall through. Maybe Jorgie will be just as cynical about the idea, or there won't be any openings at work. Though that last one is a long shot; there tends to be a lot of turnover in the non-union framing business.

Just as I'm hanging up, I feel a tug on my T-shirt. "Rosa," I say with a smile as I scoop her up to give her a tight squeeze. "How's the best daughter in the world?"

She giggles and then presses a good morning kiss to my cheek. *"Bien, Papá."* She pulls back and I drink in her dark hair and eyes that she inherited from her mother before I notice there are two more little girls waiting their turns. Setting Rosa down, I go through the same routine, substituting *daughter* for *niece* and *sister*.

"What are you girls doing up so early?"

I get some more giggling. "You're so noisy, Tío," Daniela says. I like that she calls me uncle even though, technically, I'm her cousin.

Before I can answer, my grandmother shoos them away to get dressed.

"Do they do that on their own now?" I ask, a bit incredulous. I've usually left for work by the time they get up.

"What? Get dressed?" She laughs softly. "We're working on it. Last week, your Rosa went to school with her T-shirt on backwards. I didn't notice until we were getting into pajamas later that night."

A withering noise escapes me. How I wish I could spend more time with her.

"None of that. She's going to be seven years old soon. Whether you're here or not, she has to learn to be independent. They all do."

"I guess."

She turns back to the lunches. "Can you get their cereal out for me?"

In between sips of coffee, I set the table for breakfast, including a spot for myself.

"Before they come back, mijo . . ." I know exactly what her hesitance means. She's about to ask me for money.

"Abuela, I've told you, whatever you need, just ask."

"Well, Carmen has out-grown her sneakers. I know she's not your responsibility, but . . ."

Anger rises in my gut. "Of course she's my responsibility. She's my sister." Neither of us mention whose responsibility she *should* be. My mother – and Carmen's mother – has been on the wagon for a couple of months now but nobody is interested in overturning it by putting demands on her.

Digging out my wallet, I pull out two hundred dollars and pass it to her. I wish I didn't have to give her cash, but at seventy-two, my grandmother is not going to change her ways. She thinks if it's not paid for in cash, there's something shady going on. No matter how many times I try to explain that a debit card *is* cash, she refuses to believe me.

"This is too much," she complains, though she quickly tucks the money away into her bra.

I raise my brows at her. "If one needs sneakers, they all need sneakers. I work hard so Rosa doesn't have to wear hand-me-downs."

She huffs out an annoyed breath. More things we don't agree on. But I still remember being the poor kid in school and I don't want that for my daughter.

"Okay," she acquiesces . . . too quickly.

"Okay? Now I'm really suspicious. What else do you need?"

"Well, um, I . . . you see . . ."

I hate that she's uncomfortable asking me for money. She must know that I'd do anything for her. This woman is the reason that I'm the man I am today.

"It's your sister . . . Maria del Rosario . . ."

"Mari?" I don't have a lot of contact with my fifteen year old sister. Sure we live in the same house, but like most teenagers, she's got a busy school and social life that she does her best to exclude me from.

"Yes, in July, she'd like to go to some kind of science camp."

I immediately relax. "Of course she can go to science camp."

"Yes, well, don't agree yet. You should know it costs $1500."

"Mil quinientos?" I echo, my voice on the squeaky side. Yikes, that'll take a bite out of my savings account.

"I know it's a lot of money, but Mari is going to pay the other half with money from her job at the mall."

The other half? My eyes hold my grandmother's for a moment, and I feel like we're both thinking the same thing, that maybe we're out of our league here. But I shove the idea away. If any of us has a future outside of East Palo Alto, it's Mari. She's whip smart and dedicated.

"Okay, we'll work it out."

A gasp comes from the hall and Mari rushes in. *"Gracias,* Scotty." She throws her arms around me. "Thank you so, so much."

I laugh, hugging her back. "Nothing like eavesdropping, huh?"

She plants a kiss on my cheek. "I know, I'm sorry, I was just too nervous to ask you myself. I really want to go to this thing."

"*Niños,*" my grandmother interrupts as the three little girls arrive back in the kitchen. They all eagerly parrot my grandmother's favorite refrain. "*¡En Español, por favor!*"

Honestly, I hadn't even noticed that Mari and I had slipped into English. "*Perdón, perdón,*" I grumble. "But I have no idea how to say *eavesdropping* in Spanish."

My grandmother's one rule is that we speak Spanish at home even though her English is decent enough. How could it not be? You can't live in a country for almost fifty years and not pick up the language. But I know her reasons run deep. She was here in the US illegally for a long time before she married my grandfather. I don't pretend to understand what that does to a person. And I respect her fears of not being able to communicate with her own family.

So while we all discuss how to say *eavesdropping* in Spanish, I get the girls settled around the table and pour the milk onto their cereal. Just as I'm finishing up my own breakfast, my mother wanders into the kitchen in her ratty bathrobe, holding an unlit cigarette between her fingers. After partying heavily for most of her life and having four kids with three different men, my once beautiful mother looks every one of her forty-one years.

On the way to the sink with my bowl, I bus her cheek. "*¿Qué onda, Ma?*"

She just mutters something under her breath and heads for the coffee pot. After the screen door crashes closed behind her so she can have her morning smoke in the back yard, conversation starts up again.

A round of kissed cheeks later and I'm out the door.

"Come in!"

Every Monday morning, I have a meeting with my boss. Dean is a good guy. Like Father Martín, I owe a lot to him for helping me get to where I am today. When the foreman on the job I was working a couple years ago, stopped showing up on the regular, I made sure the guys were working and kept the job on schedule.

Dean took notice. Of that and my ability to communicate in both languages. He made me a bargain that I couldn't turn down: get your GED and I'll give you a shot as foreman.

"Good, McCarthy. Come on in. Have a seat."

It's almost been a year now, and while there have been a few bumpy patches, on the whole, things have gone well with my new role. Really well. Dean gets a reliable crew and I have a job that both challenges me and pays well. Forty five grand a year may not be a lot to some people, but for a kid who grew up in East Palo Alto with a mother and a grandmother who've always worked for minimum wage, and an uncle with dubious sources of income, it's a fortune. A steady fortune that's been adding up in the bank because I'm as frugal as I can be and my grandmother's house is mortgage free.

"How're the kids?" Dean asks as I sit down in the chair in front of his desk.

"Good, thanks. How're the grandkids?"

Without any hesitation, he grabs the newest framed picture from his desk and shows it to me. He's so proud of his two-year-old twin grandsons. "Oh, you know, they keep my daughter on her toes like you wouldn't believe."

When the pleasantries are over, we start in on the week ahead; scheduling, project timetables vs progress, costs, and employee morale.

"Any more problems with Harrison?"

I shake my head. "Like you said, giving it to him straight has mostly changed his attitude." Like me, Dean started at the bottom and worked his way up. He knows rough-in carpentry inside and out and he has a ton of experience with managing guys. I think he's taken me under his wing because he sees that I'm just as willing as he was to work hard and earn the respect of those around me.

"I did have something I wanted to ask you though," I say, trying my best not to cringe. "Do we have any spots available for a guy I know?"

He sits back in his chair, observing me closely. "He got any experience?"

"No, none." I resist the urge to shift nervously in my seat.

"But he's got papers?"

"Oh, he's definitely legal. That's not an issue."

"But there is an issue." It's a statement, not a question. *Shit.*

I decide to be honest. I've got a good thing going with Dean and I can't let Jorgie screw that up for me. "He's a guy I've known for a long time. He needs a bit of help getting his life on track."

"He going to pass a criminal records check?"

Relief floods me. "He will." Jorgie may have been arrested a few times, but he's never been charged and Alejandro's lawyers have had his records sealed.

"Alright, get the paperwork from Pamela out front and have the guy fill it out. If everything checks out, he can start in a couple days. But he's on you. Your crew, your name, your reputation. Understood?"

Despite the twist of dread in my stomach, I rise to shake the man's hand. "Thank you, sir."

"Don't thank me yet. I've been in your situation before and it doesn't always work out."

After retrieving the paperwork, I head for the work site with what feels like a belly full of snakes. Damnit. Jorgie better not make a mess of this.

My anxiety level isn't helped at all by the current job site being so close to University Ave. It just serves to remind me how close I came to ruining my life on Friday night. For the millionth time, my mind skips over the events and then skids to a halt on that girl in the coffee shop. *Why? Why would she help me like that? Why? Why? Why?* It's been a drum beat in my chest for the entire weekend. I feel like I owe her something. But what? A huge thank you, of course. But there's got to be more to it than that, right?

The maddening mystery of the girl and her reasons for helping me out continues to grow over the next couple of days. Every time I imagine, *really imagine*, what could have happened if I'd gotten arrested, my chest tightens painfully. Rosa being on CPS's radar may have been my first worry, but what if I'd lost my job? Then where would my family be? The whole situation is seriously shiver-worthy.

By the time Wednesday rolls around, my need to know gets the better of me. I have no idea if she's working today, but I'm going to find out. On my lunch break, I walk the six blocks to *1001 Beans*, irrationally expecting to come face-to-face with a cop who'll recognize me. I'm so caught up in my ridiculous thoughts that I almost don't realize that it's her outside the front of the café. She's talking on her cell, pacing the sidewalk, and with every turn, her pony tail swings angrily. I'm too far away to hear what she's saying, but her body language tells me she's pissed about something.

All righty then. Now's not a good time.

After a bit of consideration, I decide to wait and see if an opportunity to approach her presents itself. Crossing the street, I lean on a wall between some kind of small art gallery and a shop selling new age crystals. Pulling out my phone to look busy, I shamelessly try to catch snippets of her heated conversation. She must be talking to an ex, because the gist of it seems to revolve around her not wanting this person to call her anymore, especially at work. Shit, maybe *I* shouldn't be bothering her at work.

She stops her pacing for a moment, clamping the phone between her ear and shoulder as she pulls out an envelope from her back pocket. A guy passes her by on the sidewalk, and I'm struck by how tall she is in comparison. I can't say I remember her being that tall, but, man, her legs go on forever in those skinny jeans. I'd roll my eyes at that irrelevant notion if I weren't watching her rip open the envelope, scan whatever's inside, then march to the public trash can to toss it. Whoever she's on the phone with really pisses her off at this point, because she abruptly hangs up and heads back inside, not noticing that the paper didn't make it into the bin.

Okay, wow. There's obviously some spark to this woman. If I don't want to get burned by her temper, I'll have to come back another time. But that doesn't stop me from crossing the street to see what she was going to chuck into the trash. It's a paystub . . . a dismal one. In the last two week pay period she worked a total of thirty-eight hours for not much more than minimum wage. I check the name: *Elsabeth Frances Summers*. Good grief, her address is on here too. She should be more careful. Any weirdo could get a hold of this.

A weirdo like me.

Cringing, I shove the paper into my pocket and promise myself I'll shred it at home tonight. I certainly can't leave it here.

When I get back to work, I find Jorgie, of all people, inside the worksite, chatting up Menendez and Harrison like they're old friends.

I can't hold back my irritation. "What are you doing here?"

"We're still on break," Harrison says indignantly, his piss poor attitude toward me making a resurgence.

Instead of telling him not to be an asshole, I stick with Dean's straight-talk approach. "You're good," I tell the two employees. "But can you guys excuse us for a minute?"

"Sure thing, boss," Menendez says amiably, sauntering away. Harrison skulks though, muttering something derogatory under his breath.

"What are you doing here, Jorgie?" I bite out.

"Don't get your panties in a twist, *boss*. I came to drop off the papers."

I let the sarcastic emphasis on the word *boss* slide. "You can't be here without the proper . . ." I gesture to him up and down, and the word *shit* is on the tip of my tongue, but I repress it. "Without the proper attire," I finish. "Anyway, I told you to take the papers to the office. If you're not going to take this seriously, I don't want you here."

His pinched expression melts away. "Jesus, did you just say the word *attire*? You really are the boss, aren't you? My mind is blown, *cabrón*."

And just like that, a smile is tugging at my lips. Anger and Jorgie have never gone together.

"Get out of here, would you? Get your paperwork in and don't come back till you've been hired and you're wearing the proper fucking *attire*."

He salutes me. "Aye, aye, captain."

I can't help but laugh. *"Ya vete." Just go.*

The rest of the day is busy, but without incident, which allows my mind to wander while I work. By the time 4:30 hits and I'm heading for home, it's not Jorgie who's burned a hole in my mind, but *her*. Of course, now she has a name and she's gone from abstractly starring in one of the most stressful moments of my life to being a real person. Since I know myself and it's clear that I'm not going to be able to let this go, I make the snap decision to get this over with.

She lives just on the other side of the 101. Her address is only about a five minute drive from my house, but it's in a much better neighborhood. It's not until I'm approaching the main door of her apartment building that it hits me that this might not be the greatest of ideas. Showing up at her home? It's creepy, isn't it? Shit, if I were her, I'd probably call the cops . . . which is ironic on so many levels.

My feet stall out on the sidewalk as I face the glass doors to her building. *Do I go through with this? Do I forget it?* Except, I can't seem to *forget it*. So, I guess if she reacts badly to my showing up, I'll apologize and leave. It's not like she knows where *I* live.

I pull her paystub from my pocket to confirm her apartment number. I've just entered it into the building's intercom system when I hear footsteps come up behind me.

Turning, I need a few seconds to piece together that the woman with the pony tail and flushed face who's approaching is the woman I'm looking for. If I didn't recognize her from her height alone, I'd remember those eyes. They're as wide with shock and surprise as they were a few nights ago. My stomach swoops with nerves and . . . something unidentifiable.

Her head tilts in question. "You?" she says, a little out of breath because she's been out jogging.

"I, uh, yeah . . . you remember me?"

The building's old intercom system finally connects and fills the air with a loud ringing noise that draws our attention to the keypad.

"Yeah, of course I remember you," she says with a slight frown. "The world must be smaller than I thought."

The intercom rings again and I search for the button that will disconnect the call as I say, "I'm actually here to see you." It rings again, but this time she reaches around me to stop the racket.

"Me?"

Hesitantly, I face her again. Her tone has a definite edge to it now.

"Yeah, I, um –"

"How do you know where I live?" she demands, her hands settling on her hips.

Chapter Four

Ellie

Initially, it had been wonder – unexpected wonder – because holy shit, my stranger is standing right in front of me, like my thoughts had magically conjured him out of thin air. If ever there was a pinch yourself moment, it was thirty seconds ago.

Now though, reality hits me with a cold slap and wonder becomes alarm.

His hands come up in a placating gesture. "It's not what you think."

"It's not?" I say incredulously.

One of his hands slips behind his back and suddenly the three feet between us is not enough. I step back, my heart rate ticking up. But it's only a piece of paper, not a freaking gun. *Good grief.*

He holds it out to me. "I went by your work today. I wanted to thank you for . . . for what you did."

That he's uncomfortable mollifies me a bit, at least enough to take the paper from him. It's my paystub from today. *What the hell?* I glare at him. "You actually thought it was a good idea to show up at my apartment after what happened?"

His Adam's apple bobs in his throat. "No. Listen, I . . . no matter how we met, I swear I'm not a criminal. I just wanted to thank you, which I'm doing now." He takes a deep breath. "Thank you so much. If there's anything I can ever do to repay you, I will."

We stare at each other for a few seconds. Honestly, he looks sincere and my inner alarm bells have stopped clanging, so when he makes to leave, I stop him.

"How do I know you're not a criminal?" I ask, only half-joking.

He considers me for a moment, then his lips tip up slightly as he pulls his wallet out and hands me a well-folded piece of paper.

"What's this?"

"*My* paystub," he says with a bit of triumph.

Unfolding it, I glance over the information. "What's this supposed to prove, Prescott?"

His eyes narrow at the emphasis I put on his name. "It's Scott, and it proves that I'm a completely respectable guy, Elsabeth."

He says my name like it's obvious I've won the worst name contest. I hold back a smile by biting the inside of my cheek. "It's Ellie, and respectable guys don't get chased by the cops, Scott."

"They do if they're in the wrong place at the wrong time, Ellie." He shifts uncomfortably. "But seriously, I just came to say thank you and I'm sorry if I freaked you out. I'll get out of your way. Have a good night."

And with that parting statement, my stranger is walking away from me. My stranger who now has a name. *Scott* is walking away from me for the third time, and something inside of me rebels.

"Did you mean it?" I call out to him.

He turns. "What's that?"

"That if I ever needed anything, you'd help me out? Because I have this thing."

His brows rise in question.

"There's this guy coming in like twenty minutes to look at some stuff I'm selling on Craigslist," I say sheepishly. "Would you mind sticking around till he's gone?"

At his seeming confusion, I go on, well, ramble really, "I know I don't really know you, but I know you a lot more than the guy who's coming. If you don't have time, I completely understand. It was just a thought. I've been kind of nervous about it all day, and then you show up here and –"

"Okay, no problem."

"Okay? Really?" I let out a breath of relief, both because our time together isn't over and because now I don't have to meet a potential psychopath alone. "Thanks." The Velcro of my armband squelches loudly as I pull it off to get my key out. Not surprisingly, the lock on the front door hasn't been fixed yet, so I have to buzz someone to let me in.

"Mrs. Stanfield? It's me, Piper. Can you buzz me in, please?"

"Piper?" she says with her usual disapproval.

"Yes, it's me."

Before she'll let us in, we're forced to listen to her complain about the landlord for a bit.

"Sorry about that," I say, heading down the hall once we're inside.

"How come she calls you Piper?"

Our eyes meet and a frisson of electricity sweeps along my skin. His dirty blond hair is a bit longer on top than it was so many months ago and his lips seem fuller and his cheekbones higher than I remember . . . and he definitely doesn't remember me.

"It's just a nickname I'm trying to shake," I explain. "Mrs. Stanfield is too old to get that I'm trying to reinvent myself." Since I'd rather not talk about *Piper*, I quickly change the subject. "Thanks for doing this. I know it's not the smartest thing to do, but I'm in a tough spot right now. You know, with money."

At the end of the hall we go right, and my apartment is the second door on the left. Luckily, I tidied up since the guy who's interested in the PS4 is coming. Plus, I finally decided not to get a new roommate, so I moved back into the bedroom. Starting this week, I'll be working full time hours, so I should be able to squeeze my rent out of my pay cheques for the next few months until I finish school. But, clean or not, when the door swings open, I'm a bit rattled by having *him* in my personal space.

I kick off my sneakers, but tell him, "Don't worry about your shoes." As Piper, I had so many parties in this apartment where nobody took their shoes off. It's not like the gray carpet is pristine or anything.

He leans down to unlace his work boots anyway. "My grandmother would kill me if she found out," he says when he straightens and sees my questioning expression.

I barely refrain from letting my surprise show on my face. He's kind *and* well-mannered? *Who is this guy?* Moving into the living/kitchen space, he sees the Playstation on the island.

"This what you're selling?" he asks. "You play?"

I like that he's not skeptical that a girl could be a gamer, but I give him the truth by shaking my head. "Not really. I like the fun ones though, Mario Kart, that kind of thing. Do you want something to drink?" I pull open the fridge, but it's as empty as ever. Slamming it shut, I give him a rueful look. "I've got water, or water . . . from the tap. Sorry."

I swear I see faint amusement on his face. "Nothing wrong with tap water, but I'm good. Have you eaten?"

"No, but I do have a date with a package of Ramen later." My brow furrows. I guess I should offer that too. "Are you hungry? Do you want some?"

He actually laughs this time. "Tempting, but no thanks. How about I order us some pizza?"

My mouth waters at the thought, but the manners my mother taught me keep my polite front in place. "You don't have to do that."

"Well, if you'd rather eat Ramen . . ."

Something resembling a strangled groan comes out of me. "No one would rather eat Ramen over pizza."

His lips still curved into a smile, he pulls out his phone. "That's what I thought," he says. "Any preferences?"

"Um, not really, but Hawaiian is my favorite."

He looks appalled. "Hawaiian? That's what my six year old daughter eats."

Right. He has a daughter. I knew that. "Well, she clearly has excellent taste," I say while casually trying to scope out his left hand. No wedding ring, but that doesn't mean he doesn't have a wife or a girlfriend. I won't be asking though. The fact alone that I'm attracted to this guy is probably bad news. I have terrible taste in men. "But since you're the one paying the bill, I'll gladly eat whatever you're buying. I'm going to change quickly." Heading down the hall, I tell him over my shoulder, "Be right back."

In my bedroom, I rest my forehead against the closed door and take a deep, steadying breath. My stranger is here, in my house! I plan on savoring every second of this incredibly surreal experience.

After I get into a pair of jeans and a T-shirt, I go back to the kitchen and find Scott running a damp cloth over the game console. "I thought you'd get more for it if it wasn't covered in dust."

"Oh, I . . . thanks." *Maybe my taste in men has improved? Because good-looking, kind, well-mannered, and thoughtful? He has to be too good to be true, right?*

"This guy's probably going to want to make sure it works. All right if I hook it up?"

I swallow. *And take-charge?* "Yeah, good idea," I stammer. "I just pulled it out of the closet this morning."

He gathers everything up and takes it over to my TV stand. "You've got a Switch, too?" he asks, noticing the Nintendo console.

"Uh, yeah, my ex was big into video games."

He's got his head behind the TV, but I see the way he pauses what he's doing, the muscles in his shoulders stiffening slightly against the material of his black T-shirt. Glancing back with a bit of a disapproving look, he asks, "You supposed to be selling his stuff?"

Annoyance pulses in my gut. *See? He's not perfect.* Instead of the *'What are you, my dad?'* that's on the tip of my tongue, I go with, "I talked to him today. He was more interested in hearing about when I was coming back to him than about his stuff. So yeah, after everything, I'm selling it."

Even I can hear the determination in my tone, daring him to contradict me, so I'm surprised when another grin tugs at his lips. "After everything? Sounds ominous."

His head slips back behind the TV and he doesn't hear the, "If you only knew," that I mutter under my breath. Talking to

Gunnar today was like breathing tiny slivers of glass into my lungs, painful and something to be avoided at all costs. The sound of his voice had flooded me with a sense of familiarity that's been sorely lacking in my life. I'd held strong though. He still wants his party-girl back, the one who was up for anything, while I want nothing to do with her. No matter how easy it would be to slip back into Piper's skin, I know the only place she'll take me is back down to rock bottom.

The jarring buzz of the building's intercom announces the prospective buyer's arrival. He's barely less sketchy than I'd imagined. It takes about fifteen minutes for him to decide he wants the console and then another five for us to come to an agreement. Scott spends the time silently milling about my living room, except when he accepts the pizza delivery. He's going through my cupboards for some plates when the guy finally leaves.

"Thanks for staying," I tell him as I pull out a piece of Hawaiian pizza from one of the boxes, settling myself on a bar stool that I pull out from under the kitchen island.

"You're welcome," he says. "Can I ask you something?"

"Sure." I moan at the cheesy goodness of my first bite. How long has it been since I had pizza?

"You live here alone?"

That gets my attention, and I consider him carefully as I chew. "Yeah, why?" I finally answer.

"Because you live on the ground floor and the lock on your patio door is busted."

I shrug. "It's been like that since I moved in. I've got that piece of wood to block the track. Nobody can get in."

I'm not sure if his half scoff, half grunt can be taken as agreement or not, but he changes the subject so I don't give it another thought. He lifts his chin at my chest and I look down at the logo of a local community college on my T-shirt. "You go to school?"

"Yeah, I'm starting my last semester next week." I'm not sure why I don't tell him that this isn't the school I go to.

"You're not in the coffee business for life then?"

With a slight grimace, I admit, "Customer service and I don't always get along."

"What are you planning to do?"

I shrug again. "I'm not sure really. What about you, are you happy at . . . what was the company name . . . something construction?"

"Dominion Construction, and yeah, I think so. I like my boss and the pay's good."

A bit of an awkward silence fills the space between us while I mull over what to say next. "So, um, do you live alone?" *I know, I know, not very subtle.* I can't resist though, I need to know.

I'm not expecting him to laugh though. "No," he says, continuing to chuckle, "I live in a house full of women."

My heart constricts.

"Four generations of them. My grandma, my mom, three sisters, my niece and my daughter."

While my mind is sorting through the list, I can tell he's mistaking my growing animation for surprise. "That's a lot of estrogen," I tell him.

"It is. But there's never a dull moment."

From that point on, there are no more uncomfortable silences. We talk about our siblings, and I tell him that I envy his close relationship with his family. It's the nicest conversation I've had in a long while and when he gets to his feet and announces that he has to go, I wish he didn't.

"Thank you so much," I say with all sincerity. "For staying, and for dinner. Here," I consolidate the remaining slices into one box, "you can take the leftovers home."

"No, it's for you."

I perk up at that. "Hey, thanks. Again. If there's ever anything I can do for you . . ." Though I can't imagine what I could possibly offer this man who so obviously has himself together.

"Actually, there is something. You don't wear glasses do you?"

"Uh, no." That was an abrupt shift. "Why?"

He groans. "My niece needs glasses and I don't have a clue where to take her."

I think it over for a second. "Don't most optical places offer eye exams?"

He blows out a breath. "I never thought of that. Thanks. That gives me a place to start."

I want to ask him why it's his responsibility to take his niece to get her eyes checked. Isn't his niece his sister's daughter? There must be more to the dynamics of his family than he's told me. But I can't ask about it because we're heading for the door and he's about to leave – forever. As in I'll never see him again. I hate how sad that makes me.

"So, hey," he says as he pulls his boots on. "Will you be around on Friday evening? I'm going to fix your patio door."

"You are?" I ask, surprised.

"Yeah, I am. And then we'll go grab dinner."

"Okay." I feel a bright smile spread across my face.

For a second his easy confidence slips and I catch a glimpse of disquiet. "Not a date or anything, just –"

"No, of course not," I interject quickly, and then my knee-jerk reaction morphs into amusement. "No dates . . . or anything," I confirm blithely. Well that settles it then. He may not have a significant other, but Scott McCarthy is officially not interested.

His eyes narrow fleetingly. "Okay, I'll see you around this same time on Friday?"

"Yep, it's my day off, so I'll be here."

With a nod, he's out the door.

I'm left standing there with myriad conflicting emotions swirling inside of me. Excitement: I'm going to see him again. Offense: What's wrong with dating me? Embarrassment: I was a tad too eager. But screw it, when's the last time I spent time with a *nice* guy? Years? Or more likely, never. I don't think anyone I've ever dated could be categorized as *nice*.

I wonder why he's not interested in dating me though . . . because clearly he doesn't remember me as that girl on the sidewalk. Am I not his type? It's true that I'm not wearing any makeup. Or maybe I'm too tall? Or it's my mouth, I bet. I've always thought that my smile takes up too much of my face. Or maybe I'm falling back into my Piper persona. Ellie doesn't need or want validation from any man – ever. And more importantly, dating anyone is out of the question at the moment. I need to stay focused on myself. If I'm going to see this guy again, I'll have to keep that in mind.

Chapter Five

Scott

I don't like it. I don't like it at all. Has this woman no sense of self-preservation? Having some random guy off Craigslist come over when no one is around? What the fuck? I shake my head as I make my way home.

And her patio door has no lock! She lives on the ground floor for crying out loud. Supposedly she has three brothers. Where are they? Why aren't they looking out for her?

It mollifies me somewhat that I could do her a solid after the way she helped me out. And there's no way I'm *not* going to fix her patio door – I'd never be able to sleep again if I didn't. I'm not sure I liked the flash of that megawatt smile though. Realizing she thought I was asking her out on a date set off all kinds of alarm bells. I don't even date Latinas let alone white chicks . . . who are almost as tall as I am, whose legs go on for days and are attached to a bouncy, perfectly round ass. Yeah, no. In any case, I hope I was clear enough to set her straight.

Pulling into the driveway at home puts my thoughts of Ellie on the backburner. I'm surprised to see my mother's car. Normally, after work, she goes out with her new boyfriend, so if she comes home at all, it's later on. On top of that, my oldest sister's boyfriend's car is parked behind my mother's.

When I open my truck door, I wish I hadn't. I can hear the argument raging inside the house from out here.

Jordan, my sister's boyfriend, is sitting on the front steps. We eye each other warily. "What's up?" he finally asks.

I sigh as I take a seat beside him. "You'd know better than I would."

"Most of it's in Spanish, so I don't know shit. They were like this when I got here," he wakes his phone to check the time, "twenty minutes ago."

"Does Desiree know you're out here?"

He shrugs. "I texted her."

"All right. Let me see what's going on."

When I don't move to get up, he laughs softly. Jordan's a decent guy, I guess. Do I like that my oldest sister – who's still seventeen for another two months – is dating a guy my age? No. But I also know she could do a lot worse. He may not have finished college, but around here, thugs are a dime a dozen, and as far as I know, Jordan's not involved in anything shady. He lives up in Redwood City with his parents who are both high school teachers.

The volume of my mother's voice escalates as does the profanity.

"Whoa, even I know what that means," Jordan says as I finally get my ass off the porch.

The scene inside the front door curdles my insides. My mother is hurling the word *puta* at her daughter like it's not a dagger capable of inflicting real damage. At least the little ones are nowhere to be seen. I slam the door.

"What the hell is going on?" I demand in English, because being pissed and articulate in my second language is not my forte.

"*Your* mother is calling me a whore for going to the movies on a Tuesday night."

"*Look* at her!" my mother exclaims. "If she's going to the movies, I'm Mother Teresa."

From their expressions, they're both expecting me to settle something that's actually an on-going war with a few words. What a joke.

I start with Desiree, who as usual, is all sass, all attitude, hands on her hips, ready to bite my head off. Her soft curls are like a halo around her head . . . but she's definitely not dressed like an angel.

"Since when do you go to the movies dressed like that?" I ask, trying to keep the accusation out of my tone. She's wearing a dress that she's been poured into, leaving little to the imagination and her makeup has been applied with a trowel.

"It's fine," she claims. "I'm perfectly safe with Jordan."

"You didn't answer my question, Des."

"I don't have to answer you, Scott. You're not my parent." When our mother takes a breath, Desiree holds up a finger that's tipped with a long, red nail. "And you don't qualify either."

"You see how she talks to me?!"

"Ma, you're not helping." I turn back to my sister. "All I want to know is why you're dressed like this, Des, and don't tell me that this movies thing isn't bullshit."

Her hackles are rising fast, I can see that. Of all my sisters, she and I are the closest. We *know* each other even if there are four years separating us. We have a lot in common; my father is white, and I'm perceived as white by the world at large, her father is black, and she's perceived as black. We've both spent our lives trying to fit in and many times we've only had each other and our grandmother. Which translates into: I care and I'm not about to let this go, and she knows it.

She sighs. "Fine, I'm going dancing."

"I knew it!" our mother screeches. *"Que puta —"*

"¡Mamá, ya párale!" I yell, because I've had enough of her. I'd had enough of her when I was five years old. Desiree and I have always taken the brunt of her crap, and I'm done at this point in my life. "Leave. Go help with dinner or something. *Por favor."*

Lips pursed, eyes flashing, she stomps her way down the hall to the room she shares with Mari and slams the door behind her.

I brush my palms down my face. "What's going on, Des?" I ask softly, resignation taking anger's place.

"You mean besides having a mother who calls me a whore?"

"Don't. We both know *she's* never going to change. She is who she is. But us? We can make choices. Tell me why you thought you had to lie."

Her chin juts out in that stubborn way she has. "I didn't want it to be a *thing*, okay?"

"What did I say about bullshitting me? You lied because you know it's not okay for a seventeen year old to go clubbing, especially when she's dressed like a twenty-seven year old looking to hook up."

Her fire re-ignites. "I'm old enough to make my own decisions, Scott."

"And you're thinking this," I gesture to her up and down, "is a good decision?"

"Yes, I do."

I feel her slipping through my fingers. I try a different angle. "Where exactly are you going at six thirty on a Wednesday night, anyway?"

"Jordan is taking me out to dinner in San Francisco first."

She must see my displeasure at that, because she volunteers some more information. "I wanted to do something special for our six month anniversary, that's all. Are you going to spoil it for me?"

"Why? Are you going to stay home if I ask you to?"

Her expression hardens. "No. I want to go."

"Well, I don't see how I can stop you unless I lock you in your room. And we both know you'll have the cops at our door in five minutes with the fuss you'll kick up. All I can do is hope you'll take care of yourself while you're out."

She scurries forward on an absurd pair of high heels to throw her arms around me. "Thanks, Scotty. You're the best."

Grudgingly, I hug her back. She feels so young, too thin, too fragile and I wish I could make her see reason. "Just promise me you'll stay with Jordan at all times, and don't take drinks from anyone you don't know . . . actually, don't drink at all, okay?"

"Okay, I'll be good." She pulls back. "I promise."

"Make sure to call if you need me. And remember that you have school tomorrow."

"Yes, Dad," she grumbles sarcastically, reaching for her coat. When she tries to slip out the front door without me following, I give her a derisive snort.

On the porch, Jordan's entire face lights up when he sees her. "Oh, you look amazing." He draws out the word *amazing* until he catches a glimpse of my scowl.

"I do, don't I?" she says with a self-satisfied purr as she turns in a circle to give him a better look at her.

Gesturing at the car keys in his hand, I tell him silently to get her to wait in the car. "You want to drive, baby?" he asks, holding out the keys to her.

"Yeah, I want to drive!"

We both watch her teeter down the steps and get in the car.

"Listen, man," he begins, but I shut him down.

"She's a kid," I say bluntly, stepping up to him. I don't normally use my height to intimidate people, but I'm making an exception tonight. In my work boots, I'm pushing 6'4", and I've got to say, I like the way he tenses as if he's about to get pummelled.

Though he's reluctant to concede my point about her age, he gives me, "I know. I . . . this was her idea. I just don't know how to say no to her. She's a force of nature."

"And that force of nature is my baby sister. I'm fucking trusting you to keep her safe."

"Yeah, why do you think we're doing this on a Wednesday? I'm keeping it low key."

My head shakes of its own accord. "I want her back in one piece by midnight."

His grimace tells me what I already know: Desiree will be home when Desiree wants to be home and not before. "I'll do my best," he says, making his way to the car.

When the tail lights have disappeared down the block, I go back inside to find my girls. They're not in their bedroom, so I go to the kitchen which is also empty. The screeching of the screen door to the back yard calls their attention.

Rosa sees me first. "¡Papá!" She comes running and throws herself on me. I hold her tight for a long moment before I put her down. "Did you eat pizza?" she accuses. "You smell like pizza."

I laugh as I give out hugs to Daniela and Carmen as well. *"Sí, comí pizza,"* I say in Spanish to get them started. *"¿Y ustedes? ¿Qué cenaron?"* What did you guys have for dinner?

"Nada," Daniela announces like it's the most scandalous thing she's ever said.

Nothing? I check the darkening yard for my grandmother. Uneasiness comes over me when I don't find her. "Where's Abuela?"

Between the three of them, I gather that the fight between my mother and my sister had been going on for most of the afternoon, and that my grandmother had gone to lie down because she wasn't feeling well. Fuck my life. I hope she's okay. Sometimes I forget that she can't be expected to manage us like she's half her age.

We go back inside and I find dinner ready on the stove. I send the girls to wash their hands and then go in search of my grandmother.

"¿Abuela?" I whisper at the door to the room that she shares with Desiree. When I don't get an answer, my stomach flips and I slowly push the slightly ajar door open. The room is dark but I can see that she's lying on the bed under a throw blanket. Until I'm able to discern the soft rise and fall of her chest, I hold my breath. She's just sleeping and the relief is both sharp and intense.

Once I get the girls eating, we sit around the table and talk about 'the fight.' When I was growing up, no one ever gave me any explanations for my mother's stinging words or her erratic behaviour. I spent so much of my childhood confused and worried. I don't want that for these girls, so we talk about the yelling and the swear words, which then leads to questions about their Tía Desiree's dress and why Mamá Lilia (which is what they call my mother) didn't like it.

I do my best to answer their questions and not to say things like 'I don't know' or 'because I said so,' but some of the conversation really makes me squirm in my seat. What do I know about the right thing to say to little girls? Or how not to damage their self-esteem? But I'm *it* in this house. My grandmother is of a completely different generation. Her parenting style revolves around children being polite, not asking questions, and respecting their elders. My mother's revolves around a firm cuff to the head. Desiree is all about female empowerment, which is good, but it's laced with a recklessness that I'm not sure I agree with. And Mari is only fifteen and shouldn't be expected to be a parent, though I suspect she's the most level-headed of us all.

Later on while I'm loading the dishwasher, I open a water bottle to rinse it out and get a good whiff of what can only be vodka. *Great.* Though I can't say I'm surprised my mother is off the wagon again, I am disappointed. This latest dry spell only lasted a few months.

By the time the girls are in bed and I'm stretched out on my foam mattress on the living room floor, you'd think my head would be full of possible solutions to my extensive list of problems, but it's not. After everything, the only thing holding my attention is a tall, beautiful woman who thinks I want to date her.

The rest of the week goes smoothly for once. Not only did Desiree make it back on time, but she arrived unscathed, sober, and happy. My grandmother got a good night's rest and was fine the next day. My mother went to work as usual. And best of all, on Thursday evening, I took all three of the girls to get their eyes checked.

Turns out that Daniela wasn't the only one who needed glasses, Carmen needed them as well. That my youngest sister, who's always so quiet, didn't mention that she was having problems with her vision is troubling.

Anyway, I was so relieved to cross *optometrist* off the list that I only had a minor heart attack over the cost of prescription glasses.

Even Jorgie starting work on Thursday went better than expected. His attitude was good, and I hope like hell that the novelty of the situation doesn't lose its lustre for him any time soon.

Unfortunately, experience tells me that this run of luck can't last – because let's face it, as soon as life gets easy, it's about to go to shit or it already has and you just don't know it yet. So, it's with a bit of apprehension that I buzz Ellie's apartment on Friday evening. I've been ignoring the odd sense of anticipation that's been building over the last few days. If I'm honest though, I like it. The feeling is new, it's different. It's *other*. That she has no connection to anything else in my life is part of the appeal, I'm sure. She's basically an island in the middle of the chaos.

She greets me with that beautiful, infectious smile that's been lurking in my imagination. "You came," she says, sounding surprised as she stands back to let me in.

"Of course I came. I said I would." She takes note of my tool box and the new lock that's sitting on top of it while I get my boots off.

"In my experience, a lot of people say a lot of things. Doesn't mean they follow through."

Her light brown hair is loose today, and I realize I've never seen it out of a pony tail. She's got it pulled over one shoulder where it sits in a curly brown mass. As I straighten, I'm again struck by how tall she is. She has to be at least 5'10". It's a bit unnerving when our eyes meet with only a foot of space between us in the cramped entrance hall.

"That's me," I say with a hint sarcasm. "The king of follow-through."

I catch a flash of another smile as she leads me into the living space. "How fortunate for me, my patio door, and my stomach," she says, her tone light. I'm satisfied to see that she's not dressed in anything . . . date-like, just a sweater . . . and jeans that are once again molded to that phenomenal ass. Right, moving on. I take another look at her sliding glass door.

When I'm not making a racket with the drill, we make small talk. It's fine. She's nice enough and the conversation isn't awkward. I find out that for the next few months she'll have Fridays and Mondays as her days off from work. My gaze flicks to where she's perched on the armrest of her sofa, watching me work. "How'd that crappy turn of events come about?"

She gives a little shrug. "My friend Vanessa is the manager and originally, she hired me as a favor, so it's nice to be able to pay her back. If I work the weekends, she doesn't have to. Plus, I make a bit more per hour when I'm the designated person in charge."

I nod. "At least you turned out to be a good employee." I tell her about Jorgie and my misgivings about getting him a job.

With all the talking, it's taken me longer to finish than I expected. Strangely, I'm not put out. I actually don't mind her easy-going personality.

"Okay, come check this out," I tell her, showing her the new locking mechanism. As she leans in slightly, the citrusy scent of her hair fills my nose and I immediately shuffle back. The last thing I need is to be sniffing this woman.

Oblivious to my discomfort, she grins over her shoulder, saying, "So, does this mean I can get rid of the unsightly stick?"

I clear my throat. "Definitely not. The unsightly stick stays. It's a good visual cue to potential home invaders that the next door over will make an easier target." Her eyes widen at my honest assessment, but I figure she deserves the truth.

"Ok, well, thanks. On that bright note, you can tell me how much I owe you for this." She waves her hand at the door.

"You don't owe me anything, Ellie." Her warm brown gaze briefly touches mine when I say her name. "I'm the one who owes you, remember? Come on," I say, grabbing my tools and heading for the door. "You can explain why you saved my ass over dinner."

"Are you sure? I feel bad that you're going to all this trouble for me." The inflection on *for me* has me turning back. It almost sounds like she doubts she's worth the bother.

"I'm very sure. And I'm hungry. You're not going to turn down a free meal, are you?"

"Not likely," she acknowledges. "So where are you taking me?"

"I don't know. Where do you want to go? There's always Applebee's."

She laughs. "Right, so I don't mistake this for a date. You know, you could probably get rid of me faster if we went to Chipotle. And the food would be better."

That makes me pause. Then I can't help but shake my head and chuckle softly. "The food *would* be better," I admit. "But I'm not trying to get rid of you."

She hums some kind of cryptic agreement before she says, "Would you mind if we stop off to pay my rent?"

"Uh, sure, no problem."

She grabs her purse and locks the door. "Thanks, the landlord's a bit of a letch. I always hate going there alone."

I'm about to ask her why her friends or brothers don't help her out when she starts chattering away non-stop like she did a few days ago. It must be a nervous thing.

"I mean, he's never actually tried anything, but I hate the way he looks at me. Like he's groping me in his imagination." She shivers with exaggerated disgust as we pass the lobby and head down the other side of the building, still on the main floor. "You know the type, right? Really creepy? But I suppose imaginary groping isn't a crime."

The landlord's door is the first on the left. Ridiculously, she jumps on the spot a few times like a boxer warming up for a fight, she even includes a few neck stretches. If she weren't so obviously uneasy, I'd laugh.

She knocks firmly and I set my tool box down while we wait.

The door swings open to reveal a middle-aged guy wearing a wife-beater that does little to cover his paunch. To complete the picture, his dandruff speckled hair is slicked back. What a nasty cliché.

"Ahhhh," he drawls. "Miss Summers. How are you?"

Sure enough, his gaze drops to her chest, though I'm not sure what he's looking at since she's pretty much covered.

"I'm good, Mr. Bostwick," she says too brightly. "How are you?"

He leans against the door jamb as his eyes slither lower. "I'm doing a little better now that you're here. What can I do

Not so Far Away

for you?" His suggestive tone has a short grunt of disapproval coming from me. He finally spares me a quick glance, but doesn't change his attitude.

"Just came to pay my rent." She pulls out a wad of cash from her jeans pocket and holds it out to him. When he doesn't take it right away, I frown. *What's with the blatant disrespect?* It's not my place to say anything though.

"*Tomorrow's* the first," he states like she's an idiot.

"I know. I'm a day early."

With a noisy exhale, he takes the money and shuts the door in our faces.

She nods absently as if acknowledging to herself that the encounter went as well as could be expected. "I just have to wait for the receipt."

"No worries. I see you weren't exaggerating his charm."

Her eyes widen as she whispers, "Right? He's such a worm."

The door jerks back open and Mr. Bostwick, the creep, is pissed. "Fifty dollars short, Miss Summers."

Ellie's shoulders shrink slightly. "I know, it's just till I get paid," her voices dwindles, "in twelve days."

"The deal is the full rent or an eviction notice. You've run out of chances."

"But it's only my third time," she pleads. "I've lived here for three years. You know I'll pay."

"No, your boyfriend used to pay. You, on the other hand, are unreliable."

I'm not sure if it's because I hate that she's being talked down to by this skeevy asshole or if I have a hero complex like Desiree claims, but I'm reaching for my wallet to put an end to this before I can really consider the ramifications.

68

"Here's the fifty bucks she owes you." My words stop whatever further insults he was about to launch at her. "And she'll need a receipt."

Chapter Six

Ellie

Mr. Bostwick glares between Scott and me before he grabs the cash from his hand and disappears back inside.

"You didn't need to do that," I squeak out, mortification flushing my cheeks.

"You'd prefer the eviction notice?" His voice takes on a teasing tone that flusters me a bit.

"No, I . . ."

"When your next check comes in, you can pay me back, okay?"

"Of course," I say vehemently. Oh my god, how humiliating. So much for my hope that Mr. Bostwick would cut me some slack in front of an audience. Why can't he appreciate the way I came *so* close to scraping the money together?

"You should see your face," Scott says on a laugh. "It's no big deal, all right? I'll get my money. I know where you live – at least for the next month."

A thin, sputtering noise trails from my throat. "Was that a joke? Please don't make fun of me. This is so embarrassing."

Mr. Bostwick is back then, pushing the receipt at me. "Come prepared next time." The sudden quiet in the hall when he's gone is nerve-racking until Scott leans down to grab his tool box and says, "Come on. A burrito with my name on it is waiting."

I hurry after him. "I'm turning out to be the most expensive charity case ever, aren't I?"

"Charity case?" His eyebrows lift as we pass through the main doors and out into the quickly cooling night. "You keep forgetting that I'm the one who owes you."

"I'm sure that's not true anymore."

"Yes, it is," he says pointedly as he pulls his keys from his pocket and unlocks the doors to a small pickup truck that's parked down the street. Tucking his tool box in the tiny extended cab space behind the seat, he gestures for me to get in.

"No one actually fits back there, do they?" I ask once we're both seated.

He starts the engine and pulls out before glancing at me. "Actually all three of them fit back there nicely."

Huh? "All three of who?"

"My daughter, my niece, and my littlest sister. They're all about the same age."

Oh, right. "How old are they?"

"Six, seven and eight."

"And why do I keep getting the impression that you're the one who takes care of them?" I wonder aloud.

"Because I do. My grandmother and I are basically their parents."

What? "Wow, that's . . . that's the nicest thing I've heard in a long time . . . and a lot of responsibility."

"Yeah, but they're pretty great, so it sounds more impressive than it is." He's almost lounging in the seat beside me with a big hand wrapped around the steering wheel.

"I'm having a hard time imagining you with three little kids."

He laughs. "Sometimes, I have the same problem. But I didn't have a ton of stability while I was growing up, so I at least try to give them that."

Holy shit. That jolt cruising through my system may have been caused by my ovaries exploding.

"Anyway," he goes on, "they're the reason that I'm so thankful to you. Having CPS sniffing around because their *primary caregiver* got arrested is not something I even want to think about."

I mull that over for a minute. "Can I ask why you're their primary caregiver?"

We're stopped at a red light and he shifts his gaze from the traffic to consider me.

"Too nosy?" I ask sheepishly when he remains quiet. "It's one of my worst qualities. That and my inability to pay the rent on time. Unless of course you ask my sister. She'll tell you that my worst quality is my lack of self-preservation. According to her, I'm way too trusting. But at least I don't constantly try to accommodate everyone, *she's* a habitual people pleaser."

As I take a much needed breath, he interjects with, "Hey, El? Does your sister also think you're too chatty?"

My mouth opens, then closes, suddenly unsure of myself. I bet he'd run for the hills if he knew that only people whose opinions are important to me turn me into a nervous chatterbox. I finally go with a harrumphing sound. "Maybe. But *chatty* is clearly not a negative. Chatty people are delightful."

He tries, and fails, to repress a laugh. "Delightful is exactly the word I'd use, Elsabeth. You took it right out of my mouth." He pulls into a parking space at Chipotle. "So do delightful types get mild, medium, or hot salsa in their burritos?"

His playfulness catches me off guard, but I recover quickly. "Burrito?" I toss back dryly like he's an amateur. "You get way more food when you order it as a bowl . . . with mild, medium, *and* hot salsa."

He looks impressed as we get out.

On a bit of high with all the teasing, I like it way too much when he holds the door of the restaurant open for me. As I scoot past him, his scent knocks me for a bit of a loop too; it's deliciously all man, with undertones of soap and deodorant. I absently wonder what he'd do if I leaned in and made myself at home in the crook of his neck. He's the perfect height for it.

Actually, as we continue with our easy banter while we wait in line, I know that he's more than simply the perfect height. He's just plain perfect, every hard inch of him. Since I'm only allowed to like him as a friend, I manage to keep the ogling of his lean frame and broad shoulders to a minimum, barely noticing how his biceps faintly strain and flex when he moves. And in no way do I acknowledge the urge to lift the hem of his T-shirt to get a better idea of the ab situation he's got going on. Although, I'm not sure if it's better or worse to leave *the situation* completely to the mercy of my wild imagination.

Once we've got our food, we snag two stools at the window and dig in. After a few bites, I can't help but moan. "I love this stuff."

He finishes chewing his mouthful and then grins at me. "So does my daughter."

It takes a second for me to make the connection to the Hawaiian pizza. "She and I are kindred spirits, then," I tell him with a smile that quickly becomes a frown. "What are you doing?" Before every bite, he's pouring bottled hot sauce directly onto his burrito. At the rate he's going, he'll have used it all by the time he's done.

"What?" he asks innocently. "I like it spicy."

"You're going to burn a hole in your esophagus."

He shrugs and then pours some more while I laugh to myself.

When we're done, he surprises me by turning my stool to face him so his knees bracket my own. "I need you to tell me why you didn't hand me over to the cops. It's been driving me crazy."

Since the truth would needlessly complicate our newfound friendship, I lie. "I don't know." He's about to object to my answer so I forestall him with a half-truth. "Okay, I do know. It was your expression. You just seemed so . . . defeated, like the world has never given you a break."

He rubs the slight stubble on his jaw. "You could have got in a lot of trouble."

"I know. But it wasn't really a conscious decision. It all happened so fast."

"Yeah, it did," he concedes.

"Are you going to tell me why you were running in the first place?"

"I told you. Wrong place at the wrong time."

I give him a skeptical look that says *really?*

"I'm serious. Fridays are my one night of the week to go out with my friends, and some of them aren't exactly the squeaky-clean types."

He seems to be waiting for some kind of acknowledgment of his innocence, so I nod. "Today is Friday, does that mean you're going to be in the wrong place at the wrong time again later tonight?"

My heart skips a beat when he unleashes a rueful smile on me. "Nah, I'm officially on hiatus. At least for a little while.

Anyway, the guy I was telling you about, Jorgie? I see him at work now, so by the end of the day, I've had enough of him."

"The guy you got a job for isn't squeaky clean? I'm not sure that was wise."

He groans. "Tell me about it."

Something through the window catches his eye, and he lifts his chin at it. "You know that guy, El?"

The pleasure of hearing the shortened version of my name on his lips is obliterated by the sight of Cody staring at me through the glass. "Oh, come on," I mutter under my breath.

"El?" There's concern in his tone.

"Yeah, I know him." *Ugh*, and he's coming inside now. "He's my ex-boyfriend's best friend."

I'm still facing Scott with my thighs between his knees. It appears more intimate than it is and I appreciate that Scott doesn't pull away from me, letting Cody draw his own conclusions.

"Piper," Cody intones.

"Cody." He's still got that preposterous, wispy goatee.

"How you been?"

"Fine." Keeping my attention glued to my nails, I refuse to ask the reciprocal question and engage with him. Under normal circumstances, I would dread this type of run-in, but with Scott here, I'm confident I can hold strong.

"Candy Cane misses you," he says, upending my attempt to remain indifferent. *Shit*. I feel tears begin to form.

"I miss her too," I admit softly.

A slight shift in his stance has me lifting my gaze to find him zeroed in on Scott. "So when you coming back?" He makes it sound like it's Scott's fault I'm not back with them already. That puts an end to the rising emotion.

I straighten my spine. "I'm not."

"Come on, Pipes. What are you doing? Don't you think this has gone on long enough?"

For a second all I can do is shake my head. When I finally find my voice, I give it to him as directly as I can. "Just leave it, okay? Gunnar and I are done. Say hi to Candy for me."

Despite my very clear cue that I don't want to continue this conversation, he lingers for another tense moment before he finally shakes his head and leaves. I do my best to pull myself together and shake off the dull ache of wounds that I wish were better scabbed over. The apology I was forming in my mind for Scott vanishes when his hand brushes my knee.

"You okay?"

"Yeah," I say, sounding brittle. "Of course. Absolutely. Should we get out of here?" Fueled by the desire to escape, I twist off the stool and head for the door. I know he follows me because outside, I hear the locks on his truck disengage, which lets me slide onto the seat.

Once he's beside me, the silence is awful. I'm about to launch into some topic, any topic, to fill the void when softly, he says, "Hey." That single word comforts and disquiets me in equal measure. I hate that he's so together, that he brims with confidence and self-reliance, while I so plainly do not. Too bad I'm not his type. Or even his equal. Too bad I'm such a mess. Maybe in another lifetime, I could have been someone to him.

"Hey, look at me," he soothes, and when I finally find it in me to meet his eyes, they're not full of pity like I was expecting, but understanding. "I'm going to go out on a limb and say your ex wasn't just a random, ordinary ex."

"Yeah, you could say that."

"Well, if it makes you feel any better, you don't have the market cornered on those. At least you don't have a kid with him . . . right?"

I give him a wry, half-smile. "No, I don't have any kids."

"Then you can make a clean break. You don't ever have to see him again if that's what you want."

I take a deep, fortifying breath. "You're right. I just wish I didn't miss them so much."

He frowns, obviously confused, which makes two of us.

"Don't listen to me," I say. "Gunnar was a terrible boyfriend. I do miss Candy though."

"You can't still be friends with her?"

I shake my head. "You have your questionable friends and I have . . . *had* mine. I'm trying to keep myself out of trouble these days and Candy definitely wouldn't help with that."

"Ah, say no more," he says like he really does understand. "But did that guy really call her Candy Cane? What kind of name is that?"

The change of subject mutes some of the unwanted emotion swirling inside of me and even brings a small smile to my face. "A made up one, just like *Piper*. We were quite the pair."

"Honestly, they sound like stripper names."

I try to smother my rising amusement with an exasperated glare, but I can feel my lips twitching anyway.

Laughing at my expression, he starts the truck. "Do you have any plans for tonight?"

I shake my head.

"Me neither. You got Mario Kart on your Switch?"

A real smile comes over me. "Yeah. You want to come over?"

"Yeah, but we're going to need caffeine or I'll fall asleep."

So that's what we do. On the way home, we stop for supplies. Two large coffees and a giant bag of potato chips for him, and a jumbo pack of Twizzlers for me.

While we're settling in on either side of the couch, waiting for the Switch to boot up, he asks me, "So who came up with the name Piper?"

"Oh, I did. I started ninth grade at a new school and I figured it was the perfect opportunity to lose the old, nerdy me. Piper was the coolest name I could come up with."

"So your stripping career started earlier than I thought. You must be really good."

I throw a half-eaten Twizzler at him. "Would you stop? We both know Piper would only qualify as a mediocre stage name. If I'd wanted to be a professional, I'd have gone with Diamond, or Ruby, or maybe Sapphire."

He chuckles. "I'm sensing a pattern."

I waggle my eyebrows at him, making him laugh harder.

"I think," he says when he's settled down a bit, "that I've got the perfect stripper name for you, way better than Piper."

"Oh, yeah?"

"Yeah. Opal."

"Opal?" I scoff. "I can't believe you said that with a straight face."

"No, no, it's perfect. My grandmother has an opal necklace. It's white and shiny, just like you."

I pull the cushion from behind my back and chuck it at him, both of us laughing like it's the funniest thing we've ever heard, especially when he enters my name into the game as Opal.

"Nice to see you again," I say cheerfully, handing the customer his change, which he promptly drops in the tip jar.

From a few feet away, where she's adding some late addition scones to the display case, Vanessa eyes me with suspicion. Sidling up, she proceeds to click her long nails on the counter. "You're going to tell me what's going on sooner or later. Why not cut to the chase already?"

With complete innocence, I say, "I don't know what you're talking about."

"Yes, you do. What have you done with cranky-pants Ellie?" Her face screws up into a frown. "You're not high, are you?"

"What?" I sputter. "No, I'm not high."

I say it a bit too loudly and Jake, who's making the drinks down the bar, begins to crack up.

"Well, you're high on life then, and I want to know why."

Ha, Vanessa doesn't know anything. I'm not high on life. I'm high on Scott McCarthy. For the past four days, I've been walking on air. I had so much fun on Friday night. I'm also absurdly proud of myself, because the fun didn't include even a smidgeon of booze, drugs, or sex. Scott is still in the friend zone where he belongs, and my self-respect is soaring. I couldn't be happier.

"Does this have to do with the fifty bucks I loaned you?" Vanessa asks. "It's not for a dealer, is it? Do you need an intervention?"

"Would you relax?" I tell her. "I'm not on drugs. I'm in a good mood. That's all."

"Okay, fine, but why is the reason a secret?"

"There's no secret. I'm just happy that my shift is over. It's one o'clock."

The bell over the door rings, announcing the next customer, forcing Vanessa to shift her attention so I'm able to slip away with only a parting wave.

In the breakroom, I grab my phone from the back pocket of my jeans and stare at the screen. On Friday, I insisted that we exchange numbers, my excuse being that I didn't like owing people money. That wasn't a lie, but my reasoning had more to do with the helplessness I'd felt at the idea of not being able to contact him. Now, with his cash in hand, the urge to text him is overwhelming.

No pain, no gain, right?

Ellie: Hey, it's me, Opal (ha, ha). I have the $ I O U.

I've already psyched myself up for being ignored. I'm prepared to wait. He's working, he's busy, he has responsibilities, yada, yada, yada. Just because he occupies so much of my mind, doesn't mean I occupy his.

My phone chirps and I snatch it up.

Scott: You didn't earn that $ on a pole, did you?

My jaw falls open. I am not going to laugh at that. I swear, I'm not. Except a giggle slips out as another message comes in.

Scott: Don't pretend u didn't laugh. Do u work tmrw? We cd meet for lunch.

My heart flutters.

Ellie: I work 5am-1pm. My lunch break is at 10, lol. After?

This time it takes longer to get a reply, but that doesn't wipe the stupid grin off my face.

Scott: Ok. After lunch tmrw. See u @ 1 @ your work.

I may have done a little happy dance.

Chapter Seven

Scott

Fucking Jorgie. Though he's still taking the job seriously, by the time he learns what he's doing, I'll either be nominated for sainthood or have an ulcer. His attention to detail is shit, and because he's constantly yapping, Menendez, who I've paired him with, isn't paying much attention either.

Luckily, I caught their mistake early. I came in this morning and something about what they had started yesterday afternoon didn't sit well with me. Going over the blueprints proved me right and we spent the morning discussing the theory behind what we're trying to accomplish here, and then dismantling and re-cutting. While it was obvious that Menendez grasped everything, Jorgie didn't have a clue. But it's early days. Right?

It's only one o'clock and I'm already exhausted. Plus, today Rosa will be with her mother from 4:00-8:00 pm. Even though her scheduled day is Wednesday, Lolita, my ex, asked to change it for today. Which is fine. But like always, I'm anxious about the visit. I never know which to hope for; that Lolita will show up so Rosa won't be disappointed, or that she won't, so Rosa will be where I know she's safe and cared for.

It's a draining state of affairs, made worse by the fact that I don't get off work until 4:30 so I won't be there when Rosa gets picked up.

I remind myself that these thoughts don't belong at work, so I squash them down in an attempt to keep my head in the game. I'm going over the plans with Thomas, my right hand man, when my phone dings with a message. Thinking it's my boss, I check it.

Huh. It's Ellie and I realize that I'm smiling when I notice Thomas watching me smugly. My face falls to neutral. "Give me a sec." I cross the room and open the message.

Opal: Hey, it's me, Opal (ha, ha). I have the $ I O U.

Just seeing the name on my screen has me chuckling softly. I type out a response.

Scott: You didn't earn that $ on a pole, did you?

As soon as I send it, I reconsider. *Shit. Do I know her well enough to make that kind of a joke?* Since I can't take it back, I roll with it.

Scott: Don't pretend u didn't laugh. Do u work tmrw? We cd meet for lunch.

Lunch? Tomorrow? What the hell am I doing? They need to invent an app that recalls hasty, regrettable text messages. This girl is going to get the wrong idea. Except I get a bit of a rush when her response comes in right away.

Opal: I work 5am-1pm. My lunch break is at 10, lol. After?

I stare at the screen. *She starts at five? In the morning?* She's got the shittiest work schedule on the planet.

"Who's Opal?"

Jorgie appears like the grim reaper at my elbow, reading my screen.

"Opal sounds like a sixty year old lady, Scotty. I know you're into older women, but I think you might be taking it too far."

His voice scrapes like sandpaper across my nerves. "Don't you have work to do?"

He shrugs. "Tell me who Opal is and I might get something done. Is she your new fuck buddy?"

"Or," I say sharply, "you can mind your own business, keep the fuck-buddy references to a minimum at work, and do what you're being paid for. I would hate for you to get fired."

"Actually, I know the boss. He won't fire me."

"Don't tempt me, Jorgie."

"Come on, tell me who she is."

"She's no one. Go get some work done."

"Fine. But I want to meet her soon. Is she hot? Hotter than Juanita?"

"Go," I growl, staring him down until he finally backs away with a suspicious scowl on his face.

Scott: Ok. After lunch tmrw. See u @ 1 @ your work.

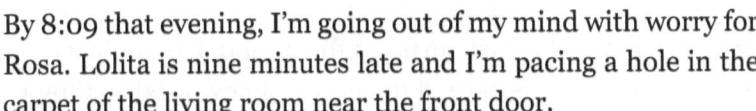

By 8:09 that evening, I'm going out of my mind with worry for Rosa. Lolita is nine minutes late and I'm pacing a hole in the carpet of the living room near the front door.

"Ven, mijo. Siéntate," my grandmother implores me. *Come and sit down.*

Not likely.

"Tell me again about when she got picked up," I ask in Spanish.

"I told you, mijo. Lolita was twenty minutes late, but she was sober."

"But she was with a guy, right? Are you sure you didn't recognize him?"

I swear, only another parent who's forced to send their child into a potentially hazardous environment can understand this awful helplessness I'm feeling. My only consolation is that Lolita is a good mother when she's not using, and when I talked to her on the phone on Sunday night and again last night, she sounded calm and lucid . . . but after what Jorgie told me about her hanging around with Richie Vasquez, I'm nervous as hell.

"I didn't recognize him because he didn't get out of the car," she says with exasperation. "And Lolita seemed fine. Don't worry."

"Okay, you're right."

I face the room directly and the familiarity of the scene calms me a bit. My grandmother is sitting in her arm chair, knitting as usual, and Carmen and Daniela are sitting on the floor in their pajamas, coloring at the coffee table. The TV is tuned to one of those awful Mexican telenovelas. Everything is as it should be . . . except my daughter isn't here. Nausea twists in my stomach.

I've made one big mistake in life: sex without a condom. In my defense, I'd just turned fifteen, and I thought Lolita was on the pill – we both did. Did you know it takes time to kick in? Unfortunately, Lolita didn't catch that critical piece of information and I'd been equally clueless. God, we'd both thought we were being so mature about the decision; we talked about it, we planned it, we were in love after growing up together, and then we went at it like only two hormonally-charged teenagers can. It took about seven weeks before we figured out our error.

The pregnancy and the following six years have been hard, brutal at times, so I don't blame Lolita for not being able to deal with it on a full-time basis. She didn't have an adult behind her, giving her all the moral support she needed like I did. But dammit, that doesn't change the fact that I'm going out of my mind right now.

It's 8:17 when I hear a car in the driveway. Wrenching the front door open, I tell myself to keep it together. Snapping at Lolita and starting a war between us is not in Rosa's best interests.

The sight of my little girl running up the driveway almost lays me out flat with relief.

"¡Papá!"

I grab her up into my arms and hug her close. "I'm back! Did you miss me?"

"I missed you so much," I tell her, foregoing the Spanish for once. "Did you have fun?"

"Yes! We went to McDonald's and then we went to Target. Look what I got!" She shows me a stuffed zebra. "And then we watched a movie at Grandma Sol's house."

"Sounds exciting," I say, my voice weak after being so worried. I plant a kiss on her cheek. "Why don't you go get your pajamas on and brush your teeth? You've got school tomorrow."

"Okay." I set her down and she turns to her mother who's coming up the porch steps. "Bye, Mom."

"Bye, Rosa. I love you."

She just nods and runs inside where I hear her squealing with Carmen and Daniela over the zebra.

"Sorry, we're late."

I can only nod.

"We had fun," she says to fill the tense silence.

Another nod.

She sighs. "I'm doing better, Scotty. Don't be all pissy."

Running a hand along the back of my neck, I meet her eyes. "Sorry, yeah. I'm not pissy. I'm proud of you, Lolis." I blow out a heavy breath. "I just worry, you know?" My gaze settles on the driver of the car and I grit my teeth. It *is* Richie fucking Vasquez.

"You don't have to worry anymore. This time, I've got this."

I manage a feeble smile. *How many times have I heard that?* Then, even though I know it's a mistake, I can't stop myself from asking, "What's going on there?" I lift my chin at the car.

Her body language shifts immediately, her arms folding across her chest as she glares up at me. "We're just hanging out, Scotty. He's nice. He drove us around today."

Instead of pointing out the obvious: that our daughter can't be hanging out with a scumbag like Richie Vasquez, I go with, "Okay, I trust your judgment." I don't trust it, but I've learned the hard way not to back Lolita into a corner, especially when there's a chance that this thing with Richie will run its course and be a non-issue. "So, the same time next week on Wednesday?"

Richie honks the horn at her, so she heads down the steps and over her shoulder, she calls, "Yeah, I'll be here at four again."

My jaw sets as I watch her go. Lolita has never grasped the seriousness of raising a child – our child. She doesn't spend enough time with Rosa to know how she absorbs everything around her like a sponge, how she imitates, how she repeats both words and behaviours. But who am I to judge? My mother and sister and their epic argument last week were beyond cringe-worthy. Sometimes I dream about starting over somewhere, away from my friends, away from my mother, away from Lolita, away from this neighborhood. Somewhere where there aren't so many constant complications.

But I don't have time for daydreaming right now. I have to check in with my kid and make sure she doesn't need to talk about anything she saw or heard in Richie's car or over at Grandma Sol's house.

The next day as I approach *1001 Beans*, I can see Ellie sitting at a table in the window. She's got her head bent over her phone one second, and the next, she's doing a mini fist pump in the air. I shake my head, trying to repress a smile.

As far as I'm concerned, the now familiar, sweet flutter of anticipation I'm feeling is a nice break from my life's usual routine.

Inside the cafe, the smell of coffee fills my senses and bumps my mood up another notch. The place is fairly busy so she doesn't see me coming. Over her shoulder, I see she's playing some kind of word game on her phone.

"Hey," I say, planting my ass in the chair across from her.

"Hey." Her whole face lights up.

"What're you playing?"

If possible, her smile gets even brighter. "Word Cookies. It's the bane of my existence."

Disbelief colors my laugh. *Word Cookies?* With her hair up in a ponytail for work, those amazing cheekbones that are devoid of makeup are on full display, and in the sunlight, her big brown eyes shine with mischief. And that wide mouth? With those full lips? Oh, fuck, I wonder what it would be like to –

"Well, hello there."

My dirty thoughts are yanked back by a woman who sets down two large coffees at our table. When her hands are free, she sticks one out to me.

"I'm Vanessa, Ellie's boss and her very best friend."

"Uh, hi," I say, shaking her hand. "Scott."

"So you're the one who's going to save this poor girl from the sisterhood?"

My eyebrows shoot up and Ellie gasps softly.

"No, Vanessa," Ellie retorts tightly, "my joining the sisterhood is still very much on." She turns a slightly exasperated expression on me. "Don't listen to a word she says."

"The sisterhood?"

"Yes, she's sworn off men if you can believe it."

I smirk at Ellie. "Is that right?"

Ellie opens her mouth, but Vanessa is already talking over her. "She thinks that when it comes to the opposite sex, her judgment is questionable at best, but I've got a good feeling about you."

The suggestive tone of her friend's voice has Ellie sputtering, "Are you serious right now? You want me to go out with him, but you're flirting with him right in front of me?"

Vanessa scoffs. "First of all, I already have a man, and second, if you think that's flirting, you're more out of practice than I thought." She turns to wink at me. "It was nice meeting you, cutie. Coffee's on the house."

"Okay, that was embarrassing," Ellie mumbles as her boss walks away.

"Nah," I say to make her feel better. "If she didn't care, she wouldn't tease you."

"I guess." She watches me take a sip of the coffee. "One cream, one sugar, right? Is it okay?"

"Yeah, much better than that crap we got on Friday from the gas station." I pause for a second, considering. "We had fun, didn't we?"

"Yeah, we should do it again sometime."

"We should. And it sounds like we should get on it since you'll be locking yourself away in a convent soon."

Pursing her lips into a thin line barely stifles her amusement. "A valid point. What did you have in mind?"

"I don't know. Maybe an adult movie for a change?"

She laughs and I like the way her whole countenance becomes happier. "An adult movie, Scott? Do you hear yourself? I don't know if we're at that point in our friendship yet."

"Ha, ha. I meant a movie that has more than a G rating. If I have to watch *Frozen* one more time, I'm going to hang myself."

"Oh, I loved *Frozen!*" she gushes. "It's not very often a heroine is named after me."

My mind draws a blank.

"Elsa?" she prompts. "Anna's sister?"

"Oh, right. Actually, I bet the girls would flip if I told them that I met a girl in real life whose name is Elsa. They never get tired of that movie . . . unfortunately."

"Poor you," she says, patting my hand with mock sympathy. "But you know what's even more unfortunate?

That there are no movies in my immediate future. Since I'm about to pay you back the money I owe you, I'm broke. At this point," she shoots me a wry look, "I'm all set for my vows of chastity *and* poverty."

I laugh. "Don't you have to be Catholic for them to let you in?"

She practically chokes on her coffee mid sip. "I think I'm offended. I'll have you know I went to a private Catholic school for my very formative elementary school years."

"What?" I tsk. "No way. I don't believe you."

"Pfft, would you like me to recite a few psalms as proof?"

My jaw hangs open for a moment. "You're telling me that you, Opal, used to be a Catholic school girl?" *Don't do it.* Don't imagine her in one of those skirts –

"Yeah, my mom was raised a hard core Catholic and so was I."

"Really? You go to *church*?"

Her lips twist. "I said I was raised as a Catholic, not that I am one. As soon as I was able to convince my mom to let me go to a regular school, I was out. Ninth grade was a new beginning for me."

Some of the pieces of her life start clicking together. "Ninth grade? When the Piper thing started?"

"Yeah. New school. New me. When I set my mind to something, I usually get it done."

"Like joining a convent?"

"Exactly. But that one's not quite set in stone yet, just under consideration."

We finish our coffees, talking in circles and making jokes. There's something about her that's so . . . charming, I guess. Her easy smiles, her laidback sense of humor, her self-confidence, they all pull me away from my usually tightly-wound self like a magnet.

"Okay, I gotta get back to work," I finally tell her as I stand. "Thanks for the coffee."

"No, thank you for the loan." She gets up and pulls the cash from her pocket, but I shake my head.

"I want you to hold on to it until you get paid, all right. I don't need it, and I don't think the sisterhood would approve of you robbing Peter to pay Paul."

"I didn't rob Vanessa, I got a loan."

"Well, pay *her* back then. I trust you not to pull a runner."

She hesitates until she finally decides to shove the money away. "Okay, thanks."

I'm not sure I like the way her soft tone burrows its way behind my sternum and takes up residence. "I'll see you Friday, okay?" I say quickly. We finally agreed that I still owe her and that I'd pay for the movie. "How do you feel about ribs?"

"No, no dinner," she says after a moment's hesitation. "I don't like being a free-loader."

"Please," I say with irony, "you're doing me a favor. Adult food *and* an adult movie? I don't remember the last time I did that kind of thing."

She wants to argue, but I cut her off. "I'll pick you up a bit later than last week."

Chapter Eight

Ellie

I'm left standing there with a stomach filled with butterflies. Dinner and a movie? Does it get more date-like than that? No, but obviously friends do that kind of thing too. Dinner and a movie can be platonic, I'm sure of it. I sit back down to finish my coffee, thinking that I may actually be getting the hang of this opposite sex, friend zone stuff. High five, Ellie Summers.

Now, if only he weren't so good-looking. Because, damn, spending time with him is a bit of a double-edged sword. Every teasing comment, every smirk, every flex of his arms further re-ignites my long-dormant sex drive. Even his hands, which are big and scratched up from his job, turn me on.

I know that doesn't mean I have to act on my impulses. Proving to myself that I can enjoy his company without complicating the situation with sex is good for me. Anyway, I'm sure sex would alter the laid-back vibe we've got going. And I don't want that. He's exactly the kind of friend I need, one who isn't interested in luring me into trouble. And he seems to like me. Me! Ellie. Ellie, who admits to playing Word Cookies, who's always sober, who loves Chipotle. Granted, he's not remotely attracted to her – but that's cool. I need my feet firmly under myself after being at sea for so long.

"Girl! That man is beautiful!" Vanessa flops down beside me.

"He is," I agree.

"He the reason you've been in such a good mood lately?"

"Probably, but don't get too excited. We're just friends."

"Uh huh."

Despite her sarcasm, I know I can do this.

The last class of my academic career starts on Thursday. I can't believe that all the requirements for my degrees are done with the exception of this one last Spanish lit class. Tentatively, I'm hoping to work in the public sector when I graduate; municipal or state government maybe. Social issues and policies are what get me going.

Before I went off the rails during my junior year, I spent a lot of my time volunteering for different political campaigns. I made a few contacts in those early years, but I'm worried that finding a real job won't be easy. There's no way I can keep paying out ninety percent of my salary in rent though. Something's got to give and graduation in June can't come soon enough.

After class, I work the late shift, so when Friday morning comes around and it's my day off, I'm grateful. I use my free time to get ahead on my reading list. At least I try to when I'm not thinking about Scott, wondering where we're going for dinner, pondering which movie we'll see, considering possible topics of conversation, ruminating over . . . yeah, it's possible I'm obsessing.

I don't hear from him until after 6:30 on Friday evening. Was I a bit worried? Maybe. Do I laugh at the text he finally sends me? Yes.

Scott: I'm out front.

Apparently, parking to pick a girl up at her door isn't part of the friend-zone package.

Ellie: Be right out.

I've kept things simple for tonight. My hair is down but I'm just wearing jeans, a T-shirt and black leather booties. On the way out the door, I grab my purse and my short black jacket. I feel good, I look decent. And I'm excited at the prospect of making conversation instead of being cooped up at home, entertaining myself.

He's double parked right in front of my building. My confidence wavers the teensiest bit when I see him. He obviously went home to shower and change. His hair is still wet and he's wearing dark jeans and a long sleeved Henley that molds just enough to his upper body to catch my eye.

"Hey," he says barely sparing me a second glance as he pulls out into traffic. "You ready?"

My confidence bounces back with his blasé attitude. This isn't him making an effort, it's just him being him. "Yeah, I'm ready. You still haven't told me where we're going though."

That gets me a quick grin that ups my heart rate. "We're going for ribs."

"You're a fan, I take it."

"Who isn't?"

"Well, as long as there's a vegetarian option on the menu, I'll be okay."

He shoots me an *oh shit* look. "You're a vegetarian?"

I laugh. "No, but I couldn't resist teasing you."

"Not cool, Opal, not cool."

"Sorry, but you didn't actually ask me."

He winces. "I didn't?"

"No, you didn't. But don't worry, when your inner caveman comes on too strong, I'll be sure to mention it."

He seems at a loss for words and I like it that I've flustered him a bit. It's endearing. Repressing my smile, I push past his sudden quiet by asking about his day at work, and he tells me about his newest employee/best friend's flagging interest in working a nine-to-five job.

The restaurant isn't far and has a definite family vibe. As we park, I wonder if it's his way of underlining our relationship status again. If it is, I'm not complaining. I could do with the reminder since following him through the parked cars, I can't tear my eyes away from his broad back that so nicely fills out the shirt he's wearing.

Inside, the waiting area is busy, but he's got a reservation. I almost want to groan. Why can't he be lame like most guys and not have any forethought? Without even knowing it, he's trying to edge his way past the friend-zone barriers I've got erected. This would be so much easier if he were less appealing.

We're seated in a booth near the back. I open my menu and am about to ask what's good when he says, "Before I forget, which movie do you want to see?"

"Whatever you want is fine. You're the one with the thing for adult movies."

He laughs. "Let's see, there's . . ." He comes around to my side of the booth, forcing me over on the bench seat, and damn, he smells like heaven; not cologne or anything, just human skin – very warm, very close, very male. With all the distraction, I'm not even sure which movie I'm agreeing to see.

He lowers his phone. "I already know what I'm going to get," he prompts, implying I should be staring at the menu instead of at him. Right!

While he's getting the tickets, I go over the menu. Clearly, he's been here before because he recommends a few things as I go.

Our waitress shows up wearing a straw cowboy hat and a red checked button down shirt tied at the waist. "Evening, y'all. Can I start you off with some drinks?" Even if she's playing a part, I like her right away.

"No, thanks," I say, but then amend with, "Well, maybe an iced tea, please."

"A Coke for me," Scott adds. "And we're ready to order."

We are?

He rattles off his choice and ends with a request for whatever extra spicy hot sauce they've got, and then turns to me expectantly.

Every good-natured caveman comment that I was going to tease him with disappears the instant our eyes meet. He's way too close to me. I wonder if he would agree to let me sit here all night and gaze dreamily at him while he whispers filthy dirty nothings into my ear.

"El?"

I swallow hard. "Yeah, I'll get this one," I say, pointing to the menu. Good thing, I'd mostly made up my mind before my brain turned to mush. Honestly, I'm expecting him to call me out on my gawping. Something along the lines of a cheese-filled *'like what you see?'* Instead, he doesn't appear to register my attraction to him at all.

Thank goodness.

"I don't mind if you have a drink," he says once our server is gone.

Finally, my brain comes back on-line. "Oh, no worries. I don't drink anymore." I smile at him wryly. "It's part of my self-improvement project. No Piper. No men. No alcohol."

His scrutiny goes on a bit too long for comfort. I'm practically squirming in my seat when he finally asks, "How long's it been since you've had a drink?"

My mind pinballs through all the ways I can avoid answering this question. I don't relish the prospect of admitting that alcohol is a problem for me to this man who seems to have his whole life figured out. But evasion would be a classic Piper move, one that Ellie doesn't make. I'm not interested in tailoring my responses to impress him. He can take me as I am, or not at all.

"It's been ten months," and then to make sure he knows I'm serious, I tack on, "and eleven days."

His eyebrows go up. "That's . . . that's impressive." Normally that kind of comment would irk me, but something about his tone tells me he's not being condescending. Something I confirm when he adds, "I wish my mom had that kind of will power."

Sympathy for both him and his mom floods my system. "Your mom drinks too much?"

His sigh is both angry and resigned. "She's on and off the wagon constantly."

We've only known each other for a couple of weeks and this feels really personal, so I'm really hoping my next words don't come across as trite or patronizing. "That must be hard, not being able to depend on a parent. They're the one person who should always have our backs."

The shadows that fall over his features tells me how close I've come to the truth. "Yeah," he agrees. "That's why I almost never touch the stuff. My daughter deserves better, and so do my niece and my sister."

There go my ovaries again, melting down to the soles of my feet.

His lips quirk at the sappy expression on my face. "Don't worry, El. You can put your tiny violin away. My grandmother has always been there for me, for all of her grandchildren."

Just then, the waitress comes back with our drinks.

"Well, I propose a toast," I say, picking up my glass once she's gone again.

"All right."

"To learning from the past, and keeping the future on the right path."

We clink glasses. "How did you get so wise, Opal?"

"Oh, you know, all that time I spend practicing my pole dancing routine allows for some seriously deep thoughts."

Around the glass, his lips curve into a smile. And then his gaze, which until this point has remained firmly above my neck, slowly slides down to rest briefly on my breasts before he sets his glass back down.

My brain screeches out: *Alert! Alert!* Okay, back to the serious conversation. "So your mom is the reason you take care of your niece and your sister as well as your daughter." I don't phrase it as a question, giving him nothing to refute. We're past that in my opinion. "Did you ever take your niece to get glasses?"

His reluctance to talk about the girls eases with the distracting question. "Yeah, I did. Turns out my sister needed them too. I don't know why she didn't say anything."

"Is she the sensitive type? She probably didn't want to be a burden, especially if there's already a lot going on at home."

He seems genuinely distressed by the idea. "I hope that's not what it is. Around our house, it's the squeaky wheel that gets the grease."

"It was the same in my house when I was growing up. I was such a pain in the ass at home that my younger sister always came across as the perfect angel."

A sudden grin comes over his handsome face. "Your sister, the people pleaser?"

Surprised, I take a moment to answer. "Yeah, you were paying attention to my rambling?"

His grin increases. "Your ramblings are full of interesting bits of information, Opal."

"Oh, really?" I laugh, though I'm incredibly pleased.

"For sure. Now tell me more about you and this angel of a sister of yours."

I groan. "Sophie has always been the ultimate good girl. I've never understood how she can agree so easily with everything my parents say. Even as a teenager, she was steady and dependable, everything that I wasn't."

"Weren't you supposed to be the older and wiser big sister?"

"Yeah, *supposed to be* is the key to that sentence. Luckily, she was always immune to my wild ways."

"The responsible type, then. She sounds like my kind of woman."

It takes everything I've got to keep myself in sync with his irreverent tone. "Yeah," I say breezily. "If she didn't have a long-time boyfriend, I'd introduce you." Because, fuck me, they'd be perfect together . . . something that appeals to me about as much as a returning to my former life. In fact, it makes me want to stab something with the nearest utensil.

He snorts. "Yeah, I'm sure your baby sister would be all over a guy who's got three kids to look after. I'm a total score."

Thankfully our food arrives, and I get some time to recover my equilibrium and then process the tail end of that conversation. He does come with three kids, doesn't he? Why hasn't that thought crossed my mind at all? *Uh, because you're just friends, Ellie. Get with the program.*

The rest of dinner is highly pleasant, wonderful even. We stay away from serious topics, joking around and enjoying each other's company. Afterwards, the movie is some blockbuster action monstrosity that barely holds my attention. I spend my time stealing peeks of Scott's profile while I munch on the Twizzlers he bought for me and ponder how sweet it is that he keeps his silenced phone in his hand so he won't miss any calls from home.

"That was awesome," he announces, when the credits are rolling. Though I'm more responding to his boyish enthusiasm than the movie, I agree wholeheartedly.

We shuffle along with the people in our row and then, when we hit the steps which are really crowded, he reaches back and takes my hand so we don't get separated. I don't know if it's because I've deprived myself of human touch for so long, or if he's got magic hands, but the energy that arcs between us sends my pulse soaring.

Emerging from the theatre into the bright lights of the Cineplex, he pulls up short and I almost crash into his back. He directs a vehement, hissing, "Shit," at his phone, which is lighting up. Towing me out of the flow of traffic, he lets go of my hand. "Sorry, I've got to take this." Turning his back on me, he takes a deep breath before he answers the call. *"¿Tío?"*

¿Tío? He speaks Spanish?

I'm unsure because Scott is mostly listening. What is clear, though, is that whatever's being said is not to his liking. He paces in the available space, tension rolling off of him in waves. When he does speak, near the end of the quick call, it's all in English. "Yeah, okay. Yeah, I know where it is." His eyes suddenly find mine. "I'm about fifteen, twenty minutes away." Pause. "Okay, yeah, bye."

Jamming his thumb down on the screen, he ends the call and then hangs his head, like the weight of the world is on his shoulders.

"Hey," I say hesitantly, "everything okay?"

"Fuck," he grinds out under his breath. When he finally looks up, there's strain written into every angle of his face. "Listen, I've got to run down to San Jose."

"Oh, okay." I blink at him. "Don't worry, I can, uh, take an Uber home." I pull out my phone and am launching the app, when he takes hold of my wrist to stop me.

"No, I don't feel good about sending you home by yourself this late."

His frustration is palpable and I don't want to add to it. "It's fine, Scott. Not a big deal."

He shakes his head. "It's not happening." Then almost like it pains him, he says, "Come with me. I'll have you back home in an hour, an hour and a half at the latest."

His tone rings with finality, as if I've already agreed. Huh. He really does have a caveman streak. Since it's clear that a flippant comment wouldn't be appreciated and I don't mind going with him, I keep my response short and simple. "Sure. I'm easy."

All I get is a tight nod as he re-takes my hand and heads for the parking lot. If I were shorter, I'd be hard-pressed to keep up with his long, purposeful strides.

He takes me to the passenger side and opens my door. I get in, but before he lets my hand go, he gives it a quick, reassuring squeeze. I watch him through the windshield as he goes around the front of the truck. Something definitely has him wound up.

It takes a full ten minutes before the silence gets to me. "You want to tell me what's going on before we get where we're going?"

"Not in the least."

Okay, then. I go back to staring out the passenger window.

"Sorry," he growls, the tightly controlled anger in his voice filling the cab of the truck. "I'm just so sick of this shit."

I wait for more, but it takes the passing of another minute before he breaks down and enlightens me.

"It's my mom," he finally admits miserably. "She's drunk off her ass and someone I know called me to come get her." He shakes his head. "Probably so the cops don't get involved."

Oh. I bite my lip, unsure of how to respond, but he saves me from having to come up with something by continuing on. "I shouldn't have to pick up my mother from some random bar on a Friday night, you know? You'd think someone else could do it for a change."

The slightly shocked, Nosy Parker in me loosens my tongue, "You've done this before?"

"Yeah," he bites out. "It's not the first time and I'm sure it won't be the last."

I watch his grip tighten around the steering wheel as I try to imagine myself in a similar situation. "I'm the last person anyone in my family would call if they needed help."

He shoots me an annoyed glance that clearly conveys *And your point is?*

"I don't know, maybe you could look at it as a compliment. Your family and friends know you as someone who cares."

Exasperated, he asks, "Are you saying you'd let your mom go to jail?"

"What? No! I don't know what I'm saying." I struggle to find the right words. "Just that it must be a nice feeling to know you're valued by the people around you."

Laughing bitterly, he retorts, "Or maybe the people around me get themselves into too many bullshit situations, and I'm the only one sucker enough to show up to bail them out."

Scott is forced to slow down as we arrive in the downtown core of San Jose where the streets are busy with the Friday night crowds.

"I guess," I say reluctantly, not at all convinced that it wouldn't be gratifying to have people in my life who thought I was worth something. But hey, I earned Piper's flaky reputation all on my own. The only way to shake it is to do better, to be better. Maybe Scott can teach me how it's done.

Chapter Nine

Scott

To the absolute depths of my soul, I'm sick of this shit. Getting the call from Alejandro who suggests I come to remove my mother from a situation described to me as *no bueno* was like taking a baseball bat to the gut.

As soon as I saw his name flashing on the screen of my phone, I knew it could only be very bad news. Though it hasn't always been that way. As my Tío Javier's best friend, Alejandro was at our house a lot while I was growing up. Javier and Alejandro used to carry me on their shoulders, hell, they used to toss me between them for fun. Both of my uncles, one by blood and one by adoption, were larger than life for a kid with no dad and an inattentive mother.

Sadly, after the drive-by, my grandmother didn't want Alejandro hanging around anymore. She didn't want me influenced by the world her murdered son had made his life in, a world of easy money and casual violence. And rightly so. Association with *Los Santos del Diablo* ultimately ends in one of only two ways, death or imprisonment.

Nowadays, Alejandro is the furthest thing from a man you want to get involved with. He's led *Los Santos* with an iron fist for the last five years; he's watchful, cunning, and deadly.

I haven't seen him in six months or so, not since the last time he called me to come get my mother from some dive bar up in Oakland. It was humiliating then, and even more so now because I have to do it in front of Ellie . . . Ellie, who tries to put a positive spin on everything. For all her self-confidence, she sure can be naïve. At least I appreciate her ability to roll with changing circumstances. She hasn't complained once.

It's busy tonight so I'm sure that parking is going to be a bitch, but I get lucky almost immediately when I catch sight of a couple getting into their car. After waiting impatiently for them to leave, I angrily accelerate into the parking spot and turn the truck off.

In the sudden muffled quiet, she says, "You want me to wait here?"

Her calm, unruffled attitude has my stress level coming down a few notches. Considering her offer, I check out our surroundings. There are plenty of people around, including a group of guys coming down the sidewalk. The same visceral rejection I had to the idea of sending her home by herself hits me again. *Not fucking happening.* She stays with me no matter how embarrassing this gets.

"No, we stick together."

Her eyebrows hitch up slightly with what I'm guessing is surprise. "Okay, lead the way."

After hiking a few blocks, we turn a corner and immediately I know we've found the right place. Down a side street, there are a couple of black Escalades illegally parked outside of a bar whose front doors are open. Light and music spill out onto the sidewalk where men mill around at even intervals. And by men, I mean *Saints*, and by mill, I mean patrol. *Jesus.* I reach for Ellie's hand. "Stay close, all right?"

I can see my mother and Alejandro sitting together on a bench out front, but as we approach, we're intercepted by a scary-ass dude with his gang tattoos clearly visible on his forearms. It takes a second, but I realize I know this guy. I haven't seen him in years though.

"I'm just here to get my mom, Niner," I say, lifting my chin to where she's sitting.

Niner takes me in from head to toe, suspicion blaring. I almost laugh as the suspicion turns to disbelief. "Scotty? *Puta madre,* when did you grow up?" Not giving me a chance to say anything, he turns to Alejandro. "*Ey, Jefe.* What the fuck, right?" He gestures to me. I've known Niner as long as I have Alejandro, which is to say, my entire life. He looks me up and down again, probably because I top him by a good five inches. *"¿Qué te da de comer la abuela, papi?"*

Scoffing, I don't bother telling him I'm sure what my grandmother is feeding me has nothing to do with my height.

"And who do we have here?" he then asks, making a show of perusing Ellie suggestively. My good humor vanishes and I'm about to tell Niner to remove his fucking old-man eyes from her when Alejandro intervenes.

"Ignore him, Scotty, and get over here."

He gets up to greet me, pulling me into a hug, forcing me to let go of Ellie's hand.

"How you been?"

I briefly scan my mother who ignores my presence by keeping her drooping gaze fixed on the double parked SUV. "Fine." It comes out sullenly. "You?"

He lifts a shoulder noncommittally. "You know how it is." He looks older than I remember. The grey in his full beard has spread and the lines around his eyes are more firmly etched.

"How's my goddaughter?" He means Daniela and my attitude softens.

"She's good," I say, wondering how much detail he's looking for. His curious expression has me adding more. "Finishing second grade soon. She's not a big fan of school work."

This has him flashing his teeth. "Takes after her old man. You got any pictures?"

"Yeah, sure." I pull out my phone, open the app, and hand it to him. While he's going through the pics, I make sure Ellie's okay. She's leaning against the side of the building a couple yards away. I give her a questioning look, and she answers with an encouraging nod to tell me she's fine.

Alejandro pulls my attention back. "This your daughter?" He shows me the screen.

"Yeah."

"She's growing up fast."

Despite the strain of the situation, I smile. "She is."

"And this?" He points to Carmen. "This Robbie's kid?"

My mood plummets. "Yeah," I say stonily. Robbie, or Roberto, is my mother's husband and Carmen and Mari's father. He's currently doing eight-to-fifteen for knocking over a liquor store with an assault rifle.

"You're a good man, Scotty," he says. "Taking on all this responsibility can't be easy." When he claps me on the back, I resist the urge to shove him away from me. None of this is his fault. In fact, Alejandro is one of the few people who helps me out from time to time. Occasionally, I'll find an envelope of cash on my windshield to help pay for anything Daniela needs. "I heard what you did for that no-good nephew of mine, too." He means Jorgie. "I want you to call me if you ever need anything, okay?"

When I don't nod, he adds, *"En serio.* You're probably the only guy I know who deserves good things in life." His eyes wander to Ellie and then he smirks at me. *"¿Quién es la chula?" Who's the girl?*

My entire body stiffens. *"Nadie importante,"* I bite out even if an unsettling note of dishonesty vibrates down my spine. I push the feeling away. She *isn't* important, not in the way he's suggesting. "It's late," I say, hoping to bring this to an end. *"Ma, ya vámonos."*

She turns a hazy expression on me as I reach for her hand to pull her up. I'm beyond grateful that it seems like she'll be able to walk on her own.

"Gracias, Tío," I say as we clasp hands and hug awkwardly because I need to keep a grip on my mother's elbow.

"De nada. Y Lilia," he says, addressing my mother. *"Si te veo con ese pendejo otra vez . . . ya sabes."*

I don't even want to know what asshole Alejandro caught her with or why he's bad news. After all the drama over the years, I couldn't be less interested in my mother's bad decisions.

We both ignore her when she drunkenly mutters something about the only asshole being Alejandro.

We shuffle toward Ellie, and I can't bring myself to look at her with all this shitty embarrassment running through my veins. She pushes off the wall to join us and I'm bracing myself for my mom's commentary, but she unexpectedly keeps her mouth shut. Ellie too, remains quiet as we make our way back to the truck. I have to catch my mother when she stumbles in her heels a few times, but other than that, she makes it under her own steam.

On the way home, the sleeping, or more probably passed-out, drunk seated between us makes conversation with Ellie impossible. The awkward atmosphere in the truck is thick and I hate that our new friendship might be affected by this twisted turn of events.

Dropping her off in front of her building isn't very pleasant either, though she's a good sport about everything.

"Thanks," she whispers over my mother's head, "for everything. I had a good time."

When I give her a sarcastic look, she smiles weakly, suddenly hesitant. "Okay, well, bye."

I know I should get out and talk to her, tell her that I had a good time too, thank her for making me laugh and going to the movies with me, but I can't muster the energy. I'm just so fucking tired. I swear, someday soon, something's gotta give.

Chapter Ten

Ellie

The little niggle of melancholy with which I begin the week, really starts to weigh on me by the end of it. Ostensibly, I tell myself it's because my period makes an appearance, but by Friday it becomes more and more obvious that Scott is at the heart of the matter. It's stupid, really. I don't even know how it happened, but somehow, somewhere along the line, I started to expect things from him, things that failed to materialize since I haven't heard a peep out of him all week.

Sure, maybe I could have reached out to him . . . but those two little words have been looming darkly in the back of my mind. Two little words I wasn't meant to understand, but ones he uttered with so much conviction.

Nadie importante.

I've done my best to be objective about it. I *am* no one important to him. I've only technically known him for three weeks. So what if we've hung out a few times? And shared a few laughs? That doesn't make us BFF's. It makes us acquaintances.

So why does it hurt? If he was just some guy, I'd cut him loose in a heartbeat. The last thing I need is another person in my life who views me as disposable or convenient. But Scott isn't some guy. He's my stranger, my knight in shining armor. I *know* he's a good person. Just maybe not good for me?

I sigh.

Pulling off my ball cap, I turn my face up into the late afternoon sun. After spending my day off with the walls of my apartment pressing in on me, I came to find some peace of mind at my favorite spot by the water. Unfortunately, sitting on my bench watching the joggers and the bicyclists go by on the San Francisco Bay Trail, and the planes coming in for a landing at SFO over the water, isn't quite as soothing as it usually is.

Beside me, my phone vibrates on the wooden slats of the bench. I check the screen and my stomach lurches at the sight of Scott's name. Damnit. There will be no butterflies – none. I forbid it.

It's 6:15. Around the same time he picked me up last week.

Scott: U feel like doing something?

Very last minute. Very casual, very acquaintance-like. Very *no one important*.

Ellie: I'm not at home.

Childishly, I like that I'm not sitting around waiting for him . . . but then the thought of not seeing him fills me with nothing but regret. The conflicting emotions only serve to annoy me. I hate it when I'm pathetic.

It's quite possible I'm being overly dramatic. Scott doesn't owe me anything. He's happy to be casual friends. Managing my expectations isn't his job, it's mine. If I boil it all down, my life is a lot less empty with him in it. I like his company. Shouldn't I be adult enough to accept that without needing more?

My ringtone sounds and I frown. It's Scott. *Calling me?*
"Hello?"

"Opal. Are you ditching me on a Friday night?" His tone is playful, and unexpected.

"Uh . . . sorry? I guess I didn't get the memo about us having plans."

"Yeah, I know. I should have asked you earlier. Busy week," he explains sheepishly. "So you're not home?"

There's disappointment in his voice, perplexing disappointment that has me thinking I missed something somewhere. "No, I'm up by Coyote Point."

"Coyote Point?" He pauses. "What are you doing up there?"

"Uh . . ." Apparently, I'm very articulate today. "Just watching the planes come in over the bay."

He's quiet for a second too long, then asks, "By yourself?"

"Yep." Who cares if I sound lame? We're only acquaintances.

"You want some company?"

"I, ah, guess. You sure you want to drive up here?" I ask doubtfully, thinking traffic would be awful at this time of day.

"I don't have anything else going on."

And there it is. What an ass.

But then he adds, "And if that's where you are, that's where I want to be."

A small moment of silence hangs between us while I grapple with my surprise.

"You eaten yet?" he goes on casually, like he hasn't pulled the rug out from under me.

"Oh, no, I haven't."

"Okay, where are you exactly?"

I give him directions, explaining that I'm not actually in the Coyote Point Park – I can't afford the parking fee – but near a smaller public park that's closer to home. "I'm right at the end of the street at the water."

"Sounds easy enough. See you in twenty."

He hangs up before I can say anything else, and I'm left staring down at my phone, nonplussed. A warm, tingly sensation seeps into my bones, making it very difficult to be stern with myself. But I've got to at least try. While I wait for him, I go over the changes I'm going to have to make to keep my friendship with Scott on an even footing. No more expectations. I need to stay cool and keep myself as uninvested as he is. Slipping out of the friend zone and into unrequited love territory would be destructive on so many levels, not to mention pitiful.

He shows up a half an hour later with his hands full, one carrying a bag of Chipotle takeout, and the other with a tray holding two Starbucks cups.

I drink in every single inch of him. He got a haircut sometime this week, and he's wearing a thin blue pullover that stretches nicely across his chest. *Why do I have to be attracted to him?*

"Hey," he says, setting everything down between us. "Nice spot."

"Yeah. You didn't have to bring all this."

"Well, I'm starving and I thought it would be rude to eat in front of you." He digs in the bag for his burrito, expertly ripping the foil from the top half, then he pulls out a half-full bottle of hot sauce.

I laugh. "Did you steal that from the restaurant?"

"No," he scoffs good-naturedly. "If there's any left when I'm done, I'll return it."

"Uh huh. Sure you will." Damn, I love the teasing rhythm that we so easily fall into when we're together. I pull my coffee from the tray and take a sip. "Thanks," I practically moan. "This is exactly what I needed."

"No problem." He looks around with interest and before he takes another bite, he asks, "You come here often?"

Holding back a burst of laughter, I adopt a breathy tone. "No, it's my first time."

He stops chewing and his head jerks around, showing me his slightly confused, slightly taken aback visage. The laughter finally bubbles from my lips as I watch understanding come over him. "All right," he says, his eyes narrowing. "I walked right into that one."

"You did. Does that line usually work for you, Scott? I had no idea you had so much game."

"Ha, ha, Opal. But you didn't actually answer my question."

I shrug, still chuckling. "I come here when I'm feeling blah, but you've come bearing some of my favorite things and some stellar pick-up lines, so I've upgraded my mood from *blah* to *eh*."

He gives me an exasperated expression. "Glad I could be of service."

From there on, it only gets better. We chat, we tease, and it's so effortless, the absolute high point of my week, hands down. It's not until the sun is going down an hour later that the mood between us shifts.

"Are we going to talk about last week?" I ask, wishing I could be satisfied with easy and superficial when I'm with him. But something I don't want to examine pushes me to ask for more.

Throwing me a wary glance, he asks, "What about it?"

"You got home okay?"

"Yeah, fine."

I nod. "And should I be concerned that you're on a first name basis with men who are . . ." I search my mind for the right adjective.

"Who are dangerous?" he finishes.

"Yes, that."

"I don't hang out with them if that's what you're asking," he says defensively.

"I'm not judging you, Scott. I was only curious. I'm the last person who would want to be judged by the people I know."

Geez, he's touchy.

His shoulders relax by a degree or two . . . and draw my attention. He's so broad and lean and I have the insane urge to strip him bare and get a good look at those tense shoulders and maybe let my fingers trace along their slope to the soft hair at his nape. *Do friends ever get to see each other naked? And didn't I just set myself some boundaries?*

It dawns on me that neither of us has said anything for too long. My eyes jerk to his in alarm, but I don't find them mocking me. I find them zeroed in on my lips. Unconsciously, I wet them and then in panic, I blurt, "How's your mom?"

And he's back to tense, but at least he's not staring at my mouth anymore. "She's fine," he grits out. He must realize how hard his tone was, because his voice softens with his next words. "I mean, I guess she's fine. She's still going to work, so that's something."

"Have you . . ." I really hope I'm not overstepping here, "Have you tried to get her some help?"

He sighs. "Yeah, of course I have, but I can't make her go to the meetings."

I hum my agreement.

"Do you go to meetings?" he asks as if it's just occurred to him.

I shake my head. "No, my problem isn't exactly with alcohol." *At least not after the initial detoxing,* I think to myself wryly. "My problem is more about the shitty decisions I make while under its influence. The alcohol itself, I could take or leave."

The skepticism on his face has me plowing forward, "As long as I keep myself away from situations where people are drinking, I'm fine. It's the fun and the socializing that I miss."

He looks out over the water, seeming to digest the efficacy of my explanation.

"If you want," I tell him with a fragile smile when he turns back to me. "You can tell your mom the best advice I've ever gotten on the subject."

His eyebrows lift in question.

"My dad once told me that one behaviour has to be replaced with another, that if you try to cut a section of your life away without filling the void with something constructive, you'll fail. And so far, that's been working for me."

"Oh yeah?"

"Yeah, since I was forced to give up my friends, I've tried to stay busy. I've been running almost every day, and I work as many shifts as I can fit into my schedule, and," I give him a self-deprecating grin, "my grades at school have never been better."

"You make it sound so easy."

The smile slips from my face. "Easy?" Of all the adjectives I'd use to describe the last ten months of my life, *easy* is not one of them – not even close. Painful, lonely, demanding, anxiety-ridden. Fuck *easy*.

"Your dad sounds like a pretty smart guy," he muses, not noticing my discontent.

My ire retreats slightly at his faraway look. "Yeah, my dad's great." I want to forget the whole *easy* comment and the bitter taste it's left in my mouth, so I push the conversation further forward into new territory. "How about your dad?"

His sudden, bitter laugh catches me off guard. "My dad? I don't have one. Well, I'm sure I have a sperm donor somewhere, but I don't know anything about him."

I blink up into the anger on his face. "Oh." I try to process that in the context of my life and fail. Without my dad, I'd probably be living in a ditch somewhere. "I'm sorry." It comes out almost as a question.

"Don't be. My grandmother's always said it's for the best. If he'd been around, he might have made me into a different kind of man." Our eyes meet and I can clearly see he's not as convinced as he's letting on. "Not that I'm a saint or anything, but what kind of a guy sticks his dick into an eighteen year old girl without a condom and then disappears." He shakes his head with disgust. "All my mom knew about him was his name, the one she gave to me."

After a moment of hesitation, I push his shoulder playfully, hoping to lighten his quickly darkening mood. "That explains the big mystery. Your mom is straight-up Latina, and you . . . are not."

"You think?" he huffs. "My whole life, I've stuck out like a sore thumb. I've always been too tall, too blond, too white."

My brows quirk. "I . . . yeah, okay, I don't think I've ever heard that sentence before."

"Do I sound like a whiny bitch, or what?" he says with irony. "I guess, I just wish I could have blended in with my family and friends a bit more when I was growing up."

"And now? Have you finally out-grown your awkward phase?"

"Opal, are you mocking my childhood trauma?"

"Possibly. But I seem to recall very little empathy for my poor little Catholic school girl routine. Anyway, you should be looking at it like you're getting the best of both worlds. Not something to be crying over."

"You and your optimism are pretty annoying, you know that?"

I give him an exaggerated smile and he rewards me with a chuckle as he concedes my point. "Fine. Being seen as white certainly hasn't hurt me at work anyway."

Surprised again, I can't help but tease him some more. "Have you been trading on your looks, Scott? You're not sleeping with your boss to advance your career, are you?"

"What? No!" It takes only a few seconds for his indignation to fade and his voice to take on a dry tone. "I don't think I'm Dean's type anyway."

"But you think Dean's been doing you favors because of the color of your skin?"

"No. Yeah. No, I don't know. I mean, yeah, I'm good at my job, but . . ."

He looks . . . vulnerable, not to mention uncomfortable with the turn this conversation has taken, so I back away from the joking around. "If you want my two cents, I think appearances can only take a person so far. You must be doing something right."

"I guess." He pushes out a breath and leans forward to rest his elbows on his knees, hanging his head. "I've never told anyone before," he confesses. "That maybe I don't deserve the job I have."

"Well, if you put half as much effort into your job as you do your family, I think this Dean guy's getting a pretty good deal."

He glances up and I can't believe the mix of hope and uncertainty in his expression. "You think?"

I nod. "Unless you've been screwing up?"

He shakes his head. "Not lately."

"Lipping off to clients?"

He laughs. "No."

"Harassing other employees?"

Having caught on to my game, he rolls his eyes, but he's unable to repress a smile. "Well, when you put it like that . . . thanks for the vote of confidence."

Secretly thrilled he seems to value my input, I just waggle my eyebrows at him. "Sister Opal knows what she's talking about."

"Sister Opal," he says, shaking his head with amusement. "I still can't believe you went to Catholic school."

"Yeah, I don't recommend it if you're not into guilt trips. Your girls don't go to Catholic school, do they?"

"God, no. It's bad enough that I have to keep my attitude positive about church on Sundays out of respect for my grandmother."

I bite my lip, holding back a snicker at the idea of Scott sitting in a pew. "You go to church?"

He groans. "I do. Even though it's torture. But I don't want to ruin it for the girls. They look forward to Sunday school and stuff. Plus, they've got choir practice on Friday nights, which lets me be here with you while you dispense your wisdom and stuff."

"Flatterer," I accuse. "Come on, it's time to show me some pictures of these kids of yours."

For a long moment, I watch the indecision on his face war with the desire to show them off.

"Fine," I pout. "No pictures. I totally get wanting to protect them from weirdos that you meet under questionable circumstances. You're a ridiculously good father."

"Now who's the flatterer?" he says as he unfolds his long body so he can get his phone out of his pocket.

I clap giddily as he moves closer to me and shows me the first picture. It's of three little girls with their thin arms around each other, their huge, happy smiles gapped at random intervals with missing teeth. "Oh," pops from my mouth in surprise. I don't know what I was expecting, but their joy is so overwhelming. I tear my gaze away to see how he's caught up in what's on the screen, his features alive with pride.

"That's my daughter, Rosa," he says pointing to the girl on the left.

"She's beautiful, Scott," I say breathlessly because she really is. Her skin is a shade darker than his, as are her eyes, but she's unmistakably a part of him. Her cheekbones, her nose. "She looks just like you."

"You think so?" He's definitely pleased.

"I do." I turn back to the screen. "Who's in the middle?"

"That's Daniela," he says just as fondly. "She's always in the middle. She's got her cousins wrapped around her little finger, always getting them into trouble."

"I can see the mischief written all over her." Daniela has more delicate features than the other two with slightly upturned almond shaped eyes. "Is she your niece?"

"Yeah."

"Your sister's daughter?"

He looks surprised, then incensed. "My oldest sister is seventeen, El."

"Well, that's biologically impossible," I joke, and then, not even knowing that I should respect his privacy can smother my burning curiosity. "Can I ask whose daughter she is?"

Though he seems reluctant, he answers me. "She's my uncle's daughter. He and his girlfriend were killed a few months after she was born. She's always lived with us."

"Oh. I'm so sorry," I say lamely, now feeling guilty. "That's terrible."

"Yep."

"Well, going by this picture, I'd say she's a very happy and well-adjusted kid."

He chuckles. "Yeah, well-adjusted is one way of putting it. She's definitely not shy."

"I bet you'll have your hands full when she gets to high school."

He rubs a palm over his face with a sigh. "Believe me, the thought has crossed my mind. I don't know what I'm going to do."

"Perhaps you could invest in a shotgun?" I suggest blithely, making him laugh. When he can't stop, I tell him, "I'm serious, Scott."

He pulls me close to rest his cheek against the top of my head briefly as his laughter dies down. "I know you are, Opal."

Leaving my head against the warmth of his shoulder, I say, "So this must be your little sister. Carmen, right?"

"Yeah." Her more obviously Latin features give her an exotic look that reminds me a lot of Scott's mom. "I worry about her sometimes," he says. "She's so quiet."

"Maybe she's just growing into her personality. Does her dad live with you guys?"

He snorts derisively. "No, that fucker's in prison where he belongs."

My surprise quickly morphs into even more respect for the man beside me. The responsibility he's taken on is staggering. It's a wonder he's not crushed by it all. "Maybe that's why she's so quiet, because she's not sure how she fits in. She still has parents, they're just absent, whereas Daniela's are gone forever."

His deep exhale shifts us more comfortably together. "Yeah, probably."

I swipe to the next picture, hoping he won't shut down my snooping. It's a picture of the four of them together, the three girls climbing over him as he sits on a sofa covered in the ugliest floral pattern I've ever seen. It's a candid shot that again, captures so much joy. I ooh and ahh, all the while trying to keep my emotions buried, because if I'm honest, the way he loves these girls has my heart desperate to overflow with . . . tenderness, I think. Or maybe it's affection. Or maybe, more worryingly, it may be longing.

We sit there, going through his pictures, one by one, while he tells me stories about his family, of growing up, taking care of his sister, Desiree, of his Mom's ups and downs with alcohol, of his love for his grandmother. I even see a picture of Scott with Rosa and her mother on Rosa's first day of kindergarten. I do my absolute best not to stare at it for too long, at how his ex could not be more different from me with her diminutive frame and short black hair. She looks so young, much younger than Scott, and I suddenly wonder how old *he* is. I always assumed he was older than I am. Before the idea can take root, I swipe to the next picture.

It's late when we agree that it's time to go. My butt is sore from sitting on this bench for hours and as soon as I move away from his body heat, I'm cold. In the dark, we gather up all our garbage and head back toward the glow of the street lights. We come to my car parked on the street first.

"Thanks for dinner, *again*. Maybe next week you'll let me cook for you." I imply that it's a given that we'll see each other next Friday night, but I hold my breath while I wait for him to reply. Something has definitely shifted between us tonight, something that makes me both elated and wary. And I know he feels it too. I'm just not sure how he's going to react to the change.

"Uh, actually, next week, I've got this thing."

The swoop of dismay in my belly feels like freefalling from the heights of a cliff. "Oh, okay," I say easily, holding myself together by little more than a thread. *I'm so stupid.* My Jetta's old door groans a bit as I get it open and slide behind the wheel.

He grabs hold of the door before I can pull it closed. "Next Friday is the girls' choir performance at the community center."

His explanation loosens the pressure around my lungs somewhat. *He isn't blowing me off.* And now his expression as he towers over me is expectant, but I'm not sure what he wants me to say. "Maybe on Saturday instead?" he suggests.

Is that hope in his voice? Because my throat is suspiciously tight. I manage a whispered, "Okay."

"I'll text you."

My head bobs in a loose nod. "Okay."

He pushes the door shut and I start the car. When I look up again, his hand is trailing off the glass of the driver's side window.

Chapter Eleven

Scott

This week I remember to text her . . . not that I forgot last week. No, last week, I *couldn't* forget her – that was the problem. The way my thoughts had been so filled with her had set my teeth on edge. Since when do I obsess about any woman, let alone a woman who's the very opposite of the one I imagine I'll eventually end up with? I'm going to need a Latina who'll understand my family life when all is said and done. And Ellie is so far from that girl it's not even funny.

So, I thought I'd skip a Friday with her just to prove to myself that I could.

Then Friday afternoon had rolled around and, after a long and stressful week, the thought of not seeing her was physically painful, as if she was the only one who could break the choke-hold life had on me. When we're together, that smile of hers somehow eases all the pressure I'm under. The pressure's not gone exactly, but it becomes manageable enough that I can fill my lungs with a few much-needed, unrestricted breaths.

And all this was before we spent what should have been a simple evening together sitting on a bench. Now that low-level buzz of attraction that's always been there between us has amped up to unnerving levels. So much so that I'd had an incredibly hard time keeping my mind out of the smut gutter that night.

I can't deny that things between us have changed. I shouldn't only be *unnerved*, I should be *scared shitless*.

But I want her.

God, do I want her.

There's nothing wrong with that, right?

Because now on Saturday, I'll be at her place. I'm thinking it's a recipe for disaster . . . but a disaster that I want with my entire soul.

But first I have to make it through *this* week, and as usual, it's full of bullshit. My mom and Desiree fight constantly, Daniela's teacher wants a meeting to discuss her behaviour on the playground, Jorgie continues to be a pain in my ass at work, and worst of all, Lolita doesn't show up for her weekly Wednesday outing with our daughter. When I call her to find out what's going on, she gives me some lame excuse about seeing Rosa at the choir performance on Friday, so she didn't think it was such a big deal to miss one Wednesday. Poor Rosa. She tries to put on a brave face, but I see how her mother's actions hurt her. Thankfully, the excitement surrounding the performance provides a welcome distraction.

A couple of years ago, Father Martín suggested the choir group for the girls, and it's worked out really well – for all of us. It's something the girls can do together, there's no cost, the girls and my grandmother love it, and I get to go out with my friends without feeling guilty. Tonight is the final performance of the season. Because there are four groups performing, it will be held at the community center, instead of the church where there's less space.

When I get home from work on Friday evening, we eat dinner quickly, then I sneak in a quick shower and climb into a fitted blue dress shirt and my black dress pants.

When I come out of the bathroom, no one is around. *"¡Ya vámonos, señoritas!"* I call.

Rosa comes out of her room in her fanciest dress, the purple one that ties with a bow in the back. *"Mira, Papá. Daniela fixed my hair."*

I hold back my snicker when I see the sloppy ponytail Daniela has managed to wrangle Rosa's hair into, complete with randomly placed bow clips.

"Wow, *qué guapa.*" I tell her how beautiful she looks with a barely straight face. "But maybe your aunt can get it a little straighter. ¡Tía Mari!" I yell. "A little help, please."

Mari is not as diplomatic and laughs outright when she sees her niece. "Bring me the brush, Rosie, and we'll get you fixed up."

My sweet daughter's face lights up and she rushes off to get a brush from her room, and comes back with her 'sisters', all of whom are dressed to the nines and have their hair in varying states of what can only be described as chaos.

"Tía Mari? Can you do my hair too?" asks Daniela and then Carmen also pipes in with the same request. Despite living in a house full of women, there's no one really who takes the time to do things like this for them. I'm grateful to Mari for being a good sport about it.

While that's being taken care of, I go in search of my grandmother. I find her sitting on her bed. *"¿Estás bien, Abuela?"* Are you okay?

"Sí, mijo, nada más cansada."

I try not to worry about her, but she's been *tired* a lot lately. When she gets up, I compliment the pearls that my grandfather got for her so many years ago, and she gives me a genuine smile.

By the time I get the three girls, with their now perfectly smooth ponytails, into their booster seats in the truck and my grandmother and sister into the front, we're not quite late, but we're not going to be early enough to get decent seats either. I don't let it bother me. Over the years, I've learned to let the little things go. Being on time is an achievement in itself.

The girls race ahead with Mari to see if they can snag us some seats, while I hang back to escort my grandmother, who hangs onto my arm with surprising strength. "Mijo," she begins. "When are you going to find a woman to settle down with?"

I snort out a surprised laugh. "Don't you think I already have enough on my plate, Abuela? Adding more would only tip everything over."

She frowns at me. "Why would you say that? A good wife would ease your burdens, not add to them."

A wife? Jesus.

Clearing her throat, she goes on, "Araceli Trujillo has a granddaughter who thinks you're very handsome."

Almost choking on my tongue, I don't even attempt to sort through all the *señoras* that my grandmother knows to deduce who the granddaughter is. "Thanks, Abuela, but I'm good. Please don't even think of . . ." My mind tries to churn up something equivalent to *setting me up on a date* in Spanish, but I come up short.

Patting my arm, she takes pity on me, apparently understanding my meaning. "Okay, okay."

Inside the gymnasium, I'm thrilled to find my mother and Desiree already sitting with Mari, saving seats for us, decent ones. "Where're the girls?" I ask Mari.

"Backstage with their instructor."

"You made sure?"

She rolls her eyes like only a fifteen year old can. "Yes, Scotty. I made sure."

I spend the next few minutes giving and receiving a million greetings to people we know from the community until my grandmother presents me to Señora Trujillo and her granddaughter, Jessica. I give my grandmother an accusatory look but she just smiles blithely. Despite being introduced in Spanish, Señora Trujillo greets me in broken English. I'm only mildly offended she assumes that my Spanish is crap because it happens all the time.

Once they deem us suitably acquainted, the grandmothers turn to give us some privacy, and Jessica, who's yet to say a word, clears her throat. "Sorry," she says, shifting self-consciously on her sky-high heels. "This kind of thing is always so awkward, isn't it?"

"Yeah, that's one word for it," I say wearily. I don't want to be rude to her, but I can already tell this is going to be painful. "So, uh, what do you do?" I ask and then almost cringe. I'd literally be grimacing if the thought of Ellie mocking *my game* wasn't keeping me in check.

But Jessica doesn't seem to notice. "I'm taking a course to be a dental assistant."

"Oh, yeah. How's that going?"

"It's okay. My mom kind of pressured me into it, but yeah, it's fine."

Her mom? How old is this girl?

"How about you?" she tacks on.

I give her some standard answers, then the conversation works its way around to why we're here tonight and she tells me about her little sister.

All the while we're talking, I wonder why there's no spark between us. She's pretty and she's got curves in all the right places . . . but . . . but what? If I were looking for someone, isn't she exactly what I've always wanted? The comment I made to Ellie the other night about being *too tall, too blond, too white* pops into my head, and I realize that I'm measuring this poor woman in the same way because I've decided she's too short, her hair is too dark, and she's not at all pasty like Opal. In fact, I almost laugh out loud at how I'm sure Ellie would get a kick out of it if I called her *pasty* to her face.

"Listen," I say when there's a lull in the conversation. "My grandmother doesn't know this, but I'm kind of seeing someone." Which isn't exactly true. Ellie and I aren't seeing each other, but what I'm doing right now just feels wrong.

Jessica nods, her lips twisting guiltily as she leans in a bit. "Don't say anything, but me too. It's hard to say no to them, right?"

Turning to our grandmothers who are pretending not to watch us, we both chuckle.

"Well, it was nice meeting you," she says.

"Yeah, same here."

As she's leaving, Jorgie approaches. "Who was that?" he asks, giving her an appreciative and almost invasive once over.

"My new wife, apparently."

His heads snaps back in my direction and I laugh, earning me a squinty glare. "What are you doing here?" I ask. "Don't I see enough of you at work?"

He groans loudly. "I've got a nephew here somewhere," he waves a hand vaguely toward the stage, "and since the thing with the cops, my mom's been sticking to me like she's my damn shadow."

"And that's my problem how?"

"No seas cabrón, Scotty. I'm dying here. If I have to listen to one more person comment on the weather, I'm going to off myself."

Okay, so I have to laugh.

"You coming out with us later?" he asks.

"No, I promised the girls we'd go for ice cream to celebrate."

"You're so lame. How long's that going to take? An hour?" And then as if he just remembered something, he whacks the back of his hand against my chest. "And what's with blowing Juanita off last weekend?"

"I didn't blow her off," I say like he's stupid. "I was busy."

"Too busy for a booty call? Don't bullshit me. Were you out with that Opal chick?"

"No," I lie. "You know where I was?" I throw a quick glance over at my mother before I tell him the story about having to pick her up, without mentioning a word about Ellie, of course. Even if this didn't happen last weekend like I'm implying, it's the perfect thing to divert Jorgie's attention.

"That's some messed up shit right there, Scotty. You know, I see you every day at work and you're only telling me this story now? I'm hurt, man. So hurt."

I scoff. "Gotta say, on the long list of my priorities, your feelings come in somewhere near the very bottom, Jorgie."

"I get no respect," he mutters, and then the lights flash, announcing the beginning of the concert. As the crowd settles in, Jorgie manages to get the seat next to me, waving to his mother across the room to let her know he's still around.

Not surprisingly, watching other people's kids sing is boring as shit and the first place my mind wanders is to an image of Ellie. Supposedly she's going to cook dinner for us tomorrow night. Grinning to myself, I wonder if she knows what's she's doing or if it'll be a debacle. And damn, I know she told me that she switched her shifts, working tonight instead of tomorrow, but why didn't I tell her I'd see her later when she got off. Why do I have to wait for tomorrow?

Finally, the girls' group takes the stage and I get my phone out to record them. They're so poised up there and I couldn't be prouder as they sing their hearts out. Halfway through, there's a bit of a commotion at the back of the gymnasium, but I stay focused on what matters. It gets louder and murmurs begin to ripple through the crowd.

"Oh, shit," Jorgie whispers beside me. "It's Lolita."

"What?" I hiss back even though I heard him. I just refuse to believe it.

Checking over my shoulder, I can't see much in the dim light, but then I hear her voice loud and clear. "I'm allowed to be here!"

Multiple sssshhhhhh's ring out from the crowd.

"Don't shush me!" she yells. "I got as much right to be here as you!"

The performers on stage start to waver, unsure if they're supposed to continue.

Motherfucker! Nudging Jorgie in the side with my elbow, I hand him my phone to keep filming and then I duck along the row, dodging knees and feet to get to the aisle.

"Get your hands off me!"

Near the back door, I see her, trying to avoid some guy who's trying to corral her out of the room.

"Lolis," I hiss. "What are you doing?"

She falters when she sees the anger on my face, so at least she lowers her voice from a shout to a regular speaking volume. It's still way too loud. "Scotty, he says I can't stay."

The guy gladly washes his hands of the situation and leaves her with me. "Let's go," I whisper tightly, jerking my head at the door.

"But she's up there! I love you, Rosa!" she yells, and again, the performers falter.

"Lower. Your. Voice." I'm about to lose it, but instead, I pull in a deep breath and gesture to the door. "Let's. Go."

For a split second, I see the indecision on her face. This could go either way. Thank goodness for small mercies when she turns and slinks through the door. In the hall, I scan over her in the light. Her pupils are blown wide open. She's high as a kite. Since it's impossible to talk to her when she's like this, I focus on how to get her home.

"How'd you get here?" I demand.

She doesn't like the tone of my voice. "What do you care?"

My anger boils over. "Are you kidding me, right now? You just humiliated our daughter in front of all those people."

Down the corridor, a woman trying to soothe a baby, shushes us, so I take Lolita's arm and pull her toward the main entrance. Once we're outside, I ask her again. "Who brought you? Is someone picking you up?"

"Don't pretend to care about me, Scotty."

She really doesn't get it. I'm missing my kid's performance for this. And I don't have a way to contact anyone because my cell is with Jorgie. "Where's your phone?"

Her blank stare irritates me to no end. "Where's your phone, Lolis?"

She finally pulls it out of the back pocket of her jeans and hands it to me. I pull up her mother's number and dial. It's a good thing she answers, because I'm at the end of my rope.

"Sol? Habla Scotty."

I get the story out in brutally concise sentences and insist her mother get someone down here to pick Lolita up. She agrees and then I'm forced to wait with her for the fifteen minutes it takes for her brother to arrive. I want to scold, I want to lecture, I want to vent every bit of twisted frustration I'm feeling right now. But it wouldn't do any good. Not when she's like this.

Once I see her brother's car enter the parking lot, I head back inside. The lights are on and the crowd is gathering up their things. I find my family waiting near our seats, but I don't get a chance to say anything before the girls come running and hurl themselves at me. Kneeling down, I manage to get all three into my arms for a group hug.

"You guys were so great up there," I tell them quietly.

"Yeah?" Daniela asks, sounding hopeful.

"You bet. The best of the night."

Despite their smiles, all three of them seem unsure, dashing my hopes that they didn't realize who was causing the disturbance. "Is Mom okay?" Rosa whispers as the others are swept up in my family's congratulations.

I stand with her in my arms and tuck her head against my shoulder. "I think so, *calabacita*." My pet name for her gets a giggle. *Little pumpkin* may be an endearment in English, but it sounds ridiculous in Spanish, which is why we like it.

Jorgie claps me on the shoulder and then hands me my phone. "See you later tonight?"

I give him a withering look.

He shrugs. "Didn't think so. See you Monday, boss."

Moving closer to my family, I ask with as much enthusiasm as I can, "So, who wants ice cream?"

Obviously, children have the ability to bounce back much more quickly than adults do, especially when ice cream is involved. The girls pick out their toppings with all the eagerness one would expect. While on the other hand, as adults, the rest of us have mostly fake smiles plastered on our faces. For the girls' sake, my sisters, mother and grandmother and I all keep quiet about what happened even though we all want to take shots my ex.

We don't get home until after ten, so we skip bath time and I get the girls directly to bed. As I tuck them in one by one, I feel like shit because at the very least, I should be talking to them about what happened tonight. But I just can't do it. Not tonight anyway.

In the kitchen, I find my grandmother drinking a solitary cup of tea. My mood further flags. "I know I said I wouldn't go out," I start. "But . . ."

"Go, mijo. Know that we're safe here"

I quickly bus a kiss on her cheek. "Thanks."

I sit in my truck for a few minutes, struggling to accept where I long to be. Logically, it's not the right decision, but emotionally, she's all I want. I need her to curb this horrible helplessness I'm feeling, to smooth my fraying edges before I unravel completely.

The drive is a quick one. Within minutes, I'm catching the front door of her building as someone is leaving, and then I'm standing in the hall, staring at the number on her door. Before I have a chance to reconsider, I knock.

The sound of the chain rattling sets my nerves further on edge, but when she opens the door, I drink down the sight of her. With her hair up in a messy bun, one satin-smooth shoulder exposed by the loose neck of an old T-shirt, and her endlessly long legs bare but for a pair of short cotton shorts, she takes my fucking breath away.

"Scott?" she says, her brow creasing with concern. "What's wrong?"

Comfort, elation, lust, all swirl together in my gut, leaving me mute.

She steps back to let me in and as she closes the door, our bodies rotate until I've got her backed up against the door.

"What happened?" she whispers, searching my face for the answers I'm not giving her.

Her wide eyes and slightly parted lips that are illuminated only by the low light coming from the kitchen, draw me closer. Between us, the air starts to crackle with the pent-up tension we've been denying for weeks. *It can't just be me feeling it, right?*

"El," I croak, my hand lifting to graze the warm skin of her jaw.

Shivering under my fingertips, she blinks up at me. "Yeah?"

Without thinking, I slide my fingers to her nape and then run my thumb along her cheekbone. She shifts toward me millimeter by millimeter until I can feel the tips of her breasts brush my chest and the scent of her hair fills my nose. She's temptation incarnate. Her lips are right there, pink and lush. She's so tall, I wouldn't have to stoop at all. Just lean in and –

Our lips touch in a feather soft caress.

Chapter Twelve

Ellie

For the entire week, I've been imagining this moment, the one where we would finally kiss. And my imagination came up short – way short. I knew there would be chemistry, but I didn't quite grasp how overwhelming it would be, how very decadent.

With his hand holding me steady, our mouths begin to play and tease until we find a rhythm that has my stomach swooping and twirling with lazy euphoria, lighting me up from the inside out. I don't think he can believe how good it is either because he's making these small, gratifying noises that cause my blood to bubble and fizz with arousal as one long kiss bleeds into another and then another and another.

Is this real? Is Scott really kissing me?

I lean into him, and his other hand joins the first at my neck. The sudden firmness of his grip sends more lust careening through me as he takes control, demanding I open to him. And if I thought his lips were good, the first brush of his tongue against mine is sublime.

"Jesus," he mutters before he comes back for another taste with an urgency that has my head swimming and heat pooling low in my belly.

Soon he's pressing himself closer, molding the tall, hard length of his body to mine. How I've wanted this. We fit together seamlessly, like an erotic jigsaw puzzle with our arms twining and his knee pushing between my thighs. He rocks his hips into me, and I gasp against his tongue as a streak of bliss radiates out from my core.

Wanting more of that, I slip my hands from his waist to his ass, trying to pull him more firmly against me. He takes the cue and surges forward again, his thigh pinning my hips to the door. I whimper at the intensity of being held down and bask in the delicious traces of the orgasm that are beginning to take hold.

"Look at you," he rasps, his eyes devouring what I'm sure is my drugged, heavy-lidded expression. "I don't think I've ever wanted anything more than you at this very moment."

I'm so busy writhing against him, longing for the bliss to coalesce that I can barely hum some kind of agreement. *God, is that his dick pressing into my hip?*

My mewls gain in volume as I squirm and buck over his thigh, but he just takes hold of my chin and turns my head to the side. "I could watch you like this all night," he whispers into my ear, his tone vibrating down my spine. "All stirred up . . . just for me."

I choke on a moan as his mouth leaves a trail of open-mouthed kisses down the side of my neck, each one searing its way down my body to settle between my thighs, joining the already all-consuming ache. The need to satisfy that ache has my hands tracing up the muscles in his back that shift and bunch under the thin fabric of his dress shirt until I reach his shoulders. I use the leverage to wrap a leg around his thigh, pulling him closer, opening myself up to him.

This time we both groan before our mouths crash back together. It's manic now, hard and ravenous. He fills a palm with my breast, squeezing, hurtling me ever closer to completion. My fingers scrabble against the back of his shirt, looking for purchase on the slippery material to pull it from his pants. And all the while, his hips continue to tease and hint at how good it's going to be to get this man inside of me.

I'd love nothing more than to live in this moment forever, high on his presence, reveling in his touch, hovering near the ultimate release, but my body insists on more.

"Scott," I whine, my frustration mounting when I can't get at all the warm skin I know is under his shirt.

"Let me," he murmurs against my mouth. But instead of working to get his own shirt off, he moves back to pull my T-shirt up and over my head.

I'm not wearing a bra, so I should probably feel vulnerable there in front of him with our chests heaving, trying to catch our breaths, but I don't. There's nothing but wonder in his expression. I'm grateful for the support of the door behind me when he reaches out to run the backs of his knuckles gently over a tightly furled and very sensitive nipple.

"Your turn," I say, so impatient now.

His eyes snap up to mine, making me shiver again at the intensely carnal yet slightly displeased look on his face. *Does he not like me making demands?* Before I have a chance to examine that thought, he's doing as I asked.

One by one, he works the buttons through their holes on his dress shirt, slowly exposing a sliver of skin down the center of his chest. I hold my breath as he finally peals it off.

My hungry gaze tries to take in the view of his bare chest all at once, racing over the beautiful caramel skin from his broad shoulders to his tapered waist. He's all lean, all muscled, all . . . perfect. The dusting of hair across his pecs is closer to brown than the blond on his head, and his happy trail takes me down to the very substantial bulge in his pants I'd gotten an inkling of earlier.

He doesn't give me much time for ogling though. In a heartbeat, his mouth is back on mine and the first feel of his soft chest hair is wondrous against my nipples.

I want him so badly it hurts.

As we kiss and kiss and kiss, we explore. My fingertips roam the exposed expanse of his back while his rough and callused fingertips trace my stiff nipples and cup my breasts until I'm a writhing, anxious mess under his touch.

"I . . . Scott, I –"

He pulls back, his gaze intense and probing, seeming to weigh what I'm asking for.

"Let's go to my room," I whisper.

His narrowed gaze tells me he definitely doesn't like me trying to call the shots, and for a second, I think he's going to deny me. But slowly, he moves back, letting cold air move between us.

Walking backwards, he starts unbuckling his belt and my jaw falls open slightly. "Coming?" he asks, his slightly mocking tone and the whoosh of his belt through the loops turning my knees to water. I push off from the support of the door despite my unsteady legs. Nothing could keep me from him at this point. I work my sleep shorts down my hips as I follow him, watching him strip off his pants.

We don't make it far. In the kitchen, our feet come to a standstill and we just stare at each other. He's truly something to behold in his boxer briefs, the black dramatic against his skin, his very hard dick outlined against the fabric.

"Fucking hell, El," he says hoarsely, reminding me we're both in the same state of undress. "Come here."

Closing the distance between us, I wiggle out of the last stitch of my clothing and then skim my fingertips over his warm skin from his collar bone all the way down to the elastic of his underwear. Our eyes meet and hold as I slowly free his straining erection. I want to hiss out a triumphant *Yes!* when I get my first look at him; nature did not cut any corners when Scott McCarthy was constructed. He's long and thick, and the way the V of his hips frames the sight is mouth-watering. I don't know what I want more, to drop to my knees or demand that he fuck me this very second. Neither of those choices are on his radar, though, because he wastes no time before one of his hands threads into my hair so he can plunder my mouth, while the other pushes between my thighs to cup me. The base of his palm bears down on my clit, and the pulse of bliss is so strong it buckles my knees.

He hums his approval, catching my sagging weight. And all the while his lips never break from mine, devouring my pleasure like it's the most appetizing thing he's ever tasted. Once I'm a bit steadier on my feet, he shuffles me back until my butt hits the edge of the counter. He props me up and my hands find his biceps, trying desperately to give myself an anchor. Pulling back enough to focus on me, he strokes a finger along my slit and my whole body tenses with anticipation.

"Oh, Opal, you're so fucking wet," he says, his voice suffused with lust and appreciation.

"Scott," I whimper when he strokes me back and forth. "Please . . . just . . ."

The grip in my hair tightens. "Just what?" he taunts. The finger pulls forward to press slippery circles to my clit and I gasp, my eyelids sliding shut.

"Uh uh, El. Keep your eyes on me."

I pry them open and our gazes clash before they both slide down our bodies to witness my breasts rising and falling with my ragged breaths and then to his fat cock resting against my abdomen, smearing precome across my skin. It's obscene and thrilling and divine.

Something akin to a gasp spills from my lips as he slowly pushes his finger into me and I clench around the invasion. My grasp on his arms intensifies as he pulls out only to return with two fingers. The stretch is delicious. Over and over, he slides in and out of me with an exasperating amount of patience, his mouth nipping at my lips and jaw and throat.

"Scott," I whisper urgently, my head falling to his shoulder. "Come on, please."

"Please what, beautiful?" he replies, his thumb nudging at my clit.

Two can play at this game. I slide a hand down his chest to gently caress his cock, and a shot of triumph hits my bloodstream as a strangled sound fights its way out of his throat.

"Please, Scott." I grip him tighter. "I want you inside me."

"El," he groans. "We really doing this?"

Irrational panic flares in my chest. *How can he doubt it?* "God, yes."

A moment later his hands are disengaging themselves to reach for his wallet and a condom. I watch greedily as he rips the package open and rolls it down his length.

From there, lust takes over; our lips and hands are everywhere. We struggle a bit, both of us having different ideas of how this is going to go down. In the end, his strength wins out, and I'm both ecstatic and disappointed to find myself bent over the kitchen island, his palm in the middle of my back holding me down, and his dick notched at my entrance.

I'm practically keening with anticipation as I claw at the counter top, wishing I could see his face, that I could touch him, that I could watch that glorious cock slide into me.

He surges into my slippery pussy and it's so good that I almost come on the spot, the length and breadth of him stealing my breath.

"Fuck, fuck, fuck," he whispers, stalling out inside of me. "You good?"

"Yes," I moan, my pussy fluttering around him.

The hand on my back slides up to curl around my shoulder, the other grips my hip, both of them squeezing before he shifts back a little and then . . . Sinks. Himself. Deep.

I make not a sound, my mouth open in a parody of a scream of surprise and delectable discomfort. The feeling of fullness is irresistible to my lust-ridden mind. So. Incredibly. Good.

"Too much?" he huffs out, the strain in his voice obvious.

"No," I gasp.

The slow retreat of him is almost as incredible as the thrust that follows, parting my flesh, driving heaven right into me. Over and over again. And after all the foreplay, that heaven quickly doubles down on itself, allowing the pinnacle to rush me from all sides, splintering me apart in ecstasy in no time at all. The strength of my orgasm compels a strangled scream from me as my body clenches around him again and again.

"Fuck, yeah," he grunts, still sinking his dick into me at a slow and steady pace.

His continued strokes set off round after round of luscious aftershocks, leaving me utterly spent. Here, spread out on the counter, limp, moaning, taking his cock is quite possibly the most wanton experience of my life. The embers of my next climax are slowly kindling themselves into open flames, but when he hisses, "Oh, shit, gonna come," all I can think is *yes! yes! yes!* The knowledge that I'm making him come, that he's finding completion buried deep inside of me is all-consuming – there's nothing I want more.

When he finally stills, his heavy body collapses onto me, covering my back. We pant together like we've just finished a marathon until slowly, groaning as he goes, he pushes up and away from me.

Over my shoulder, I watch him take a deep breath then exhale, his head tipped to the ceiling, eyes closed, the earlier tension in his shoulders gone. I did that to him, I think, delighted and full of pride, but that quickly disappears when his chin dips back down. The devastation on his face as he pulls the condom off is alarming.

I get myself upright and open the cupboard door under the sink so he can toss the condom in the trash. "You okay?" I ask softly, reaching up to cup his cheek.

Instead of answering, he leans into my touch.

Unsure of what to do next, I say the first thing that comes to mind. "Let's go lie down for a while."

Taking his hand, I lead him into my bedroom, a little surprised by how compliant he's being, especially when he gets into bed without a word. It's definitely a relief when he holds the covers up, inviting me to slide in beside him. Not that I was expecting rejection or anything, but I won't deny that I was a little worried he'd regret our actions. Pulling me close, he settles my head on his shoulder, and the feeling of rightness that washes over me is mirrored by his contented sigh.

Silence descends on us, but it isn't uncomfortable, it's peaceful. The post-orgasm glow has me firmly in its grip; my limbs are weak and my mind is sluggish in a most agreeable way. And after a short while, I feel his breaths even out, making the glow burn brighter because he feels enough at ease to fall asleep beside me.

As my brain slowly comes back on line, I bask in the wonder of it all. Scott and I . . . did it. *It.* And it hadn't felt cheap or dirty like so much of my past. I feel wanted, and my heart is about to burst with sappy happiness. I mean, holy crap, Scott McCarthy and I did it and now he's naked and sleeping in my bed. I haven't felt this light, this content, in so long.

When I feel him stir under me some time later, I lift my head from his shoulder to watch him wake, loving the soft, relaxed look on his face.

"Hey," he rasps.

"Hey."

He reaches a hand out to trace a line across my cheekbone. "How long was I out?"

"Not long," I whisper, melting under his touch. "Maybe an hour or so." His hand flops back to the bed and he stares up at the ceiling.

"Do you want to talk about it?" I ask hesitantly. The skin under his eyes is bruised with fatigue and I wonder again what happened tonight.

He focuses back on me, a slow grin starting to form on his lips.

"Oh, no," I say quickly, realizing he's misunderstood my meaning. "Not about *that*. I mean, uh . . . I mean, about what happened." His brows tick up even farther and his smug grin expands, the bastard. I prop myself up on my elbow as I push at his chest playfully. "I mean about what happened *before* you got here?"

His teasing expression dims, and suddenly I'm uncertain if I'm supposed to be asking this kind of a question. Is this thing between us meant to be superficial? I don't want that, but maybe he does. My brain ping pongs between all the ways I can play this . . . and then I balk. I don't want to *play* this at all. No games. If he can't handle my asking questions, it's better to know now.

"I feel like I failed tonight," he announces, pulling me from my thoughts. "My daughter's so young, you know? And I should be able to protect her from the world's bullshit."

I give him a long look. "There was bullshit?"

He goes back to studying the ceiling. When he doesn't answer me, the quiet begins to sink my mood.

"Well," I say hesitantly. "Whatever happened, I hope your daughter's okay, and I'm sure she knows it wasn't your fault."

He gives me a faint smile, but there's melancholy etched into his features.

"You're a good father, Scott," I tell him truthfully. "I know because of the way you talk about those girls. You love them and you want the best for them. No child could ask for better."

His lips thin into an angry line and my stomach turns nervously, leaving me afraid I've said the wrong thing. "She *could* have better," he insists. "She could have a mother who puts her first. Instead, she has one who shows up high and makes a scene in front of everyone she knows."

Oh. Damn. Without a doubt, his heart is bleeding for his little girl. "You're not responsible for other people's actions."

He swallows. "No, but that doesn't mean I don't feel useless."

"True," I concede. "I guess all you can do is not let that feeling change how you love and support your daughter."

He frowns, then looks exasperated, then tsks in defeat. "Again with the wisdom, Opal?"

My heart lurches in my chest at his approval. "That's me, Sister Opal the Wise."

Grudgingly, the corner of his lip tugs up. "Sister Opal, huh?" He pulls me close and nuzzles into my neck. "How does Sister Opal feel about sin?"

A sigh sounds between us as he kisses down my sensitive throat. "She's very recently come to recognize that certain types of sin have their appeal."

"Oh, yeah?" I feel his lips pull into a smile against my skin. "What kind of sin are we talking about here? Not excessive pride, I hope."

Stifling a giggle, I manage to say, "No, nothing like that. Sister Opal would never allow something as mundane as arrogance to bring her down."

He laughs and raises his head. "Mundane?"

"That's right. If she's going to Hell, she'll be doing her sinning in a much more carnal fashion."

"Damn," he says, leaning in to nip at my lips. "Sister Opal isn't only wise, she's hot, too."

I'm sure I could have come up with a few more pithy rejoinders, but the heat of his slow kisses has my mind emptying of anything but the pleasure of his tongue against mine. And his hands are everywhere, caressing, fondling, groping. By the time he's pulling me on top of him with his palms filled with my ass cheeks, I'm about ready to combust.

"El?" he groans. "We gotta stop."

Like hell we do.

"I'm serious," he whines even though his hips curl into mine in imitation of what we're both dying for. "I only had the one condom."

Is that all? With effort, I push myself up so I'm sitting, straddling his thighs. The hunger in his expression almost makes me forget what I'm doing. "Condoms, right," I mutter barely able to tear my gaze from his lips as I get up on my unsteady legs and go in search of what we need.

Chapter Thirteen

Scott

"**A**re you saying you have some?" I call, my eyes glued to that ass of hers as she saunters out the bedroom door. The desperation in my voice would be funny if it wasn't for how badly I want back inside of her. Just the thought of it has me shuddering.

Sitting up, I arrange the pillows behind my back and do my best to distract myself from my very insistent dick. Her room isn't very interesting though, just four empty walls, a dresser and a closet that could pass as the site of a bomb blast. *She's not exactly a neat freak, is she?*

She comes back, digging through an enormous box of assorted condoms, reading the labels as she goes. I'd ask her why she thinks she needs to get her condoms at Costco, but the woman is naked and all my brain cells are currently gorging on the display in front of me. She has the body of a goddess. She's a dream, a fantasy girl, and I'm completely obsessed with the flair of her hips and her long, toned legs.

"Jackpot!" she announces, holding a single condom up in triumph and chucking the box off to the side.

She straddles my thighs, pushing the condom to my chest until I take it. With a predatory glint, she runs her gaze over me, settling on my rock-hard dick that's shamelessly straining for her attention. But I can only stare at her, ogling the acres and acres of flawless skin.

"Need some help with that?" she asks cheekily when I become fixated on her exposed pussy.

That's another thing, she has a confidence level I've never come across before. Nothing seems to faze the woman. And to my dick's delight, she wasn't shy about begging me . . . in that lust-drenched voice.

Watching hungrily as I get my dick suited up, she doesn't waste any time before getting up on her knees and running my length along her pussy a few times, groaning as she circles her clit.

This is beyond surreal. It's gotta be a dream.

Except it must be real because we both moan as she slowly begins to take me into her body. I don't know what's better, the way she struggles to take all of me or the bliss on her slack features as she gets it done.

Forehead to forehead, we pause to savor the moment, but then like clockwork our mouths come together, open and wet as she starts to move. Shit, I can barely concentrate as she pushes up, then sinks down. Pushes up, sinks down. It starts to feel too good and my head falls back against the wall. Her fingers thread their way into the longer hair on top of my head and yank me back forward.

"Want you to watch," she purrs, sending a jagged thunderbolt of lust directly into my already aching balls. I follow her gaze down my chest to where her pussy is stretched wide around me. The sight of my dick disappearing and reappearing in and out of her is crude in the best possible way and just adds to the unbelievable urge to come.

I need a distraction or this is going to end much too quickly. Though I'm not sure if her swaying tits count, I run my thumb over a tightly-furled, pretty pink nipple, which gets me a very sweet little noise for my trouble. I go back for more, this time with a wet thumb and forefinger to roll the peak gently. She inhales sharply and her body clamps around me in response. From between clenched teeth, I push out, "Like that, huh?"

I don't get a verbal response, only a mewl, so I roll both nipples at the same time with a bit more pressure. Her rhythm falters and I'm so grateful for the reprieve. I'm already so close, but I refuse to come before she does. I don't care how good she feels.

I slide my hands to her hips to hold her still as my mouth closes around a nipple. She tastes of sunshine and joy and raw sexuality. And she sure loves the suckling because it kicks off some serious squirming and moaning. Jesus, she may as well be riding me for how good it feels. I move to the other side and now both her hands are in my hair, holding me down on her breasts.

Her breathing ramps up and a thrill runs down my spine. I want her to come, just as hard as she did earlier. Releasing one side of her hips, I caress my way to where we're joined, running my fingers over her drenched and straining pussy lips before I nudge at her swollen clit. She jerks, her inner muscles clamping down hard around me. "Oh, Scott," she gasps, writhing in earnest now. Damn, she's magnificent. With one arm wrapped around her waist to hold her steady, I stroke and fondle that bundle of nerves until I figure out what works best. In the end, it's pressure that brings her off and produces one of the most exquisite experiences of my life. God, watching her lose herself in the ecstasy, her lips parting, her eyes sinking shut as her hips buck and her pussy convulses around me is insanely intimate. I swear, the image will forever be engraved in my memory. And it only gets better when she opens her eyes again and lets me see how they're glazed and brimming with emotion. She's gorgeous and wild and overwhelmed, and it has reciprocal emotion quickly rising in my chest. A single tear streaks from the corner of her eye, and I catch it with my lips. "My beautiful girl," I whisper.

We can't look away from each other. Her hand caresses my face, her thumb dragging across my mouth before I pull it inside and suck, the rhythm matching the throbbing of my dick that's still buried so deep within her. Pulling her free of my mouth, I wrap one hand under her ass, the other behind her head. As gently as I can, I rock us up and get my legs under me so I can maneuver us over onto her back.

We're so close now with her long legs wrapped around my waist, her breasts pressed into my chest, her breath on my neck. I drive into her with long, powerful strokes that blur my vision. I've never felt anything like it and I can't resist setting a stronger pace than before. Soon, I'm tilting her hips with the hand under her ass to get myself in deeper.

She's trembling underneath me now, I can feel it. "Let it come again, beautiful," I rasp in her ear. "I want to feel it."

Her knees slide up my chest to grip my ribs, opening herself up more for me. "That's it," I grind out, feeling like I'm pushing into her very soul. "Just like that."

I'm almost there, barely hanging on when she starts chanting almost unintelligibly, "Ohmygod, ohmygod, ohmygod, ohmmmnnnnnnnnn."

She comes again and everything in me lets go, all of it. Everything is right with the world. Holy shit.

Everyfuckingthing. I come and come and come until I'm light-headed and completely wrung out.

When I finally come back to my senses, I find that while I'm not completely squashing her, I've only got myself propped up on one side with my other hand still lodged under her ass. She doesn't seem to mind at all though. She's practically comatose, loose limbed and heavy lidded, her lips caught in a tremulous smile that registers somewhere between awe and fulfillment.

Her disapproval when I start disentangling our limbs has me leaning in to kiss her sweet lips. "You're okay," I whisper to her before I get off the bed. "I'll be right back." I find a trashcan in the corner for the condom and then I work on getting us both under the covers.

This time it's her that conks out first. With my arms around her, satisfaction hums in my chest in a steady, comforting timbre. The way she responds to me is something I could definitely get used to. The memory of her pulsing around me has a too-soon, semi-painful surge of arousal stirring my dick. *Down boy,* I think wryly. There's plenty of time for that.

I float in and out of a light sleep until she shifts slightly and brings me more fully awake. I'm annoyed when the hamster wheel in my head starts spinning like it usually does when everything is quiet. Soon a sliver of worry starts to poke at me. I do my best to push it away, to concentrate on Opal's soft warmth next to me, but soon my sensible, pragmatic self really pushes to take over.

What am I doing?

Ellie isn't some random girl that I'm hooking up with. This isn't fuck-buddy stuff. Any idiot, including myself, can tell the difference between this and the kind of fun I sometimes have with Juanita. I don't just casually like Ellie, and I don't think she just casually likes me.

Shit, what am I doing?

I can't fall in love with anyone, let alone someone like Ellie. She's obviously all wrong for me. I need a woman who understands the meaning of family, not a recovering alcoholic who's riding the poverty line. She'd probably turn out to be just another person I'd have to take care of. And god knows I'm officially maxed out on dependents.

Carefully, doing my best not to wake her, I get up to find my clothes which are scattered all over the apartment. Once I'm dressed, I go back into her room. Seeing her peaceful and so lovely in sleep has every reason I had for getting out of her bed fading away.

Am I really not going to see her again? My face pinches with disgust. Of course I'm going to see her again.

Am I really going to skulk out of her apartment without saying goodbye? I'm not skulking out, I'm letting her sleep.

Am I really in danger of falling in love with her? My heart beat starts to thump painfully in my chest at the thought. Falling for her isn't a good idea. I know it's not. But . . .

God, I can't think when I'm near her. I need a bit of distance, a bit of perspective. I'm sure it'll all make sense tomorrow.

I get almost no sleep that night. Arriving home at 2:30 in the morning, I lie on my uncomfortable, makeshift bed and stare at the living room ceiling for what feels like hours until I hear the girls creeping around the living room, trying so hard to be quiet and failing completely. I crack an eyelid.

"¿Ya ves?" Daniela whispers loudly. *"Está despierto."*

Well, I'm awake now.

"Buenos días, Tío."

Three bright smiles greet me, and I mumble something that sounds like *buenos días* back.

"¿Desayunamos waffles, Papá? ¿Por favor?"

"Waffles?" It is Saturday, and it's my responsibility to get the girls fed on the weekends, so, "Okay. Just give me a chance to shower first."

While the girls and I are making breakfast, my sisters and grandmother straggle out of their beds one by one and seat themselves around the kitchen table to drink their coffee. After last night's choir fiasco, I like that we're able to bury our differences enough that there's no squabbling. For once, spending time with my family soothes some of my worry – not only about Ellie, but also about the situation with Lolita.

In the end, the girls and I make a crazy mess in the kitchen, but we're left with a big batch of pink, chocolate chip waffles, enough for everyone. It's after noon by the time everything is put to rights, and slowly my family starts disappearing out of the house. Mari to her job at the mall, Desiree out with her boyfriend, and my grandmother out with her knitting circle. I wonder vaguely where my mother's gotten to, but it's fleeting. The girls and I are trying to decide what we'd like to do for the day when Jorgie texts me.

> **Jorgie:** My mom's having a *comida*. Bring the girls. The back yard is full of nieces and nephews. Mikey will be here. No arguments, see u soon.

Actually it sounds like exactly what I need. Distracting adult conversation while the girls play with other kids.

The five-block walk over to Jorgie's brings back so many memories of being a kid. It's a miracle that I ever made it to adulthood considering the things Jorgie, Mike and I used to get up to. Then, nostalgia hits me even harder as we go in the door at Jorgie's mom's house. I spent a lot of time here as a kid. Jorgie's mom, Nora, was almost as much of a mother to me as my grandmother. Nora is so welcoming as she squawks over how tall I am, how big the girls are, how thankful she is for my help in getting Jorgie the job that I almost feel a knot forming in my throat. Good grief, I'm a bit of wreck today.

I catch up with people I haven't seen in forever – and it feels good. The lilting sounds of Spanglish, the smells of Mexican food, and the easy laughter have me forgetting everything for a while.

We eat around 3 o'clock; *tacos de cochinita, rajas con crema*, and *picadillo*. I try to make sure that the girls are eating, but the women in the kitchen shoo me away after they assure me that they're taking care of it.

Shortly thereafter, Alejandro, of all people, sneaks in, much to the delight of his family. He could pass for a normal guy without his entourage, in jeans and a long-sleeved button-down that covers his tattoos. I think he likes the same things that I do about this place; it's a nice reprieve from everyday life.

Alejandro makes his way around the room greeting his brothers, sisters, cousins, nieces and nephews. When he finally gets to me, he pulls me up from the sofa into a hug.

"Scotty."

"Tío."

"What's it been? A week?" he jokes. "Hey, is my goddaughter here?"

"Yeah, she's around. You want to say hi later?"

"You bet."

He's about to move on to Mike beside me when he says, "Where's your *chula*?"

My face falls a bit and Alejandro chuckles. "You screwed it up already?"

I dip my head, embarrassed for some reason. "No, uh, not exactly."

When I glance back up, he gives me a hard stare. "Not exactly? She didn't strike me as the type to let you give her the run-around. But I guess you know what you're doing."

I scowl as he moves his gangster-ass on to greet Mike. *What does he mean by that?* I look around the room, trying to picture Ellie here beside me, but I can't do it. She wouldn't fit in at all. The language barrier would be tricky enough, but the cultural barrier would be the real killer. Ellie lives alone for fuck's sake. It doesn't seem like she even sees her family regularly, let alone has them all up in her business on a daily basis. She wouldn't be comfortable here and I would be even less comfortable having to babysit her. Just thinking about such an unpleasant scenario is depressing as hell.

A few minutes later when Mikey gets up to get another beer, he asks, "You want one this time?"

"Yeah, sure," I agree. "Why the fuck not?"

I'm just so tired of life.

Chapter Fourteen

Ellie

I'm not at all surprised that Scott's gone from my bed in the morning. I'd known he couldn't stay. He had to be home when his girls woke up and I'm completely on board with that.

Despite his absence, I'm all smiles. Last night was incredible. I may be sore in certain fabulous places, but I feel like I could take on the world – and win. It's as if our connection has buoyed everything inside of me, and it's a total trip, feeling like this; fearless, invincible, all in.

And if that wasn't enough, I spend the entire morning lazing around in bed, snoozing, daydreaming, texting with my sister about him, just generally being a bum on a rare morning that I don't have to be at work or school. It's wonderful.

Around noon, I head over to my parents' place to pick up the supplies that Amelia has readied for me so I can cook dinner for Scott. We agonized over it all week and finally decided on a Tex-Mex casserole since he likes spicy. There are quite a few steps to it, but Amelia assured me I could handle it.

"Oh, *mi amor*," Amelia gushes, embracing me with gusto when I walk into the kitchen. "How happy you look. You really like this boy, don't you?"

I'm sure I'm glowing under her scrutiny. "I do. I know we're just starting out, but there's something special about him."

She laughs. "Well, I didn't think you would *cook* for just anyone."

"Hey, I cook," I say, mildly indignant. "Kind of."

"Yes, of course, of course. You're a regular Martha Stewart."

I give her a mock glower that melts when she continues to laugh at me. I love Amelia so much. I ask about her family – they're all fine. I ask about my family – they're all fine. My mom and dad left for their place in Palm Springs this morning.

We go over the recipe again and I ask a million questions to be sure I've got a handle on it. Now more than ever, I want tonight to go well.

"You're all set then," she says happily. "I wish you luck."

"*Muchísimas gracias.* I couldn't do this without you."

She waves me off. "That's what I'm here for."

I hug her tightly to me, not thanking her for what I really want to, for being a mother to me over the years. She doesn't like any of us kids to focus on how our 'real' mother has never had much time for us.

"So, hey," I say hesitantly as I pull away. "Before I go, I was wondering if I could ask you something."

"Of course."

"Do you think I have the right kind of personality to deal with kids?" I pause to pull in a steadying breath. "I know I don't have a ton of experience with them, but . . ."

"Kids?" She's suddenly concerned. "Does this boy . . . this man have children, Ellie?"

I nod my head nervously. "Yeah, he has one biological daughter, but there are three girls who see him as their father."

I bite at my thumb nail. I don't want Amelia of all people to tell me that I've lost my mind, so I rush on. "That he's such a good father is one of the things that I really admire about him."

Amelia's mouth opens, then closes, then opens again, as if she's not sure what to say. She finally comes out with, "You've given this some thought?"

I must look like a bobble head doll with all the jittery nodding I'm doing. "Yeah, I have. I'm worried that my willingness to hang out with little girls isn't going to count for much. What if they don't like me? Or . . ." At this point I swallow hard, because here's my real fear. "Or what if Scott doesn't think I'd be a good influence? I'm not exactly a poster child for good morals."

Her only response is a furrowed brow, so I give her more. "I mean, I want to be the kind of person who's good for kids. But what if I'm not?" I hear the raw emotion that's leaking into my words now, and Amelia is quick to speak this time before I can work myself up any more than I already have.

"*Mira, mi amor,* I think those girls would be lucky to have you in their lives. You've become a strong woman. You're living proof that we can all change and work towards our goals and achieve them, right?"

I just blow out a heavy breath.

"Have you talked about this with him?"

"No, we haven't gotten that far yet. He's very protective of them."

"Oh, my Ellie, he sounds like a wonderful man."

I smile with relief. "He really is. I can't wait for you to meet him."

"I can't wait either. And I wouldn't worry, mi amor, if it's meant to be, all will be well."

"Okay, yeah. You're right. I'll take it as it comes."

Feeling much better about this storm cloud that's been looming on the horizon for the last couple of weeks means there's almost nothing tethering my mood to the ground. At home, I work on the recipe, reading and rereading the instructions carefully as I go. I even send my sister a picture of myself in front of the stove. Briefly, I consider sending Scott the same picture, but for some reason, that feels really intrusive. I know Saturday and Sunday are his days with the girls. He'll be all mine tonight at 7:00.

When I finally get the casserole in the oven, I check my phone for the hundredth time and start to wonder why he hasn't sent me anything all day, at least to see how I am, or to confirm our plans, or to say hi. But then it occurs to me that I haven't contacted him either. I never was one for double standards, so I decide to put on my big girl panties and text him.

Except my thumbs hang poised over the keyboard without a clue of what to say. I start with the obvious, *Hey.* But then what? *Can't wait to see you*, or *you rocked my world last night*, or maybe a simpler, *hope your day is going well.* Ha, ha, that last one sounds like something out of a Hallmark card. I'm backspacing furiously when I accidentally hit send. Oh shit. I stare down at it and laugh.

Ellie: Hey.

Short and sweet. I consider adding more in another message, but ultimately leave it as is. If he's busy, then he won't feel obligated to answer.

While the food bakes, I jump in the shower. When I get out, I frown slightly at the lack of a response. I really thought he'd answer, but then I chide myself. It's not a big deal.

I get dressed in my favorite jeans and an off the shoulder blouse. Last night, he'd clearly liked the exposed skin and I want a repeat of the experience. When the timer on the stove goes off and it's only twenty to seven, I decide to take the straightening iron to my hair to pass the time.

By seven, my apartment smells amazing and I look great. I'm unreasonably nervous and excited. I can't wait to see him.

By seven fifteen, I'm more nervous than excited. He's never been late before.

At seven twenty-five, my phone dings and I snatch it up. But it's my sister responding to the picture I sent earlier.

By eight fifteen, I know something is wrong, and I do my best to scrub images of car accidents from my mind.

I text him.

Ellie: I hope everything is ok.

He doesn't respond. By nine thirty, I'm climbing the walls. Is it wrong that I'm hoping that *something* happened? Some kind of family emergency maybe. Because the thought of him blowing me off for no reason is painful in ways I don't want to even contemplate.

I jump up from my place on the couch when I feel the sting of tears. No, no, no, no. Not happening. I don't cry over men anymore.

By ten thirty, the walls are officially closing in on me and I'm desperate. I text Vanessa.

Ellie: Hey, you guys still going out tonight? Can I tag along?

Though I fully plan on giving Scott the benefit of the doubt, there's no way I can continue to sit here all night, waiting and wondering and worrying.

Vanessa: Why? I thought you had big plans.
Ellie: They fell through.

It's a relief when she texts me the address of a local salsa club that I've been to plenty of times in the past. Well, Piper's been there, but I have confidence in Ellie now. She's much stronger than she was even a month ago. I certainly won't be drinking. I'll take my car so if Scott needs me, I can be ready to go at a moment's notice.

As I'm putting my driver's license and my money into my phone case, I'm hit with a very unsettling case of déjà vu. Maybe this isn't the best of ideas. But the thought of staying here is suffocating. I just can't.

Arriving at the club near midnight, I balk at the lineup outside. Piper has never, in her life, waited in a lineup. I make my way up to the front.

"Hey, Chico," I say to the bouncer.

"I know you, honey?" he drawls, his giant arms crossing over his equally giant chest as he scans me from head to toe without a trace of recognition. Do I really look *that* different as Ellie?

"*¿Cómo que no te acuerdas de mi?*" I say, thickly laying on my lisping Spanish accent that so many Latinos here in California find amusing. *How can you not remember me?*

Chico's eyes bug out and I laugh.

"Piper?"

I throw my arms up and spin for him. "In the flesh."

His face lights up. "*¿Dónde andabas? Tenía mucho que no te veía.*" *Where have you been? It's been a long time.*

"Around, Chico, I've been around. How've you been?"

"Without seeing your beautiful face on the regular, bored."

"You're too sweet."

He lifts his chin at the door. "You going in?"

"If you'll have me."

"You've got an open invitation to any club I work, *mami*, you know that."

"Thanks," I say, getting up on my tiptoes to kiss his cheek.

Though I could hear the music from outside, it's not until I'm inside the doors that the rush hits me; the thumping beat, the smell, the hum of voices, the lights, the press of the bodies – it's all like coming home and falling into welcoming arms. It feels amazing.

Somewhere in the back of my mind alarm bells are ringing, but as I make my way through the crowd, my hips bouncing to the rhythm, they're muffled at best.

"Piper!" Vanessa screeches when I make it to her table, drawing everyone's attention and setting off a wave of exclamations of welcome. These aren't exactly the people I used to hang out with, but I know all of Vanessa's friends from over the years, and they're eager to talk to me – or to Piper. All the attention is gratifying and for the first good hour or so I'm inundated with girls who want to catch up, and guys who want to flirt – and the reverse; guys who want to catch up and girls who want to flirt. After eleven months of self-imposed isolation, it's a heady experience. I can't fathom why I ever left.

After the initial excitement, though, the lustre slowly starts to wear off. The same old conversations surface: *Remember the time we were so wasted that we . . . ? Did you hear that so-and-so cheated on so-and-so? Omg, did you see what she's wearing?* And the selfies. *Should I post this one?* Yet I still chatter on with them like a dam has broken inside of me and I can't stop words from pouring out.

To distract myself from the ever-growing squirming sensation in my gut, I invite guys to dance. The first couple of songs are great. Just like the socializing, the immediate high is a welcome rush. I've missed dancing like you wouldn't believe. But it's salsa and some of the guys are a bit too . . . overenthusiastic. Having strange guys' semi-hard junk pressed up against me isn't as sexy as I used to think it was. It might even be a bit nauseating.

The disquiet grows.

By the end of the second hour, everyone around me is having a blast . . . and I'm feeling brittle and left out, because when you're not drinking, things aren't as funny or interesting or acceptable as when you've had a few.

Maybe just one. To take the edge off, to help get me back to the magic I felt when I first got here. It can't hurt, right? After all, it's not the booze that's my problem, it's the choices I make under its influence. And one drink is not going to get me drunk.

Once the decision is made, the tension eases from between my shoulder blades. I immediately start scoping the place out for the lucky guy who's going to buy me a drink – and freeze. *Forget that.* If Ellie wants a drink, Ellie can buy her own. Ellie is not Piper.

I push my way up to the bar and throw my best smile at the bartender. It reels him in and, again, I'm hit with the heady sensation of being in my element, one I know how to navigate and manipulate to my own ends.

"What'll you have, baby girl?"

Tilting my head and gently biting my lip, I pretend to consider my options. Alarm bells sound a little louder this time. *Why am I flirting?* I shut it down and very calmly order a dirty martini like a normal person.

The bartender throws out innuendo laden banter as he mixes, but I don't respond to it, which sours his mood. "Twelve

LL MEYER

bucks," he says flatly when he places the drink down in front of me.

Twelve?! Twelve dollars for one drink? How did I not know that? I hand him my only twenty and wait for the change. My outrage dulls considerably as I raise the glass and get a whiff of the most glorious smell in the world; it's good times, laughter, sex, joy, euphoria all rolled into one. I bring the glass to my mouth and the anticipation all but strangles me. There's a short pause in the beat of the song that's currently playing, and in that second, two things happen. One, the liquid heaven hits my taste buds, and two, I hear a high-pitched exclamation of excitement, a name, over the general din.

"Escotty!"

It's pronounced in Spanish, but my brain easily pulls it apart and identifies it. It came from upstairs. My mouth still full of alcohol, I look up at the balcony. His height and his sandy blond hair make him easy to spot, right there against the railing.

My entire world screeches to a halt. I spit the mouthful of alcohol back into the glass. Every question imaginable crams its way into my mind as I watch him bend to receive a kiss on the cheek from one of his friends. He's laughing with her, his profile relaxed, a beer in his hand, like he's having the time of his life.

And I'm . . . holy shit . . . I . . .

With a trembling hand, I very carefully place the martini glass back on the bar.

Oh my god.

All the questions in my head become realizations, realizations that crush and choke and set my heartrate into a painful, body quaking, erratic thump. I clutch at my chest,

165

light-headed for a moment. Then the burn of the alcohol registers on my tongue. It tastes like horror.

I almost took a drink.

I'm suddenly blind and deaf to everything except the mind-tearing truth of what I almost did.

I almost took a drink.

Heedless of the complaints, I push my way through the crowd toward the doors, stumbling out into the night air, struggling to control my panic and my quaking limbs. Chico, the bouncer, calls out to me, but I wave him off.

The walk to my car is a blur, but once I'm seated in the driver's seat, how close I came to betraying myself swamps me. Horrified beyond all recognition, I take some deep breaths in an attempt to calm myself. I need to get home, but my hands are shaking so badly that I worry I won't be able to drive. Forcing my shoulders down from around my ears, I hear myself whisper, "You're okay. You didn't do it. It's fine. You didn't do it."

I turn the key in the ignition and take comfort in the familiar rumble of my car.

"You're okay," I repeat.

But I can feel it gathering inside of me like a dark tempest; the self-recrimination, the disgust, the soul-squeezing disappointment. I stare at the brightly lit, yellow check engine light on the dash in a daze.

A horn sounding brings me back to myself. "You leaving or what?" some guy hanging out the window of his car yells.

Right. Home.

I make the drive swiping away tears and swallowing back the bitter tastes of alcohol and reproach. At home, the first thing I do is rush into the bathroom. Slathering my toothbrush with toothpaste, I scrub my mouth out over and over again.

Oh my god, I almost took a drink.

When I'm finally satisfied, I force myself to look in the mirror.

"You almost fucked up, Ellie," I say unsteadily to my reflection. "But you didn't. You're fine."

Fine?! I'm not fine?!

I can't stand the sight of myself. Shaking out my hands, I take deep breaths as I leave the bathroom to pace the living room. My attempts to calm down fail utterly when I notice that goddamned casserole sitting on the counter.

Wrenching open the cupboard under the sink, I chuck the entire thing into the garbage.

How dare he treat me like that?

But then, almost immediately, his betrayal is burned away by my own.

How dare I almost give up? How dare I almost fall back into that empty, life-sucking black hole?

Staring down at the casserole that's oozing over the edges of the pan in the trash can, I can't help but imagine how this mess could easily have resembled my new reality, how I could have gone back to being that self-disrespecting train wreck I'd come to loathe.

A stilted laugh hits me. *What am I doing?* I can't throw Amelia's pan out. Angrily, I grab a spatula and with jerky, staccato movements, I get rid of the casserole and then let the empty pan clatter down into the sink.

My phone buzzes in the back pocket of my jeans. With trepidation, I pull it out and find a message from Vanessa.

Vanessa: Hey, did you leave? R u ok?

Ellie: Yes, sorry I didn't let you know. I'm home now.

I check the time. It's 3:05am. I have to be at work in less than four hours. I should sleep.

But sleep is a pipedream. I wish I could go for a run, but that would be stupid at this time of night. I settle for a shower. Then I pace and only allow myself to think about the why's and how's of my almost fall from grace. Tonight was a huge wakeup call. I've been right all along to restrict my exposure to those kinds of places. It's a lesson I'll never forget, and I'm so grateful that I didn't take that drink . . . something good Scott did for me. From there, my thoughts hit a brick wall. I refuse to think about him or acknowledge the deeper sadness under all the self-flagellation.

At work, I wish it was busier, but it's Sunday. There's not the same rush that happens on weekdays. Jake asks if I'm okay and I give him what I'm sure is a pathetic smile. *Why wouldn't I be okay? Because I almost ruined my life? Or because Scott doesn't think I'm worth a simple text?* Well, fuck that! I didn't take that drink and I don't need a text, simple or otherwise, from anyone – ever. I'm a strong, independent woman who knows how to save herself when she needs it. My goals and aspirations don't involve anyone but myself.

By the time my shift finishes at three o'clock, I'm exhausted. I'm running on no sleep and I can feel sorrow seeping into my blood like an infection. It doesn't matter that I refuse to acknowledge it, it just keeps spreading.

And *still* he hasn't contacted me.

When I get home, the stench of the casserole is everywhere, ingrained into the very walls and carpet, and what little I've eaten today threatens to make a reappearance. Yeah, I can't stay here. I haul the garbage out to the dumpster behind the building and then go for a run.

I'm five miles in when the music on my phone is interrupted by the ding of an incoming text message. Somehow, I know it's him.

Scott: Hey. Sorry I didn't get back to you yesterday.

Anger surges inside of me, crushing down on all the emotion that's been threatening to spill out of me over the last eighteen hours. I like it. Anger I can deal with. I'm already searching for an emoji to flip him off, when I stop myself. He doesn't even deserve that.

I drag my ragged ass back home. After a shower, I get in bed and sleep like the dead for the next few hours.

When I wake up at three in the morning, it's with a heart that's weighed down with the loss of him. All the hope and affection and awe that had built up over the last few weeks has turned to dust, and I can no longer ignore the gaping hole it's left in me. Is it possible to choke and die on sadness? Because that's what it feels like. I just don't understand how I got it all so wrong, how I didn't realize I meant so little to him.

My beautiful girl.

I scoff at the memory and at the tears welling in my eyes. But those three whispered words feel like they've been stabbed between my shoulder blades. They sting and burn and ache, and I'm not sure how I'm going to dig them out of my flesh.

Except, the more I think about it, the more foolish I feel. Beauty is not respect. Beauty is not loyalty. Beauty is not even affection. Beauty is only skin deep. He was never interested in *me*.

The weight in my chest grows heavier. I'd glimpsed something great inside Scott, I'm sure of it. It's so unfair that what he'd seen in me hadn't meant the same to him.

I've often wondered if there's something intrinsically flawed about me. Is it just my poor judgment of character or is there some essential piece of me that's missing? The piece that motivates people to care about me on a less superficial level.

I know better than anyone that wondering and wishing do nothing to change the unfairness of life. I'm going to have to tough it out . . . but lying here in my bed with only the light from the street to keep me company, I know that toughing it out is going to be impossible. If I'm going to get around this . . . setback, I'm going to have to grieve.

The tears start to fall and they're soon joined by pathetic sobbing. God, it hurts so bad to know that I'm going to have to forget him, that I'm going to lose his laughter, his touch, his warmth.

Hours later, the dinging of an incoming message wakes me from a restless sleep.

Scott: Please talk to me.

I blink. And I blink again. *What? What would we even say to each other? Does he think I'd sleep with him again? Is that what he's after?*

Rolling off the bed, I hold my temples that throb with the ache of crying my heart out. In the bathroom, I find some ibuprofen and stand under the scalding water of the shower for an eternity, trying to erase the last month from my memory.

Standing in front of my closet, I dig out *the* gray hoodie. The one that he covered me with so many months ago. Initially, I'd worn it all the time – slept in it even – until I'd felt stronger. It had served as a much-needed reminder that there are good people out there who are willing to help others . . . that there was a good person out there willing to help *me*. Today will be the last time I put it on. Today I'll purge Scott McCarthy from my system and then make plans for the future.

I'm going to need coffee though. Lots of it. So once I'm dressed, I get in my car that's pitifully low on gas and stop off at work.

When Vanessa sees me, her eyes widen with alarm. "Oh, no, Sweetie, what's wrong?"

I only have enough energy for a half-hearted shrug. "Eh," I tell her, waving her worries away because I don't want to get emotional here in front of her and Jake. "Nothing that a little caffeine won't fix. Will you make me up an extra-large double shot latte to go?"

"Of course I will," she says, full of concern.

"Hey, El," Jake says. "You seemed kind of down yesterday, so I got these for you." He slides a package of Twizzlers across the counter.

"I . . ." Shit, tears are rising. "Thanks, Jake," I whisper as I take the candy and put it in my purse.

And damn it, it's after the morning rush and before lunch, so they're not busy and they're both coming around the counter to give me hugs and tell me that everything will be okay and that if I want to talk they're here for me. Despite my embarrassing tears, it actually makes me feel better.

"Thanks, guys."

So, armed with my coffee and my candy, I drive up to my spot near Coyote Point and make every attempt to reconcile myself to life without Scott. When he texts me again, I know I'm going to have to block his number. Soon, I tell myself. Tomorrow. I'll do it tomorrow.

Scott: You're pissed at me?

Another tear leaks down my cheek as I shake my head. *Pissed?* I place my phone face down on the bench beside me and go back to staring out over the water with another licorice in my hand.

Twenty minutes later, my phone is ringing. *For fuck's sake.* Turning it over, I hit decline and then toss it back down.

"So, there's nothing wrong with your phone, then."

I jump at the sound of his voice. The glare I'm going to level him with falters when I look up. There he is, standing over me, his beautiful face serious in the natural light. His very presence sends a knife piercing through my chest.

The hurt of it has me turning away like a coward.

"You're not going to talk to me?" he asks quietly, sitting beside me.

I feel my shoulders curl in to protect myself. "Don't see what there is to say," I tell him, hating when the end of the sentence hitches.

He just sits there for a minute completely oblivious to my fervent wish he'd just leave me in peace.

"Just listen then?" he asks, sounding uncertain. "I, uh, I'm sorry I ghosted."

Maybe he'll go if I assuage his guilt. "Okay, apology accepted." Because he needs to go . . . the hemorrhaging around this knife in my chest isn't letting up.

But after more strained silence, he keeps talking. "I've got a lot of stuff going on right now, and uh . . . yeah, a lot of stuff."

"Fair enough." My voice is flat, not showing him an ounce of the pain he's causing me. I refuse to give him any more of myself than I already have.

"Look at me, please."

His pleading tone yanks the cover off my simmering emotions. "Let's not make this any harder than it has to be, okay?" I whisper, hating that I feel a tear sliding down my cheek.

"I said I'm sorry, El." His earnestness twists the blade in further. "I really am. You just don't understand how much pressure I'm under."

I huff out a disbelieving breath and turn to him, a spark of indignation fueling the steadiness in my voice. "I do understand, Scott. I understand perfectly. With everything you've got going on, I don't rate."

I watch the beginnings of alarm register on his face. Good. It goads me to continue.

"I don't even rate a simple text to cancel our plans. You've made yourself very clear."

He's completely taken aback. "What? Of course you . . . rate. And what plans?"

I snort with derision. "We're done here, Scott. I'd like you to go, please."

"Done? What does that mean?"

He can't really be this obtuse, can he? "It means that we're at an impasse. You feel that I'm not worth your time and effort and I disagree. Let's leave it at that."

He's offended or horrified or maybe shocked, but I don't know why.

"That's not true. I just got overwhelmed, I –"

"Stop. Please stop." Taking a deep breath to steady myself, I decide to explain my point of view, so there'll be no room for later re-interpretation. "You let me go all day Saturday thinking that everything was fine." I swallow hard. "No, not *fine*. You let me believe that everything was wonderful. *That* was shitty." I'm on my feet now, the rawness of my emotions swirling with the humiliation and the anger I've been stewing in for the last day. It's potent and it drives me on. "I wasn't expecting a marriage proposal or anything, Scott, but I thought . . ." I falter ". . . I thought it was good between us."

I start walking down the path. I don't want to do this, I don't want him to see me cry, I don't want to pretend I'm fine.

"El," he calls. "El, wait."

I don't make it very far before he's stopping me with a hand around my elbow. I yank away from his touch. "Listen," I tell him forcefully before he can come up with more excuses. "I get that it's my fault. I built it up in my head. I obviously saw things that weren't there, felt things that weren't real. I even heard it from your own lips. *Nadie importante.* That's what you said, right? That I'm no one important."

His head jerks back with surprise. "You speak Spanish?"

My mouth twists. "That's really not the point here. The point is that you're not interested in a relationship and I'm not interested in being a booty call."

By the look on his face, I've hit the truth dead center, which twists the knife in my chest viciously.

After a few moments of silence, I wipe my cheeks free of the tears before I zip off the hoodie. "I want you to have this back." I can't get my voice above a whisper and when I hold it out to him, he scarcely notices it. Pushing it at him, I say, "You asked me why I didn't turn you over to the cops that night and I didn't tell you the truth."

That registers more with him as he takes the sweater, his strangely vulnerable expression jiggling the knife some more.

"I didn't turn you over to the cops, Scott, because I wanted to repay you for what you did for me."

"What?" he croaks, completely confused.

"Do you remember that girl on the sidewalk in Mountain View? About a year ago? Her phone was dead and she had no money."

He blinks, and then I watch as the memory comes back to him. "The one with the ripped dress?"

I flinch. "Yeah, her." He still hasn't put it together, but he's about to. I look away so I'll never see his disappointment, never witness his disgust.

"El?"

I clear my throat. "That was me." Dead silence. "Well, it was Piper, but same difference, right?"

Shuffling closer, I kiss him on the cheek still without meeting his eyes. "I want you to know that it was an important moment for me," my voice cracks, but I force myself to continue, "and that I'm so glad it was you who found me that day. So thank you."

I walk back to the bench, grab my phone and leave him behind for good.

Chapter Fifteen

Scott

It didn't go how I planned.

Yeah, I knew ignoring her texts on Saturday was a grade-A asshole move, but I didn't want to deal with any of it; not her and definitely not any of what I was *feeling*. I needed a breather. I needed to let off some steam before the pressure of my life caused more than just the usual hairline fractures.

When she didn't return my Sunday night/Monday morning messages, I knew she was upset. It worried me enough that I asked Dean for a very rare half day off to get things sorted out, to apologize or whatever. I fully expected her to accept my explanation and let me off with a warning . . . or something.

It was supposed to be easy.

I figured since it was her day off, she'd be at home. When she wasn't there, I went by her work, where I got an extremely stony reception. Admittedly, that worried me, but I managed to get enough hints out of her friend, Vanessa, to a make an educated guess where to find her.

Then, the sight of her made the bottom of my *still* slightly hung-over and queasy stomach fall out. She'd been crying.

My self-assured, steady, full-of-life Ellie had been crying – because of me. And then, she'd hit me with a ton of shit.

Since leaving the shore, my brain's gone from being stuck in neutral to fifth gear. Initially, I didn't have a clue how to start sifting through it all. *She was that girl on the sidewalk? And the Spanish?* It struck me as . . . lying and tendrils of betrayal had started to work their way into me, like the roots of a weed that manages to take hold in unexpected and impossible places. And once the roots were embedded, my indignation and resentment didn't just bud, they flourished. Apparently, I'd never known her at all.

"Mijo?" My grandmother's surprise when I walk in our front door at two o'clock in the afternoon on a workday quickly turns to concern. "Is everything okay? What are you doing home?"

I expanded my half-day to a full day off, but I don't tell her that. "Everything's fine," I say neutrally. "I had something to take care of, that's all."

"I see."

Her expression is suspiciously similar to the one she wore all day yesterday while I pretended that I wasn't hung over like a mother fucker after going out with my friends on Saturday night after leaving Jorgie's mom's house. For all my effort, she saw right through me. A roiling stomach, an aching head, and a bitter mood aren't things I'm very adept at concealing.

"What time do the girls get out of school?" I ask, trying not to be aggravated with her silent censure. I'm an adult and I do *not* need this right now. "I'll go pick them up."

She gives me an infuriating sweeping gesture with her hand that seems to say, *by all means, go. You don't need my permission.* I grit my teeth and head back out the door.

Standing in the hot sun while I wait for the dismissal bell does little to improve my outlook and I rebuff all the moms who try to engage me in conversation.

"*¿Papá?*"

"*Hola, guapa,*" I say, bending to scoop Rosa up, backpack and all. "*¿Cómo te fue?*" How'd it go today?

"*Bien.* Is Abuela okay?"

"She's fine."

"Okay," she says cautiously, her big brown eyes round as she kisses my cheek. "I'm glad you don't smell like Mamá Lilia today."

Shit, if that's not a kick to the gut, I don't know what is. "No, and I'm sorry about that."

The smile that spreads across her face makes me feel a little less guilty. "Let's go get your sisters."

As soon as Daniela's teacher, Ms. Josson, spots me, I wish I hadn't come. "Mr. McCarthy, a word please if you have a few minutes." Shit, that's right, she wanted to talk to me about something that happened on the playground.

I muster up a pleasant expression. "Yeah, okay. Just let me get Carmen." Ms. Josson was Carmen's teacher last year; she's strict, but she's fair. It's not like I dislike the woman, but it sure would be nice to have a partner sometimes, someone to tag team with so I don't have to take every blow.

When I've collected all three of them, I crouch down. "So you guys want to tell me what Ms. Josson wants to talk about?"

I get silence. Their reluctance to spill the beans can't be good.

"It was my fault," Carmen finally blurts.

"What do you mean?" I ask, pulling her close when I see she's close to tears.

"Claire kept making fun of my glasses."

"Yeah," Daniela scoffs. "Claire wouldn't shut up about Carmen's glasses, so I helped her."

I almost laugh at my little gangster-in-the-making, but I can't because I'm supposed to be the adult. "Helped her how, Daniela?"

"She's just a big cry baby," she evades.

My eyebrows rise. "Helped her how?"

"I only gave her a little shove, nothing serious. But she went crying to the teacher."

"It's true, Papá," Rosa adds solemnly. "Claire deserved it."

It's unbelievable how much I love them. "Okay, I'm glad you're sticking together, but you know what Ms. Josson's going to tell me, right?"

Their gazes scatter, suddenly finding the pavement under our feet extremely interesting. "We've talked about this. The school has a zero-tolerance policy. You don't want Daniela to have to go to a different school, do you?"

"No!" they squawk together, shocked by the idea.

"Then you guys have to find a way to use words instead of pushing or hitting, okay? I know it's hard, but that's what we've got to do. ¿Sale?" Agreed?

"Sale," they repeat in unison.

Getting to my feet, I take Carmen and Rosa's hands, wishing I had another one for Daniela. Then after that ridiculous thought, another more practical one hits me. "Carmen, why aren't you wearing your glasses?" Unlike Daniela, who only needs them to read the board, Carmen needs to be wearing hers all the time.

"Oh, uh, I forgot them at home," she says so quietly that I almost don't hear her.

Frowning down at her, I wonder how many times she's 'forgotten' them in the last few weeks. I suppress a sigh. First things first. Ms. Josson gives it to me straight and I listen politely and keep my mouth shut until it's time to reassure her that this kind of thing won't happen again.

The rest of the day doesn't go particularly well either. Homework time, during which I'm usually at work, is stressful. Daniela seems baffled by the concept of subtraction and doesn't take kindly to my attempts to explain it to her, which leaves me frustrated. The mounting tension lessens when Carmen takes over the explanation. That is until I realize that Daniela is just getting Carmen to do the work for her. When I start to lose my temper and insist she do it herself, there's a total meltdown with noisy tears and sobs.

Then later, Mari and Desiree get into it over a missing sweater, and I lose my shit again, telling them both to grow up. But worst of all are my grandmother's eyes which follow me around, heavy with what feels like suspicion and disappointment.

Then, to add insult to injury, none of it is enough to keep *her* from my thoughts. Ellie's always there, lurking, lying in wait for me to lower my defenses and jump to the forefront. The ambush comes when the house is quiet and I'm supposed to be sleeping. Instead, I'm staring up at the dark living room ceiling, hating that resentment isn't fueling me anymore.

Without that fuel, there's only a sick feeling in my gut telling me that maybe she was right about a lot of what she laid on me. That I was more of a douche than I realized, especially when it finally comes to me that we *did* have plans that night. She was going to make me dinner and I'd been so caught up in my own shit that it hadn't even crossed my mind, not when I was at Jorgie's place and not when I was out getting wasted with my friends. If only I hadn't been so careless and self-absorbed, I could have avoided putting that wrecked expression on her face with a simple phone call or even a fucking text message.

The sick feeling only grows when I get a call on Tuesday afternoon from Pamela at the office, telling me that a nice girl came to drop off an envelope for me. At first I'm stumped. When I question her further, she tells me conspiratorially that she thinks there's money inside. The fifty dollars Ellie owes me. She's really going to cut me out of her life.

It gets worse as the week goes on. I barely sleep, and when I do, my dreams are full of her. She's so beautiful, under me, over me, coming on my cock in every possible position my brain can come up with. I don't know how many times I wake in the night with my hand wrapped around my very hard dick, jacking myself and then feeling like shit about it after the euphoria fades. But it's not only the sex. I miss *her*; her company, her laugh, her advice. God, the guilt for screwing things up so badly and the resulting exhaustion grate on me to the point that I'm snapping at my guys at work and my family at home. I can barely stand myself.

By Thursday evening, I guess my grandmother has had enough of my bad temper because while I'm loading the dishwasher, she gets my attention with a firm, *"Mijo."*

I look up.

"Please, sit down." She gestures to the kitchen table.

Groaning internally, I slide onto my chair, sure I'm about to get a lecture. I should have guessed something was up when she sent the girls out to the back yard to play after dinner.

"Tell me what's going on."

I blow out a tired breath. "Nothing's going on, Abuela."

"Is it your job? Is it not working out?"

"The job is fine."

"Then what is it? You've been peevish all week. Are you worried about Lolita? Because I —"

"Definitely not," I say with finality, because the situation with Lolita, who I haven't heard from since the girls' choir debacle, is the last thing I want to think about right now.

She sighs heavily as if she doesn't appreciate my lack of cooperation in her quest to get to the bottom of my *peevishness*. "Is it Jorge? Is he causing problems for you?"

I shake my head impatiently, already weary of this. "No more than usual."

"It's a woman then," she announces.

My eyes flip up to hers in surprise. "What? No!" Except I can feel an embarrassing flush creep up my neck.

Inexplicably, my grandmother grins like I've given her the world. "That's *wonderful* news, *mijo*."

Despite the further denial that's on the tip of my tongue, my disbelief at her reaction gets the better of me. "How's that?"

"A woman is exactly what you need."

Say what now? My grandmother and any *woman* that I *need* don't belong in the same thought, let alone in a sentence that's spoken aloud.

"Yes," she says, her enthusiasm gaining ground. "A *novia*. So wonderful."

Good grief. *Not just a woman, but a girlfriend now?* "There's no *novia*, Abuela."

"I suppose not. Not with the way you've been moping around all week. What happened? Does she not care for you as you do for her?"

I balk. "Who said anything about caring?"

"Please, *mijo,*" she says like I'm twelve. "If you didn't care for her, you wouldn't be this out of sorts."

Exasperated, I tell her, "I'm not *out of sorts.* I'm . . ." I don't know. *What am I?* "It doesn't matter what I am. We're not right for each other."

"Oh? Why do you say that?"

"I . . . we're . . ." I flounder.

"Why don't you tell me about her? What's her name?"

A heavy pause hangs between us. I don't see what good can come from talking about this, but my grandmother is not a woman who can be put off. "Her name's Ellie," I finally admit.

She smiles. "And?"

"And she works in a coffee shop while she goes to school."

Her eyes widen with what can only be described as dismay. "High school?"

"No," I laugh. "She's in her last semester of college."

Her relief quickly becomes interest. "Really? What does she study?"

My shrug has us both frowning. *Why don't I know that?* In fact, as my grandmother quizzes me about the only woman I've felt a connection with since Lolita, I don't know a lot of the answers to her questions, not even her birthday, or exactly how old she is or where she grew up.

"I don't understand, *mijo.* If you're not sure about so much, how do you know she's not right for you?"

"She's not Latina."

The surprise on my grandmother's face is unnerving. "So? What does that have to do with anything?"

My mouth opens and then closes as I try to come up with a reasonable explanation for the one person I'd never thought would need one.

"You want her to be Catholic?" she supplies.

"What?" I scoff. "No. Not that. She just wouldn't fit in around here."

Her head rears back. "You think we wouldn't accept her?"

"No, I . . . I just don't see it happening."

I squirm under her scrutiny, wishing she wasn't so obviously searching for more specific information, information that I can't seem to come up with. "Have you told her about the girls?"

Picking at the tattered edge of the placemat, I avoid her gaze. "Yeah, she knows."

"And she didn't receive the news well?"

"Oh, no. I don't know why, but she isn't put off by the idea."

After a moment of consideration, her next words take on a very adult to child tone. "Listen to me, Scotty. If there's one thing that life has taught me over the years it's that race is meaningless. There are good and bad people in all walks of life."

I nod because of course she's right. But I can't quite shake the unease my grandmother's unexpected liberal attitude has sparked in me. If Latin heritage is not important to her, why is it so important to me? "It's not only that though," I say, feeling like I need to defend myself. "She has problems . . ."

"We all have problems."

"No, she has problems with alcohol."

My grandmother's demeanor instantly shifts, as if the word *alcohol* changes everything. Almost as quickly, I'm jumping to defend Ellie before she can say a word against her.

"It's not like *that*. She's not . . . She doesn't . . . I don't even know what I want to say."

"But you wish to shield her?" She's surprised, shocked even. Probably because we both loathe the impact alcohol and drugs have had on our lives.

The word *shield* resonates with me. "Yes, exactly. I already want to shield her, but I can't. I can't take care of a single other person, Abuela. I've hit my limit on people being dependent on me."

Her brow puckers as she absorbs my words. "Dependent? You mean financially? I thought you said she has a job."

I huff impatiently. "Yes, she has a job. But I don't want to have to be responsible for her."

Her frown deepens. "You don't see her as an equal then?"

I recoil. There's so much wrong with that sentence that I don't even know where to begin with my denials.

"Scotty," she says sternly before I can get a word out. "You said something similar the other day. Do you think women in general are incompetent? Or just her?"

"What?! No, I don't think that at all!"

"Then I don't –"

"– don't understand. Yeah, I don't think I do either." Scrubbing at my face, I haul in a deep breath, trying to collect my thoughts. "I think the only thing I do know is that I miss her like crazy," I finally say.

"Then go to her, *mijo*. Tell her that."

"I can't," I say miserably. "She doesn't want to see me."

She reaches for my hand. "I don't want to know why this is so, but if you feel this much for her, you must apologize and put some effort into getting to know her."

"But . . ."

"No buts."

Even though I can feel my resolve crumbling, I grunt with frustration. "I told you she doesn't want me anywhere near her."

"Regardless, you must try. Use your charm," she jokes. "Convince her that your intentions are good."

When I don't answer, she squeezes my hand. "They are good, aren't they, *mijo*?"

And here we have the million dollar question. *What do I want from Ellie Summers?* The answer comes to me with startling clarity. *I want it all.*

Chapter Sixteen

Ellie

My attempts to dodge my sister's calls finally fail on Friday morning. Her pre-emptive strike comes in the form of a text.

Sophie: I know it's your day off. If you don't answer your phone, I'm calling Dad to tell him you're partying again.

My phone rings ten seconds later.

"Soph!" I exclaim indignantly.

"So you're still alive."

I throw her sarcasm right back at her. "And what would make you think otherwise?"

"Because I haven't talked to you in a week," she retorts. Then she goes on more gently. "I assume your cooking date didn't go well."

"You assume correctly." Great. All the effort I've put into *not* thinking about that asshole begins to slough away with her words. Exactly why I haven't wanted to talk to her. "But I don't want to talk about it."

"Of course you do. You're going to tell me every single detail because I'm your sister and your best friend and you value my input above anyone else's."

Despite her light-hearted tone, a knot of emotion starts forming in my throat. "That's true," I say softly.

"Oh, Els. What happened?"

I sigh. "He blew me off."

Mortification rising, I tell her the story and I'm hit with an awful sense of familiarity. Why am I always telling my sister the same story? The details may be different, but at its core, the scenario is depressingly similar. Poor Ellie/Piper likes a man more than he likes her. Or poor Ellie/Piper wants more from a man than he's willing to give. Ugh. So pathetic.

And worse, by the time I finish my sad, woe-is-me tale, I have tears running down my cheeks again after a week of trying to keep a stiff upper lip. The only bright spot is that Sophie proves once again why I can always count on her. She doesn't feed me pitiful platitudes, she gives me, "You want me to come up there and give him a shot to the balls for you?"

Around my sniffling, something approximating a chuckle slips from my lips.

"I'd do it, you know? I have a class to TA this afternoon, but I could drive up and be there before midnight. Do you know where he lives?"

I laugh, outright this time. "Thanks, sis, but I don't think that'll be necessary. I'm already moving on. I spent the week applying for paid internships for when I graduate."

"That's great," she enthuses.

"There's one position in the Chicago mayor's office that I'm really interested in."

There's a moment of silence. "Chicago? You're applying out of state?"

I blow out a breath. "Not all of them, but yeah, I'm aiming for out of state. There's nothing really holding me here."

"Uh, excuse me, what am I? Chopped liver?"

"Ha, ha. Of course not. But it's not like I see you that often. And you'd come visit me, right?"

"I guess. But Chicago, Els? You wouldn't last five minutes in the winter. Doesn't it go down to like minus a million?"

"That's the whole point of a fresh start. That everything is new and different."

When I get nothing but dead air, I pull the phone away from my ear to check the screen to make sure she's still there. "Soph?"

She sighs. "Yeah, I'm here. I'm thinking the eight hour drive is going to be necessary after all. This Scott guy really did a number on you."

"Nah, come on. Even without that jerk, there's nothing here for me – just Amelia, and I'm sure that she'll come and visit me too. Anyway, enough about me. What's going on with you?"

When we hang up, I feel better than I have all week. Though I've managed to keep myself busy with school, work, internship applications and long runs through my neighborhood, last weekend's events have left me feeling drained. No matter how much I'd like to pretend I'm fine, I know I still need time to recover.

It's not until I'm putting my nightly Ramen noodles in the microwave that my relative levity fades with the jolting sound of the building's intercom.

The clock on the stove says 5:40 . . . on a Friday evening. *He wouldn't. Would he?* I slam the microwave door and fire it up, ignoring my rising dismay. It doesn't matter if it's him. I'm not going to answer.

The intercom jars me twice more while I pace, waiting for my soup to cook. *Damn him. What could he possibly want?*

Anger starts to mix with the trepidation. *He's got a lot of nerve coming here.* I grab up my phone and check the screen before I remember that I blocked him.

My nerves calm a bit when a few minutes pass without the intercom going off. Maybe it was Mrs. Stanfield needing to be buzzed in.

A soft tapping at my door has the dread surging back. *Who let him in the building?* I'd haul the door open and give him a piece of my mind if the thought of seeing him weren't so terrifying.

More knocking, this time loud enough to echo through the apartment.

"Come on, El. I know you're home."

My pulse stupidly spikes at the sound of his muffled voice.

"Please? I just want to talk."

Before I can stop myself, I pad my way to the door and peer through the peep hole. My heart leaps at the sight. He's as beautiful as ever, but with a slight slant to his brows, showing his consternation.

He knocks again, loudly, and I jump about a foot in the air.

"Please, El?"

Behind him, I see Mrs. Stanfield's door open just enough to be caught by the safety chain. "Young man, if you don't leave, I'll have to call the police."

The back of Scott's head fills the view as he turns to face her. "I'm really hoping it doesn't come to that." He turns back and knocks again. "El? You don't want me to get arrested, do you?"

"Well, don't say that I didn't warn you," she says indignantly.

Oh shit. I quickly unhook my own safety chain and turn the deadbolt. "It's okay, Mrs. Stanfield. I didn't hear him knocking."

The half of my neighbor's face that's visible through the six inch gap shows her suspicion. "You're sure, Piper?" she asks with what almost sounds like concern.

"Yes, thank you so much for looking out for me."

The old lady harrumphs and bangs her door shut.

I finally bring myself to look at Scott and the anxiety in my stomach pulls lower and starts to heat. "What are you doing here?" I mean it to be an angry hiss but it comes out more like a pathetic whisper.

His big brown eyes swirl with entreaty. "I only want to talk."

"There's nothing to talk about," I say, dropping my gaze so I won't be swayed by the look on his face.

"Yes, there is."

My shoulders sag. There's only two reasons he could be here. One, he's sorry and he wants a second chance, or, more likely, two, he's here to assuage his conscience. Either way, I'm not interested.

He takes my momentary silence for uncertainty because he goes on, drawing my eyes back up. "If you don't like what I have to say, you can throw me out." His lips twitch into a sad, fleeting grin. "Please, I only need five minutes."

Trying to ignore the ache in my heart at his apparent sincerity, I wonder if he'll show up again if I deny him this chance. I step back to let him in. "Okay," I whisper. "But FYI, I'm *not* sleeping with you."

His palms come up in surrender. "No, of course not, I mean, I wouldn't . . ."

With a frown on my face, I lead him into the kitchen. *Is he nervous?* I don't think I've ever seen Scott nervous. It's almost as if he has something to lose. The idea does little to shore up my resolve as we square off at either end of the island.

For a long minute he doesn't say anything and I fiddle with my phone on the counter to avoid looking at him.

"I was a dick," he announces like it's news.

"Yes, you were."

"I want to apologize."

Irritation chips away at my patience. "We've already had this conversation."

"It got cut short. And I've still got four minutes left."

His tone has my hackles rising. "Fine. I'm listening."

"I'm sorry that I didn't call," he says earnestly. "I panicked. Because you were right when you said it was good between us."

He has got to be kidding me. "You blew me off – after you fucked me – because it was *good between us*?"

"Yes," he says, maddeningly meeting my sarcasm with calm equanimity. "And we didn't *fuck*, and you know it."

"Well, I'd hate to see how you treat the women you *do* fuck, because you left me feeling like trash."

He winces. "I was selfish. I admit it. But you have to know that I didn't intentionally hurt you."

I scoff. "Not intentionally because I didn't figure into your thinking at all." I turn away, sighing heavily. "Why are you here, Scott?"

"I want to make things right between us, El. I've been miserable."

"Is that right?" My irritation boils over. "*You've* been miserable? You're not just selfish, Scott, you're a complete narcissist. You have a family to go home to. You have children who love you. You have friends. You have –"

"I don't have you."

That damned knife is re-plunged into my chest, trying to rob me of the breath that I need to get rid of this guy. "Which is the way you wanted it," I remind him with as much force as I can muster. "You told me so from the very beginning."

"Don't pretend that things haven't changed."

I close my eyes against the throbbing ache in my chest. "They haven't changed enough, Scott. I can't be your . . ." my mind searches for the right word, ". . . your *whatever* girl, the one you call up when you've got nothing better to do."

"That's good. Because I don't want that either."

"Oh, really? What is it you want then? What is it that you're envisioning for us?"

"I don't know. I –"

"You don't know?" I mock.

"Let me finish," he grits out, his fist clenching on the counter in front of him. "Please."

I fold my arms over my chest, hating that this is just a painful waste of time, one that's going to leave me gutted when he's finished. But I'm determined that he'll take this nasty knife with him when he goes.

"I know," he says pointedly before his voice gentles, "that I want to get to know you. This thing between us is not something that happens every day . . . or ever."

Shit, are those butterflies forming in my stomach?

"I feel good when I'm with you, El. You make me want more from life. And that scares me because I've already got more going on than I can handle. I don't know how to sort that out in my head, but I want to give it my best try."

Irrational hope starts to crest inside of me. But I can't allow that, I need to keep this real. "That's all well and good for you, Scott, but I'm not in a position to let you experiment with what does and doesn't work for you. When you disappeared, it felt like getting hit by a truck while I was looking the other way, and I'm not interested in repeating the experience." He wants to defend himself, but I hold up my hand to stop him. "I think we both got in over our heads. Let's just move on."

"No."

My expression twists. "What do you mean, *no*?"

"I mean, no. We may be in over our heads, but we're good together, El. You can't deny that."

True, I think weakly, my resistance starting to melt and pool around my feet, like the wax of a candle left to the mercy of its own flame. "You'll do it again," I say, my voice barely above a whisper.

"Do what?" he huffs out half-heartedly. "Fuck up? I'm sure I will."

Indignation flares. "This isn't a game, Scott!"

"I know it's not! I truly never meant to hurt you. I didn't think it was a big deal to take a couple days to wrap my head around everything. You're always so confident, El, like nothing fazes you. I never considered that *you'd* ever need anything from *me.*"

That pulls me up short, and it must show on my face because he adds more.

"Believe me, I understand now how selfish I was."

"Do you?" I ask, still a bit stunned. "Because I think we're playing for different stakes here, Scott. God, I almost took a drink last weekend."

His head pulls back an inch in surprise. "What?" Clearly that was the last thing he expected to hear tonight. "Are you serious?"

I nod, avoiding his gaze for a moment. "When you didn't show, I couldn't stand just sitting here by myself, so I went out with Vanessa and her friends."

Watching his face drain of everything but shock and remorse only adds to the heat staining my cheeks at hearing the confession spoken aloud.

"Oh, El, I . . ."

I cut off his unwanted apology. "I'm not blaming you. I really thought I could handle it. It wasn't like I was setting myself up to fail, or anything, but it was a close call."

"What stopped you?"

I laugh, a bitter, self-deprecating sound. "You did. You were there. With your friends at the bar. It's ironic when you really think about it."

"I . . . El. . . I'm. . ."

I wave him off. "So you can see why I can't take the chance that the next time you have a selfish impulse, you won't ruin me completely."

Chapter Seventeen

Scott

For crying out loud. *Again*, this is not going how I planned. This time, not only am I getting blindsided, but I'm sinking in quicksand. That I almost drove her to drink is nothing I ever want to hear again.

Just how badly I screwed up hits me, and for an instant, I consider that maybe she'd be better off without me. But the thought disappears as quickly as it came. I'm not giving up on her or myself. It's just not in my nature. When my mind's made up, it's made up. Now I have to convince her I can get my head out of my ass and treat her with the care she deserves. If only I can find the right words.

"I . . . yeah, I can see why you wouldn't want to take that chance. I got so caught up in my own damage that I ignored *you*." Rubbing the back of my neck nervously, I force myself to go on, to lay it all out there. "I'm used to depending on myself, El. Over the last few weeks, I've been doing my best to ignore the feeling of *needing* to see you, of missing you when you aren't with me. I thought it was a problem, or a weakness. But these last few days without you have finally shown me the truth."

Her watery, owlish brown eyes shine up at me. "They have?"

"Yeah," I admit. "The truth is that when I'm with you, everything is right with the world, and when I'm not, I feel like I'm drowning. I realize now that needing you and missing you don't make me weak . . ." my stomach flips and twists, ". . . they make everything so much better." My voice drops to a whisper then. "I know now that I care about you – a lot."

Her gaze drops from mine as her hands clasp and unclasp on the island counter. God, her silence makes me feel exposed, completely vulnerable and unprotected. If I could, I'd claw my chest open with my bare hands to stop the rising of this horrible, on-edge sensation. Finally, I can't stand it any longer.

"I've got my head on straight now, El. Please give me another chance."

The sound of her pulling in a breath to speak coils my stomach into a double knot. "So, let's say I forgive you," she says softly. "Then what?"

Then what? "Then . . . we move forward." I almost cringe at how it sounds like a question.

"What does that mean to you, though, moving forward? You have kids."

My defenses immediately rise and spring thorns at the mention of the girls. "I never hid that from you. Are you telling me it's some kind of deal breaker now?" I can't keep the incredulity from my voice.

Her brows, which had been pinched in concern, re-align themselves to show confusion. "What? No, Scott, I'm saying that you have *kids*. Before you knew how we really met, I could pretend that my past didn't exist, that Piper isn't Ellie. But we both know that's bullshit." She nervously pulls the elastic from her hair and re-ties her ponytail. "If I'm the sum of my parts – and I am – I'm not fit to be around children, especially not yours."

My insides freeze. *What, exactly, is she saying?* For long, excruciating moments, we just stare at each other. For the life of me, I can't think of how to respond to that.

"See?" she finally says hoarsely. "This is what I'm talking about. I'm not right for you, Scott, and I don't want to be a placeholder until you find someone who is. No matter how much I love being with you, no matter how good you make me feel, I can't do that to myself."

I watch, horrified as she swipes at a tear that's now rolling down her cheek before she goes on. "It would be so easy for me to slip into that role for you, but I can't be that girl anymore. Piper is dead."

"El. Why are you . . . please don't cry." I can't stand it anymore, I need to touch her, but when I start around the island, she matches my steps in the opposite direction. I blow out a heavy breath of frustration and stop. We've now got the short side of the island between us. "I don't want Piper, El. And I definitely don't want you to play some role or be a . . ." my mouth curls with disgust, "placeholder. I just want you."

She's shaking her head at me. "How can you say that? If you knew half the things I've done in my life . . ."

Her distress hits me like a punch to the gut, and before she can react, I make it around the island and wrap her up in my arms. "Hey," I tell her gently as she pushes at my chest, feebly attempting to free herself. *"Oye, escúchame."* Spanish gets her attention where English didn't, and her forehead comes to rest on my shoulder, followed by the rest of her.

"Whatever you've done, Opal, it can't be as bad as you're thinking."

She sniffles. "That's because you don't know."

"Come and sit down then." Pulling her toward the couch, I sit her down on the cushion beside me. "Tell me."

"You won't like it," she says miserably as she picks at the nail polish on her finger nails, studiously avoiding my eyes.

Taking her chin in my hand, I turn her to face me. "Tell me anyway."

She heaves a sigh. "Well, I, uh, kind of fell off track at the end of my sophomore year . . . you're sure you want to hear this?" My poor girl. It's like she's being led to the gallows.

"Yes."

She nods at the firm tone of my voice. "Okay. So at the end of my sophomore year I found out that my long-term boyfriend had a wife and kid back home."

Okay, not what I was expecting. "The fuck?"

Our gazes clash, and I see so much sadness reflected there. "Yeah, Nathan was a grad student from Ohio, doing his degree here. It really messed me up when I found out. I mean, we'd been together for almost a year, we'd even talked about marriage and having kids together. I just couldn't wrap my head around the kinds of lies he'd spun for me."

She seems even more worn out now than when I arrived, as if dredging up these memories is exhausting. "Anyway, after it all came out, I needed to escape, so I applied to do a year abroad in Spain . . . and I got accepted, but not until January. It was such a disaster, my junior year. I barely managed to pass my classes here at Stanford and when I finally got to Madrid, I didn't do much better. Then, over the summer break, I went to Ibiza with some friends . . . and I, uh, never looked back."

I can feel the frown on my face as I try to untangle what she's telling me. I say *try* because my mind is tripping over words like *Spain, Stanford,* and *Ibiza,* and how they apply to *my* Ellie.

"After that, all I did was hang out and party for almost two years."

She sounds . . . ashamed, and that further confuses me. *Wouldn't hanging out in paradise like that be amazing?* Then my practical side comes up with, "Wasn't that expensive?"

A rare blush starts to bloom under the dismayed expression on her face, confounding me even more. "I . . ." She flounders for a second, then re-starts. "So, there are a few things Ibiza isn't lacking. Alcohol, drugs, and rich men, and I basically played that scenario out until I . . . couldn't anymore."

Huh? What scenario? "You're saying . . . You're saying what?"

"I'm saying I hooked up with guys who liked to party." She then starts shaking her head jerkily. "No, I'm sugar-coating this," she says more to herself, rubbing at her forehead anxiously. She hauls in a deep breath and starts again. "I slept with rich guys in exchange for a place to crash, all the booze and drugs I wanted, and gifts; designer bags, shoes, clothes, jewelry. Stuff I would pawn when I needed a break. Some 'relationships' would last a few months and some only a few weeks."

Jesus. What?

My brain spins, trying to digest her words.

Because . . . What?

"In the beginning," she continues, her voice reduced to a whisper. "I didn't realize that I was chiseling away at tiny parts of myself. All I focused on was the ego boost after Nathan's betrayal. Men wanted me and I didn't like being alone with my thoughts. With everything being blunted by the booze, it seemed like a perfect solution to all my problems."

I can only stare at her and note how she starts to hunch in on herself.

"It took a while, but I finally pulled myself together," she says, uncurling her spine slightly as if she's gathering the vestiges of her self-respect around herself.

It's that change in her that shakes me from the shock. I'm not going to pretend that what she's telling me hasn't taken me by surprise. Because, what the fuck? But I haven't heard anything that needs to be forgiven.

"So you can see why I . . . I'm not . . . it wouldn't be appropriate for your girls."

"Oh, El, come here." I pull her onto my lap and tuck her head under my chin. "You don't think my girls would benefit from knowing a woman who pulled herself out of a situation she recognized as damaging?"

"Scott —"

"Hang on. A woman who's strong enough to completely remake herself and quit drinking? A woman who — if I understand correctly — is about to graduate from an Ivy League school? You don't think she'd be appropriate?"

"I . . . no, I . . ."

"How many times have you told me that Piper is your past, not your future, El?"

"I guess, but —"

"Is there a reason I shouldn't take you at your word?"

"No! I'm done with all that."

"Okay, I believe you."

"You do?"

"Yeah, I do. I'm the only one here who's done anything that needs to be forgiven. And I'm still hoping that you're going to give me a second chance."

"I want to, so much," she whispers.

"I know I'm going to have to work to earn back your trust."

She lets out a contented sigh and I smile into her hair.

"Does that sound mean you're going to forgive me?"

"Are you sure that's what you want?"

"A million times yes, Opal, as long as you promise to be patient with me. I have zero experience with being a boyfriend."

She stills in my arms. "You have a daughter. How can you not have experience?"

I squeeze her tighter as if I'm afraid she'll bolt. Considering everything that she's confessed tonight, I have no right to keep this to myself. "I don't think the experiences of a fifteen year old count."

"Fifteen?" She looks up at me, obviously confused. And rightfully so, since I've told her so little about myself.

I grin at her sheepishly. "Yeah."

"But your daughter is . . ."

"Almost seven," I finish for her.

"But that would mean you're only twenty-two." She sounds a bit horrified.

"Only?" Even if she took two years off of school she can't be that much older than I am.

She lets out a strained, disbelieving laugh.

"What?" I ask, perplexed.

"I'll be twenty-seven soon."

Uh? After a few beats all I can do is laugh, though it holds a lot more joy than hers did. Almost immediately my amusement cuts off as she wriggles her way off my lap.

"Opal," I call as she disappears down the hall. "Come back. Let's talk about this."

I'm about to go in search of her when she reappears holding a roll of toilet paper. Flopping herself down on the opposite end of the couch, she proceeds to wipe her tears. Then, leveling me with a dejected glare, she demands, "You mind telling me why you find this funny?"

I give her a bright smile. "My best friend, Jorgie, is convinced I have a thing for older women. And now I've proven him right. He's never going to let me live this down."

She studies me for a moment. "It doesn't freak you out?"

"Not at all," I tell her honestly. "Does it freak you out?"

"I guess not . . . it just doesn't make much sense. You're so together. When I was twenty-two I was a complete disaster."

"Ha ha," I say, the sarcasm dripping. "Clearly, you overestimate me. I almost messed up one of the best things that's ever happened to me."

And she's back to wide-eyed hurt.

"Hey, I meant what I said," I say softly. "I won't disappear again."

She's still worried, but she looks a lot more like herself than she did when I arrived, seeming to take me at my word after a few moments of consideration. "Will you tell me about fifteen year old Scott?"

"That's a pretty self-explanatory story," I tell her ruefully. "My girlfriend and I both thought she was on birth control. It hadn't taken effect yet. We were stupid. But I wouldn't change a thing even if I could. Rosa means the world to me."

She nods, like it makes perfect sense. "Which is why you're so responsible and work so hard."

"Yeah, probably. I'd do anything for her."

"It might sound crazy, but I envy that kind of motivation. I've always felt . . . adrift, I guess."

I reach for her hand and she lets me pull her back into my arms. I hate seeing her sad and defeated. With her head tucked under my chin, I promise myself I'll do everything in my power to avoid hurting her in the future.

Chapter Eighteen

Ellie

I expected excuses from him, I got confessions. I expected trite and superficial, I got heartfelt and deep. Then after confessing *my* worst sins, I expected him to make a bee line for the door. Yet somehow he's up-ended it all.

I'm worried I should still have my guard up, but after the aching emptiness of the past week and tonight's emotionally exhausting heart-to-heart, I don't have the energy. For now, I'm going to allow myself to soak up the warmth of his presence and the strength of his arms . . . and the way his dick is beginning to press against my thigh since I'm sitting on his lap. The idea that maybe he's not off-limits anymore sparks to life inside of me, but I ignore it. I meant it. I'm not sleeping with him tonight.

"What should we order for dinner?" he asks a bit tightly, trying to shift my hips away from his without being obvious.

"Are you going to stay for a while then?"

He kisses my temple before planting me on the couch beside him so he can dig his cell out of his pocket. "I told you, you're not getting rid of me."

An arc of longing begins to twine between us. God, he's as beautiful as ever, his jaw still strong, his lips still inviting, his dark eyes still expressive, framed by his bangs that brush his forehead.

"Opal," he says, his voice low. "Don't look at me like that."

"Like what?" I whisper.

"Like you want me to strip you naked."

"That sounds . . ." *completely delicious* ". . . like a bad idea."

"Yeah, the worst."

Oh, shit. *Is he leaning in?* I scramble back. "We agreed," I blurt.

He lounges back on the sofa cushions, barely repressing a smirk. "Chinese okay?" he asks casually like he wasn't about to kiss me.

I want to be as laid back as he is and say something flirty but all I manage to get out is a squeaky, "Sure, thanks."

While he orders the food, I dispose of my now congealed soup that's in the microwave. When he comes up behind me, I'm facing the sink, lost in a choppy sea of hope and despair. "You really think we have a shot at this?" I ask carefully.

His arms curl around me, and again, I can't resist the offered reassurance.

"Yeah, I do." He nuzzles into my shoulder, chuckling softly before he goes on. "And now that I know about your cougar status, you're more under my skin than ever."

"My what?" I choke out in surprise, though a second later, I'm repressing a laugh. "Take that back. I'm at least a decade short on cougar status."

"Fine. Cradle robber then."

My low shriek of outrage is corrupted by more laughter. "You make it sound like you're a teenager. When exactly do you turn twenty-three?"

"Not until November."

"We're only four years apart."

"*The end* of November," he says, needling me further. "That's way closer to five years."

"And your point is?" I ask, slightly exasperated as he lets me go so I can turn and face him.

"My point is," he says, his brows arching, "I think it's hot as fuck."

I bite my lip to stop a pleased smile from starting. "Is that so?"

"Uh, yeah. You going to tell me when exactly your birthday is?"

"On Thursday."

That surprises him.

"I'm going to need presents," I announce with mock arrogance, liking him off kilter.

Slowly a grin spreads across his face. "Oh, I'm sure I've got something I can give you," he says suggestively, reaching for me once again. I'm saved by the intercom's shrill buzz that announces our dinner. Slipping down the hall, I grab the receiver off the wall and let the delivery driver into the building just as rough hands grab my waist and turn me.

"Tell me I can kiss you."

"I . . ." My mind blanks as his palms slide along my jaw, one of his thumbs brushing my bottom lip.

"Please," he whispers, his mouth already so close to mine that I feel his breath on my face.

"Okay." The syllables are barely formed before he's kissing me like his life depends on it, giving me sure, strong strokes of his lips and tongue that have my insides turning to liquid fire.

A minute later, when the delivery guy knocks on the door beside us, we pause briefly, but my soft whimper has him plundering my mouth again. The knocking is louder the second time.

Scott grudgingly releases his grip on me to open the door. Glaring at the poor kid, he passes me the food, while I try to hold in my laughter. Why is his irritation so endearing?

While we unpack the food, the air shimmers around us with potent, unfulfilled desire. God, if I'm going to stick to my principles, I've got to find a distraction.

"So, um, where is your family from originally?" I ask, sitting on a stool at the island to fill my plate.

He eyes me like he knows exactly what my game is. "My grandfather was born in Texas, but his parents were from Sinaloa, and my grandmother grew up in a small town near Acapulco. So, Mexico. You?"

Stop watching his mouth, Ellie. "Well, I told you my mom was born in Poland. And supposedly, my dad's family practically came over on the Mayflower."

He considers me. "You want to tell me how a half-Polish Catholic school girl speaks Spanish?"

"Oh, um, I –"

He holds up a finger to stop me. "Tell me in Spanish?" He poses it as a question. As if he doesn't quite believe I'm fluent enough to do it. This time it's me with the smirk on my face.

"Pues . . ." I start telling him about one of my first wars with my mother, who was adamant that I learn French. I didn't see why I couldn't study Spanish so I could practice with my beloved Amelia. Even at ten years old, I chafed against her prejudice. At the time it was only a partial victory; I could learn all the Spanish I wanted as long as I learned French as well. In the end, it helped me get into college, so I can't bitch about it too much.

All through the story, his jaw has been clenching and unclenching. When I get to the part about how I learned all the really filthy swear words in Madrid and then on the beaches of Ibiza (because no one wields a curse better than a Spaniard), he interrupts me.

"Opal?"

"Yeah?"

"Unless you want me to take you up against the wall behind you, you need to stop talking."

"What?"

"That crazy accent of yours is making my dick hard."

"¿No te gusta mi acento español?" I ask him with more than a little sass. *You don't like my Spanish accent?*

He laughs. *"No, me encanta tu acento español."* No, I love your Spanish accent.

I feel my mouth go lax at the incredible sound of him speaking a language I adore. After a much needed moment to recover my equilibrium, I agree with him. "Yeah, okay, we'll save it for another time."

Turning my attention to my plate, I can't stop the dirty girl in me from wondering just how extensive his vocabulary is and if he'd be willing to whisper dirty things in my ear.

His low chuckle catches me mid chew and does nothing but add to the desire that's growing inside of me. "What's so funny?" I demand after I swallow my food.

"Just that you're so transparent."

Even if I don't have a clear view of his lap, I drop my gaze suggestively. "No more than you," I purr, loving it when he shifts in his seat.

"Okaaay, next question. What's your major?"

I take a breath. "I have two. Poli-Sci and Spanish."

"Poli-Sci? As in . . . as in politics? You want to be a politician?"

The dawning horror in his voice has me smiling. "No. I'm more interested in social policy . . . things like immigration and education reform, social programs for women, homelessness."

Now he's the one who's stopped chewing, looking at me like I've grown horns and a tail. He's quiet for longer than I'd like and just as I'm on the verge of worry, his lips tilt up ever so slightly. "I thought we agreed to lay off the sexual innuendo."

"Huh?"

"I knew you were smart, Opal, but not that smart. I never stood a chance against you, did I? I mean, how is it fair that your brain is probably hotter than your ass?"

"Is that supposed to be a compliment?"

"You're damn right it is." He puts down his chopsticks. "So let me get this straight. You're fun and funny, you're about to graduate from Stanford with a double major, *and* you're more beautiful than . . . any woman – ever."

I'm unsure how to respond to so many compliments, but he doesn't notice.

"I'm going to ask you straight up, El. What the hell are you doing with me? I just got my GED last year. Plus, I've got an entire family to support."

Though he's trying to joke, I can hear the unease that's scratching at the edge of his tone. His vulnerability has him inching his way further into my heart. "You're also a very decent human being, Scott, and a wonderful father. And don't even get me started on the situation we've got going on here," I say, waving my hand at him.

He shakes his head slightly. "I'm not Stanford smart."

"Please. Everyone knows book smarts don't equal intelligence." I jerk my thumb at my chest, like I'm the perfect example. "At least you have a moral compass that's fully intact and operational."

"There's nothing wrong with your moral compass."

How can he say that after everything I've told him? I give him a look that says *give me a break*.

"I'm far from perfect," he says like that's the real issue here.

"No one's perfect. If you knew how many pretentious assholes I've met in my life, you'd have no problem understanding what I find so attractive about you."

He ducks his head a bit, pleased, I think, by my words, possibly even embarrassed. If I'm not careful, he'll win me over so completely that I won't be able to keep a clear head.

He stays with me until late. We talk some more, we endure another agonizing make-out session, and then, because I've had such an exhausting day, I fall asleep on his shoulder while we watch a movie.

I wake up as he places me on my bed, tucking me under the blankets. He smiles at me in the light from the streetlamps outside my window.

"Sorry I woke you," he whispers. "But I have to go." He pushes my hair back from my face and I press my cheek into his palm. "What time do you work tomorrow?"

"Mmmm? Early. Six to two."

"Your phone's here," he says, lifting his chin at the night stand. "Is your alarm set?"

I sigh with happiness as I nod. "Yeah"

"Okay. One more thing, will you go on a real date with me tomorrow?"

My sleepy smile must be as wide as the Cheshire cat's. "Really?"

"Yeah, really. I'll pick you up around six?"

"Okay."

I'd be lying if I said I didn't love the approval on his face as he leans in for a quick, sweet kiss. "I'll see you tomorrow then. Sleep well."

"You too."

Chapter Nineteen

Scott

The next morning, weekend breakfast with the girls once again leaves the kitchen resembling a war zone, but we're happy. The time and effort to clean up is well worth it; cooking is an activity that we can do together, one that I'm thankful for because it doesn't involve dolls or ponies. I really want to be a good father, but that uber-girly stuff grates on my nerves like you wouldn't believe. Also, I like that we work together as a team to put the kitchen to rights afterward. The sense of accomplishment suits all four of us.

Of course accomplishment is not the only thing giving me the warm fuzzies this morning. After the huge ups and downs of last week, I've made things right with Ellie – mostly. Things aren't perfect, but for now I'm focusing on the only thing that I know for sure: I want Ellie in my life. And not just on Friday nights. To do that, I need to broach the idea with the girls.

I've come up with a tentative plan.

I sit them down on the couch, three in a row. They look like baby birds with their curious expressions, waiting expectantly for whatever I'm about to tell them. Pacing in front of the coffee table, I run a hand through my hair in a sudden bout of nerves. "So, um, I need your guys' help with something important today."

"Really?" Daniela says, showing the same surprise as her sisters.

"Yeah, I want you to help me choose some flowers that I want to send to someone."

"Flowers?" Daniela asks. She and Rosa begin to vibrate with sudden excitement.

Carmen, on the other hand, is now suspicious – smart girl. "To who?"

"To . . ." A girl? A woman? A lady? Or maybe just a friend for now? Shit, *woman* is probably the right answer but I don't like the way it sounds in my head. Snap decision. "To a girl that I really like."

Rosa sucks in an audible breath. "You like a girl, Papá?"

The next words on the tip of my tongue are: *Yes. Is that okay?* But I can't let that out of my mouth. It can't be their decision whether I date a woman or not. Do I ever want their approval though. "Yeah, I really like her."

"Like . . ." Rosa's eyes are huge in her face. "Like a *girlfriend*?"

"Yes, like a girlfriend." And then I hear myself say, "What do you guys think about that?" Damn it. But I suppose it's better than *is that okay?*

Daniela claps with glee. "I think it's amazing. What's her name, Tío? Is she beautiful? I bet she's beautiful. Anne Marie says her mom thinks you're so handsome, so she must be beautiful."

Shit, I think I might be blushing. I take a deep breath to give myself a chance to gauge the others' reactions; Rosa: shocked, but not horrified. Carmen: unhappy. All righty then.

"Yes, she's really beautiful. And . . . " I say, drawing it out, "you won't believe what her name is. I'll give you two guesses. It's from your favorite movie."

Daniela's excitement can't be contained. "Her name is Anna?!"

"No, but close."

"Her name is Elsa," Carmen says reverently, her displeasure now forgotten.

"It is." All three of them squeal and I laugh. "Can you believe it? But she likes to be called Ellie."

Rosa, who has a practical streak to rival my own, dives right in with the pertinent questions. "Are we going to bring her flowers *today*? Do we get to meet her?"

My stomach clenches. "Um, well, no. We'll get them delivered."

"Awww," Daniela complains. "Why can't we meet her? We'll be good."

"It's not about you being good . . . anyway, you guys are always good. If things go well, you can meet her in a couple weeks. Deal?"

Even Carmen, with her obvious reservations, is nodding in agreement.

"So, go get your sweaters and we'll go pick out some flowers."

In the truck, I marvel at how well that went. Even though I didn't think any of them had it in them to hate Ellie on principle, if they wanted to, they could really make life difficult for me on this.

At the flower shop, the girls *oooh* and *ahhh* at all the selection.

"*¿Papá, le vas a comprar rosas?*" Rosa asks cheekily.

Laughing, I agree, "We should definitely get roses. You guys can choose the color."

Surprise, surprise, they choose pink. When the owner of the shop informs me that pink signifies admiration, I grimace. "Are you sure you don't like the red ones?" I ask them hopefully.

"Ellie is a *girl*, Tío," Daniela informs me. "She likes pink way better than red." The word *red* comes out sounding like she's describing roadkill and I have to smile.

The florist sympathizes with me. "How about eleven pink with one red in the center of the bouquet?" she asks, handing me a pen to fill out the card.

"I like it," I tell her, relieved, but then I hum and haw over what to put on the card until I come up with:

Dear Opal, I hope you like the flowers. The girls chose the pink ones and I chose the red. See you tonight at 6. Scott.

I have to pay a premium to have the flowers delivered to her work before two o'clock, but it's worth it.

The energy around the house that afternoon is different – good different. As soon as Abuela arrives back from her knitting circle, the girls tell her the whole story. I've gotta say it's a little embarrassing to have my kids watch my grandmother pinch my cheek and say how proud she is of me.

They go through the same process when Desiree gets home from work, then again with Mari, both of whom tease the shit out of me. I don't really care, I'm thrilled to see my family happy and laughing. Well, happy and laughing until my mother makes an appearance.

When she arrives, there's no clamor to include her in the family gossip. She does, however, realize that something's up.

She leans against the door jamb, assessing us suspiciously where we're gathered around the kitchen table.

"What's going on?"

Mari snorts. *"Scotty está enamorado."*

I tsk. "Shut up. I'm not in love." I shove her shoulder playfully.

"With that tall girl?" my mom asks, and everyone turns to her and then back to me.

I consider my answer, wondering what her angle is. I can't see any harm in not denying it, so I give her the truth. "Uh, yeah."

"¿La conociste, mija?" my grandmother asks curiously. *You've met her?*

"Yeah, I met her. She's whiter than Wonder bread."

My mouth opens but nothing comes out. I think we're all surprised by the spite in her tone. Desiree recovers first. "What are you trying to say, mother?"

"Nothing. It's typical, that's all."

My back is definitely up now. "What does that mean?"

"Just that it figures you'd choose some white chick who looks like a model instead of a regular Latina."

I don't have a single clue what to say to that. Again, Desiree comes to my rescue.

"Yes, mother, we all consciously choose who we fall in love with," she says caustically. "Just like you. That's you and Robbie, right? Till death do you part? Oh wait, it's not death keeping you apart, it's prison."

Carmen, who's sitting on my knee, recoils at the mention of her father. In fact, everyone does and before my mother can fire back, I put a stop to this bullshit. *"Ni una palabra más."* *Not another word.* I look from my mother to my oldest sister, who opens her mouth anyway. I cut her off. *"Ni una,* Des. This conversation is over."

I put Carmen on her feet. "Come on, girls. Let's go to the park."

We make the walk to the playground near our house in silence, and I wish we'd left before my mother arrived. She has this uncanny ability to suck the joy out of any situation. I hate it, but I don't see any way around her presence in my life or the lives of my kids. That dream of mine, the one where we move away and start over, seems as far away as ever.

Keeping an eye on the girls from the bench where I park my ass, I pull out my phone and smile at the excited texts Ellie sent me earlier when she got the flowers. It's not quite enough to erase my mother's comments though. My mother's not a racist . . . is she? I suppose she's always had a bit of an attitude toward white people, or more specifically, one white person . . . my father.

A sense of horror comes over me. All this time, have I thought I was supposed to be with a Latina because it's what my mom wanted? Has her prejudice against my father influenced me? After some consideration, I decide on *possibly* or maybe even *probably*. But I also realize that's not the whole story. I've always wanted a Latina because I figured she would somehow legitimize my claim on my heritage, somehow make up for my pale complexion and ridiculous height.

It all seems . . . silly now, weak even. I am who I am, no matter who I choose to make a life with.

I stare down at the last message that Ellie sent me, which is just a series of emojis that show her delight. It goes a long way to draining some of the stress from the base of my skull.

"Hi," Ellie breathes when she opens her door a few hours later, her happy smile almost blinding me.

"Hey," I return.

She takes my hand and pulls me inside. "Come see."

In the kitchen, she gestures with exaggerated grace to the roses on the island like they're a prize on *The Price is Right*. "Aren't they awesome? When the delivery guy announced they were for Opal, I almost fell over."

"I'm so glad you like them."

"I *love* them. Thank you."

"You're welcome."

The air between us thickens and her lips show me something much more sinful than a smile. The idea of kissing her, of touching her, starts to consume me. I refuse to act on it though. I'm determined to do this right. "We should go," I say, a bit embarrassed by the hoarseness of my voice.

"Okay. Is this all right for where we're going?" She indicates the jeans and flowy blouse thing she's wearing.

"Yeah, you look great."

On closer inspection, I notice the blouse is see-through, showing me the skimpy tank top she's got on underneath. We definitely need to go. If I'm not careful, I'll be wincing all night at the pressure in my pants.

She grabs her purse and her keys to lock up.

"You've never come inside to pick me up before. This *must* be a real date," she teases.

I pause. *I haven't?* "Well, if you promise not to make fun of me, I'll admit that I've never been on a real date." I hold the truck door open for her while she just stands there, studying me like I'm full of shit.

"I'm the first?" she asks, a slow smile spreading across her face. "That's kind of adorable."

"Get in the truck, Opal." My exasperation only serves to increase her smile.

"Such a caveman."

At least she doesn't seem to mind my overbearing side.

Once we're on our way, she says, "The card said the girls picked the roses . . . did you . . . what did you tell them?"

"Yeah, so I Googled it, and –"

"Wait, what? Googled what exactly?"

"How to tell your kids you're dating someone."

"Are you serious?" I can hear the underlying laughter in her voice.

"Yeah, I'm not taking any chances. I don't want to mess this up."

She must decide there's some logic to the idea, because she says, "Fair enough. What exactly did you find?"

"Well, I'm supposed to talk about you in a positive way, so I told them that there's this girl I like and then I tied it in with the flowers."

I glance her way to see if she agrees with the brilliance of my plan, but she's just biting at her thumb nail.

"And?"

"And they were pretty excited," I say, reaching for her hand to interlace our fingers.

"Really?"

"Yeah, really. Well Daniela and Rosa mostly. Carmen was . . . concerned until we got to the part about your name being Elsa." I grin at her. "I hope you know how to sing and dance."

"What?" The word comes out with half-choked amusement.

"Hey, we'll be using every possible advantage. I don't want this to get ugly."

Her happy countenance slips. "You think it could get ugly?"

"Sorry, wrong word. Listen, for now, we don't need to worry about the girls. I'm pretty sure I've got us covered, okay?" She watches me pull her hand to my lips for what I hope is a reassuring kiss.

"Okay."

The restaurant is a nice Italian place that Desiree told me about with candles on the tables. We get a booth and she seems pleased when I slide in beside her instead of across from her.

Over dinner we get to know each other better. We talk and talk and talk, mostly about the future and where we see ourselves in five or ten years. Ironically, neither of us brings up what we'd like out of a long term relationship. I can't speak for her, but for me, things between us feel fragile at this point, like they're not yet strong enough to hold up our combined hopes and dreams, no matter how tentative they are.

While we both avoid discussing the obvious, she has no reservations talking about her life plan, which she has every intention of implementing as soon as she finishes her degree in a little over a month from now. She says she's hoping for some kind of job in municipal or state government, or maybe a charitable organization. It kind of . . . awes me. I love to see her like this; strong, confident, so sure her lofty goals are attainable.

The tables turn though when she starts putting the same questions to me. For reasons I find hard to pin-point, talk of the future unnerves me.

"I don't know," I say evasively. "In ten years, the girls will be finishing high school." I shudder, not able to contemplate them as grown women, let alone as teenagers with minds of their own. "And my grandmother will be eighty-two. Neither of those things is something I like to think about."

Her head tilts as she considers me, and I'm struck by how beautiful she is with her big brown eyes shining in the candlelight. "But what about *you?*" she asks.

I blink. "What about me?"

"What do *you* want for your life in ten years?"

Even after I think on it for a few seconds, I can only shrug. "I'll obviously still be working my ass off. Teenagers are expensive. And I'm sure a couple of them will want to go to college." I say it flippantly, but the cold, hard truth of it hits me a second later. "Jesus," I whisper. "What if a couple of them want to go to college?"

Her expression turns apologetic. "I didn't mean to stress you out, Scott."

"Oh, no? How do you pay for *Stanford*? I can't even imagine how much that costs."

"You're right. It's outrageously expensive, and I'm lucky that my dad is still willing to pay my tuition."

That gets my attention. She almost never talks about her parents. "Why do you say *still* willing to pay?"

She looks rueful. "I'm not exactly a teenager fresh out of high school, am I?"

I feel my lips twitch. "True."

"After I ditched school in Spain, I disappeared for a while. It understandably freaked my parents out. Then, once they found out I had no intention of going back to school anytime soon, my mom pretty much disowned me. Two years later when I came home, she said I was crazy if I thought I could just show up and continue on as if nothing had happened."

Her eyes dart away, but her voice is still steady when she continues. "And she had a point. I see that now. But at the time, we both had our pride."

Pride? "What does that mean?"

"My mom wanted me to prove myself worthy of . . . being their daughter again, I guess."

Say what? My face must convey that question because she goes on, almost sheepishly.

"Yeah, she had a whole list of rules I had to follow, including living with them. She wanted to control everything. Who I dated, who my friends were, what I wore . . . even what causes I gave my time to." She sighs. "I was almost twenty-four years old and I couldn't do it. Even if it meant I had to give up school permanently. So I did the only thing I knew how to. I hit the clubs. That's how I ended up with my ex, Gunnar. I barely saw my parents for another two years even though they only lived twenty minutes away."

My poor Ellie. She seems so lost when she talks about her past. "I can't imagine not seeing my family for that long," I tell her. And I mean it. They're my support system. Without them, I'd be . . . *lost*. Realization hits me.

She lifts a shoulder with nonchalance, like it's no big deal. "My mom's not a very nice person. It was no great loss, believe me."

Except it is. Because no one has Ellie's back. She faces everything on her own. But I let that go for now. "So, how did you end up back in school?"

She rearranges her napkin in her lap nervously. "I, uh, hit rock bottom." Her gaze flashes to mine. "After you found me on the street, I had no pride left, so I went to see my father at his office a few days later."

The sadness lacing her words causes a wiggle of anxiety in my gut, so I pull her close and kiss her temple. "And all the conditions?"

She shakes her head against my chest. "My dad didn't tell my mom until later. His only condition was that I had to pay for my own living expenses, which was way more than fair."

"Fair," I agree. "But not easy." California is an expensive place to live.

She pulls back. "No, not easy. But I was done with easy. And I think my dad had that figured out. He's a pretty smart guy."

"Sounds like it. What does he do?" I ask, wondering how one pays for an Ivy League education.

"He's a lawyer."

"He must be pretty successful if he pays for you *and* your sister to go to college."

She fidgets in her seat, uncomfortable again. "You could say that. He, uh, owns a corporate law firm that handles a lot of Silicon Valley. My two oldest brothers are partners."

Sitting here, studying the smartest, most beautiful woman I've ever met – who currently looks like she's confessed to something heinous – I can't keep an ironic grin from my face. I think she's telling me that her family is loaded.

"So, Opal?"

"Yeah?"

"You and I . . ."

Her brow creases. "You and I what?"

"We've got a lot stacked against us, huh? I'm too young for you, too poor for you, too uneducated for you, and I've got three too many kids for you."

She pales a bit. "That's not true."

"It's very true."

"So what are you saying?"

"I'm saying it's a damn good thing that you're not into *easy* anymore."

She gives me a solid thump on the arm.

"Hey, what was that for?" I rub at the spot dramatically.

"Don't scare me like that."

"What? It's true," I say with mock innocence, loving the fire in her eyes. "This thing with us isn't going to be easy."

"But you still want to try, right?"

I was only teasing, but now I don't like the uncertainty in her voice. "Come on, El." I run my fingers into the hair at the back of her neck and squeeze gently. "I want to do more than try. I want you. I want us. Don't ever doubt that, okay?"

She nods cautiously, like it's too much to hope for. Then, her eyes flicker to my lips and my dick perks up, taking an interest as if it's his job to prove to her just how serious I am. Shit, how did the mood change like that?

"Let's go to my place," she whispers as I loosen my grip on her.

Oh, yeah. My pants are officially too tight. Let the wincing begin. "That's not a good idea. I'm trying to do this right."

"*Right* by whose standards? Because I'm thinking *right* involves you taking me home and making me come."

I make some kind of strangled noise. "I . . . you're sure?"

"Oh, I'm sure, Scott. I want you inside me more than I want my next breath."

Chapter Twenty

Ellie

The ride home is tedious in the hottest, most delicious way imaginable. The anticipation is killing me. In between squirming in my seat and wondering if he'd care if I stuck a hand down my jeans to ease the ache, I worry if I'm being too hasty about re-initiating our sex life. My conclusion? I don't care. If it's not going to work out between us, then it's not going to work out. Allowing him to put his hands all over me won't change that.

At a red light, his gaze rages over me like wild fire. "Stop your wriggling, would you?"

The soft command echoes between my thighs. "Or what?" The idea that we have so much to discover about each other's sexual boundaries makes me light-headed.

The glare he levels me with is unexpected . . . in the best possible way. It's like he's pouring kerosene onto the wild fire, easily burning away the last of my will power. Loosening my clamped-together thighs, I very deliberately lower my hand and press a hard circle into my clit through the denim. I groan at the surge of pleasure.

His firm hand wraps around my thigh, pulling with steady pressure to further splay me open, twisting me slightly in my seat. I meet his eyes as he tells me, "I swear to god if you come in my truck . . ."

He'll what? I'm desperate for him to finish that thought. But I'm not sure he even knows the answer. *Is this assertiveness new for him?* More desire pools low in my belly.

A horn honks behind us, but he ignores it, continuing to glower, filling the cab with menace. Goosebumps raise along my arms. "Eyes on the road, Scott," I taunt. "The sooner we get home and all that."

The horn sounds again. Still we sit here.

I huff out a disbelieving laugh. "Fine, I'll keep my hands like this." I interlace the fingers of both hands and rest them in a parody of a kindergartener between my spread legs. "Happy?"

The pressure on my thigh grows tighter for a second. "Not yet," he grits out, but we finally start moving again.

By the time we find a parking spot, I'm giddy with lust; my nipples are hard and rubbing against the inside of my bra and my panties are wet and clinging.

On the sidewalk with my hand firmly anchored to his, our long strides match, though mine are much more animated than his. He makes an attempt to stop me from swinging our arms and I practically swoon. His need to control the situation bodes very well for me.

When the key to the front door of my building actually turns in the lock, I laugh. "It's our lucky night." I throw a smile over my shoulder as we enter the lobby, but his stern expression remains, reflecting just how wound up he is.

As soon as we're inside my apartment, I find myself pressed up against the wall with his demanding mouth on mine, and his hands all over me, rough and seeking. I meet him head on, riding his thigh, groping his ass, sucking on his tongue. I've never wanted a man more.

"I want skin," I rasp, pushing at his shoulders, trying to create some space between us so I can get at the buttons on his shirt.

"So fucking bossy, aren't you?" he says before his lips are back on mine, ignoring my request.

I push at his shoulders again, but all that gets me is my wrists encircled and lifted over my head. My attempts to free myself from his grasp fail and nearly short circuit my brain. I'm quickly becoming a moaning, hot mess.

He pulls back, transferring my wrists into one of his big hands and uses the other to caress down my throat to trace along my collar bone then move lower. I love how his eyes follow the movement, but the soft touches are maddening, with no real pressure behind them. I wriggle and push forward into his hand, wanting more.

He leans into my ear. "Maybe you're right," he says, slowly increasing the force of his fingers on my breast until he tweaks my nipple through the layers of fabric, making me cry out. "Maybe skin is exactly what we need."

Gradually, he moves away, releasing my wrists, leaving me panting softly, propped up against the wall. As he works the buttons on his shirt, his eyebrows arch subtly as if to ask me, *isn't this what you wanted?*

Fumbling with my own buttons, I undo enough of them to get my blouse over my head and chuck it to the floor. My tank is next, followed by my bra. As we watch each other undress, I revel in the indolent satisfaction of knowing what's coming.

I brush past him and head for my room.

I barely make it to the hall on the other side of the living area before he's got me by the waist of my jeans. "Where you going?" he demands, the warmth of his arms wrapping around me, one hand sliding up to grip my throat, the other delving into my jeans, under my panties. "Shit," he rasps into my ear as if he's surprised by how wet I am. "I'm so going to fuck you."

Despite being pretty much putty in his hands, when he starts to maneuver me toward the island, I drag my feet. *Uh uh, no way.* I'm not going over the counter again. And my refusal to go has every muscle in his body straining. The power and strength running through him feels so good that, for a second, I'm tempted to let this happen how he wants.

But no.

I lift a foot and plant it on the side of the island to stop his forward momentum. "We're not doing this with me face down again."

"Oh, yeah?" he scoffs, pulling me back enough that my foot comes away. "Says who?"

"Says me. This time I'm going to watch that big dick of yours slide into me."

He pauses and then lets out a sullen grunt against my neck before loosening his grip so I can turn in his arms. With only the light coming in from the street through the patio door, I can't make out his exact expression. Which is a good thing because I'm sure if he could see the triumph on *my* face, it would only re-incite him to try to get his way.

Placing a sweet kiss on the corner of his mouth, I lead him into the bedroom where I flip on the bedside lamp.

I turn and my breath catches. He's standing there in only his jeans, his chest bare and glorious, all smooth lines of long, lean muscle. My gaze trails down to his abs where that thin line of hair disappears into the just-visible waistband of his boxer briefs. Somewhere along the way, he lost his belt and the button of his jeans came undone, leaving them slung low on his hips and doing little to disguise the outline of what's beneath them.

I watch transfixed as one of his hands moves to slowly lower his zipper, each tick of the metal teeth sounding lewd in the quiet room. The jeans and the briefs come off together, and for a moment, I can't help but stare at his bare feet – because when did his shoes and socks come off? An asinine thought, really, considering he's now naked in front of me, letting me ogle every square inch of him.

"Opal," he says, his voice low and rumbling as he takes hold of himself and gives one leisurely stroke. "Unless you want to watch this sliding inside of you somewhere else . . . *up close*, you're going to have to finish getting rid of your clothes."

But the scenery is so very distracting. Is there anything sexier than a man touching himself? He strokes again, base to tip, this time running the pad of his thumb over the head, forcing my pussy into a greedy little clench that makes me whimper.

He smirks cockily at my reaction as he reaches down into his jeans pocket and pulls out his wallet to get a condom. Seeing the foil package shakes me out of my deer-in-the-headlights funk. I shimmy my way out of my own jeans with as much grace as possible without taking my eyes off of him.

He closes the distance between us, throwing the condom onto the bed behind me.

Leaning in to my ear, he whispers, "You bare, here," he runs the backs of his fingers down my belly to graze my clit, "is the hottest thing I've ever seen. And these," the fingers roam back up to my breasts, his knuckles whisper softly against the tight tips of my nipples. "Are perfect."

I've been paid my fair share of compliments over the years. I did trade on my looks for a long time after all, but I've never been more pleased than to receive them from him.

His bobbing cock knocks against my belly as I raise my arms to encircle his neck. His hands land on my waist to pull me close and our lips meet.

We kiss, tongues dueling, long and slow, our hands caressing, fondling, groping until I can't stand it any longer. I get bolder. Hitching my leg behind his thigh, I raise myself on tip toes, trying to find the right angle to get him inside of me. He groans into my mouth. There are definite benefits to being so tall, I think vaguely as his dick slides against my core with delectable ease.

A hand circles my throat and carefully pushes me back. Gasping in surprise, I grab onto his wrist to steady myself. My insides further liquefy at the lust in his expression as he backs me up another step and the backs of my knees hit the mattress. He prowls after me onto the bed, driving me back until my head hits the pillow.

Kneeling between my thighs, he gestures for me to sit up, adding another pillow behind my back. "You wanted to watch me fill you up, right?" he says, somehow making the question sound like a threat.

"God, yes," I croak, doing as he wants, pulling my knees up, spreading myself wide.

Watching him roll the condom down his length has me holding my breath in anticipation. "Well, then, let's see how much you can take before this pretty little pussy of yours starts protesting."

A shiver rolls through me from head to toe.

He guides the head of his cock to my entrance to tease me, gently running himself along my slick heat until he's embedded himself at just the right spot. Leaning over me, he places a palm beside my shoulder and the other takes hold of my jaw. "I want you watching every single inch go in."

I can only blink at him, wondering where this deliciously overbearing attitude has been hiding. My lack of a response prompts him to squeeze slightly. "Yeah," I whisper hoarsely, "I'm watching."

Satisfied with my response, he lets me go and then we both take in the sight of his fat cock lodged between my pussy lips, spreading them wide. Holy shit, when he pushes forward, sinking into me inexorably inch by inch, the slide of him triggers a glorious whoosh of pure hedonism. I turn insensible to everything except the high of my climax that goes for what feels like an eternity.

"I'm sorry," I finally breathe, still loopy and smiling.

"Sorry?" he laughs with disbelief. "Are you kidding? That was spectacular."

Then his hips flex and he starts pushing into my sensitive flesh in long, sure strokes that set off little aftershocks of rapture. I reach up to cup his cheek with wonder, watching the intensity on his features grow until it all spills over. I swear, I can actually feel his pleasure as he comes.

We end up mostly horizontal. His elbows have most of his weight, but his head rests on my shoulder, his breaths coming hard against my collar bone. I nuzzle into his hair and run my hands up his back, encouraging him to put more of his weight on me. Instead, he raises his head to give me a tired grin.

"Give me a sec," he says quietly, dragging himself from the bed to toss the condom in the trash can by the door. He stops on his way back to grab another condom out of his wallet and throws it on the nightstand.

I'm on the verge of saying something teasing like *someone's optimistic* or *a little presumptuous, aren't we?* but he makes some kind of tsking sound to stop me as he motions for me get under the covers. He gets in beside me and we lie face to face.

"Don't pretend," he says with humor, "that that was it for the night. You came after five seconds, and I barely managed two minutes."

I giggle as he leans in to kiss me.

"I plan on fucking you again," kiss, "much more thoroughly," kiss, "and taking my time about it."

Humming with agreement, I pull myself closer.

"I can't believe I almost lost you," he whispers into my mouth. "That I almost lost this."

"Please, don't remind me." I bury my nose in his neck, inhaling his scent, internalizing it, memorizing it.

He sighs. "Thank you for giving me another chance, Opal."

"Thanks for not giving up on us."

From there we take our time, exploring each other with lips, tongues, and fingertips, learning the spots that make the other moan and squirm, testing our limits, seeing what pushes us over the edge. He discovers how sensitive my neck is and how to suckle at just the tips of my nipples and then to pinch them with the perfect amount of pressure. And I learn that he loves the light drag of my nails over almost any patch of skin, but over the head of his cock drives him wild.

I'll be tired tomorrow at work, but never has lack of sleep bothered me less.

Chapter Twenty-One

Scott

When the alarm on my phone sounds at 3:30 in the morning, all I want to do is ignore it and snuggle back down with Ellie in my arms while I breathe in her sleep-warmed skin.

Five more minutes, I tell myself.

If not for the snug fit of my dick against Ellie's ass setting a whole whack of ideas loose in my head, I'm sure I would have conked out and not gone home at all. Instead, she ends up impaled from behind on my latex wrapped cock, while we lazily bring each other off, still half asleep. *Life is good.*

She watches me with heavy, sated eyes as I get dressed. When I sit next to her to kiss her goodbye, I feel a pang of displeasure; I wish I didn't have to leave. But I push it away as a useless thought. No sense in being frustrated over something that can't be helped.

"I'll text you," I whisper before I head home.

The streets are empty at this hour and soon I'm creeping in the front door, trying not to wake anyone. In the dim light, I can see that my foam mattress has already been laid out on the floor in the living room. Despite the incredible night I've had, I get another flash of frustration. Again, I push it down. Not having a proper bed can't be helped either.

Thankfully, the resentment doesn't linger. After all, I've got better things to spend my time focusing on, namely the memory of us tangled together in her sheets. Making love to Ellie is a revelation; the connection between us, the need to see her happy. All of it is so new to me, including that overwhelming urge to control everything. It was unnerving at first, at least until I realized that whenever I gave into it, we were both happier.

I must have finally fallen asleep because the next thing I know it's broad daylight and I can smell bacon.

Close by, someone whispers something I can't make out, someone small and sweet who can only be my daughter. I try to pull the covers over my head, but *someone* giggles and pulls them down again. "We saw you, *Papá*."

Without opening my eyes, I reach out to see who I can grab. I get nothing but air and squeals of delight. All three of them are peeking over the back of the couch when I look up. I have to rub the sleep away to take them in. "Are you guys ready for church?"

Carmen nods proudly. "Abuela said we had to let you sleep."

"How come you're so tired, Tío?" Daniela asks.

"Yeah, Scotty, how come?" Desiree is curled up in my grandmother's chair with her phone, presenting me with the very definition of cheeky insolence.

I snort out a laugh. I love my sister, but she's a serious pain in my ass. "I was so tired because, I, ah, came home late from my date with Ellie."

"Oh, did she like the flowers?" Rosa asks.

"Yeah, she did. She told me to say thank you to you guys."

"Really?" Carmen asks, always suspicious.

"Yeah, she did." I drag myself up to sit with my back against the couch.

"Papá, can Ellie come for Sunday dinner?"

"Huh?" I need some coffee before I answer something like that. "What, tonight? No, she has to work."

"Next week?"

"Uh, no, sorry, she has to work every Sunday."

I'm surprised by the disappointed rumblings all three of them make. Are they already invested in Ellie? Or I guess, they're invested in the idea of her. I swallow hard. I do not want to mess things up. Not only for Ellie and me, but for the girls too.

"Ok, chicas," Desiree says, interrupting my growing discomfort. "Go help Abuela set the table for breakfast, please."

There's a few muttered complaints, but they do as they're told and Desiree comes to sit next to me on my crappy bed. "You really like this woman, huh?"

I push the heels of my palms into my eyes to try to clear my head. "I do."

Desi's smile takes me by surprise. "I'm glad, Scotty. You may be annoying, but you're not a bad brother."

I shoot her an incredulous look. "Are you on something right now?" My sister rarely hands out kind words. "How many times have I told you to say no to drugs?"

"Shut up. I'm allowed to be happy for you."

"It's worse than I thought then. You having problems with Jordan? Do I need to kick his ass for you?"

The disgust on her face makes me laugh. "Please. If his ass needed kicking, I'd do it myself. Actually, I wanted to make sure you're not thinking of taking off."

"Taking off? What?" I shake my head, trying to clear it. I definitely need coffee.

"You've had this look in your eyes for a while now, Scotty, like you're trapped in a cage or something."

"What are you saying? I'd never leave Abuela."

"Even for this girl you're dating? You know you can't live with your grandmother forever."

I glare at her, my mind tripping over things I have yet to consider.

She keeps talking, "And what happens if she isn't into kids? It's not like our own mother didn't leave *us* behind for guys over the years."

My jaw clenches. "And you think I'd do the same? What in the actual fuck, Des?"

She studies me, not even remotely put off by the fact that she's seriously pissing me off. But that's my sister for you, completely fearless. "No," she finally says. "I don't think you would. I just . . . wanted to make sure. We haven't known a lot of men who stick around."

"And you're lumping me in with them?"

"Your chromosomes lump you in with them, and I've never seen you . . . in love before."

I scoff loudly, but she doesn't give me a chance to set her straight. "And," she goes on, "love isn't known for going hand-in-hand with rational decision making."

"Mijo!" my grandmother yells from the kitchen. "Are you going to shower? Breakfast is ready."

"Okay," I yell back absently, fully intending to give my sister a piece of my mind, but when I turn back to her, she's already getting up. *"Oye,* where do you think you're going?"

Throwing me a smile over her shoulder, she says, "Good talk, Scotty. Have fun at church."

What the hell? I haul my tired ass up and put my bed away all the while doing my best not to dwell on how I'd love to strangle Desiree.

Mari is just coming out of the bathroom. "Is there any hot water left?" I demand.

She shrugs.

"For fuck's sake," I mutter, angrily locking the door behind me. As I put my cell down on the counter, it vibrates with a message. My mood does an immediate one-eighty when I see it's from El.

Opal: Thinking of you.

The words are attached to a selfie of her still in bed, her hair a bit of a mess, her eyes sleepy, her lips pushed together in a soft grin that tells me exactly what she's thinking about. She's sexy as hell and my dick is now tenting my sleep pants.

Scott: Well, if I wasn't thinking about you every second before, I am now.

Scott: GOOD morning, sweetness.

She answers with a string of kiss emojis and I grin stupidly.

Scott: Aren't you supposed to be at work?

Opal: I start in 25 mins. The only way I'll make it on time is if I keep my hands off myself in the shower.

My dick jerks at the mental picture.

Scott: Stop torturing me. I have to be in church in 25 minutes.

Opal: lol, perfect. You can confess all your sins.

"Tío!" comes through the door. "Abuela wants to know why the water's not running."

"I'm coming!" I grouse. "Start eating without me."

Scott: I gotta go, sweetness.

Opal: K, see you later?

Scott: Yeah, after the girls are in bed.

Before I get in the shower, I change the passcode to my phone. I'm never sure who's seen me punch it in. The last thing I need is for anyone in this house to be stumbling into my private life.

Ellie and I fall into a pattern that week. During the day we go about our regular daily routine, but every night I'm at her place by nine or so. Things are going . . . well. So well.

Thursday is a long day for her; she has class in the morning and then she works late, until ten, but since it's her birthday, there was no way I could let that day go by without seeing her.

Though she must be tired, she hits me with that incredible smile of hers when she opens the door. After a quick kiss, she asks, "Is this all for me?" I love her excitement. "You know you didn't need to do anything, right?" She takes the big gift bag that's hanging from my hand, careful not to jostle the cake box I'm carrying.

I blow out a breath of mock annoyance. "Are you kidding? The house went into an uproar this afternoon when they found out it was your birthday."

"It did?" I almost laugh at how skeptical she sounds as I follow her into the kitchen and set the cake down on the counter next to her roses which are still in full bloom.

"Yeah. The girls," I take the gift bag back from her and reach inside, "made you birthday cards." She takes them with hesitant fingers. "And my grandmother made you a flan," I indicate the Tupperware container that rests on top of the cake box, "but that was *after* she informed me that getting you a cake was mandatory."

"She did?" she says, genuinely confused.

"She did," I confirm. "But I want you to know that I came up with the present all on my own." Digging out the little black velvet box from the bottom of the gift bag, I place it on her palm, watching her face closely to get a sense of her reaction. I've been having a few second thoughts. *Am I overstepping? Is it inappropriate when we're still in the early stages of this relationship thing?* In the end, I'd said fuck it. I don't care if it's inappropriate or not, I want her to have it so I'm giving it to her. That doesn't mean I'm not nervous though.

When all she does is stare down at the box, I lift her chin with my finger. "Too much?"

A slight frown creases her brow. "No, it's . . . it's so . . . thoughtful."

Well, that's not cryptic. My continuing nerves manifest themselves as a laugh. "You don't even know what it is yet. Open it." I shove my hands into the pockets of my jeans and rock back on my heels.

"It's an opal!" The elation in her voice and the pleasure on her face has warm satisfaction expanding in my chest.

She pulls her gift out of the box, unwrapping the chain of the necklace from the velvet insert, and holds it up to study it before lifting her emotion-filled eyes to mine. "I *love* it. Thank you so much." She holds it out to me and then spins to give me her back. "Help me with the clasp?"

Once I've convinced my clumsy fingers to cooperate, she turns back. The pearlescent teardrop-shaped stone sits against her sternum, brightly polished and glowing. I remember back to when I teased her about the color of her skin, but now I realize it's more of a match for her personality. Still, I can't resist a bit more teasing. "It really suits you, Opal."

Instead of whacking me like I'm sure I deserve for making fun of her, she surprises me by throwing her arms around my neck. "It's the best birthday present I've ever gotten, Scott."

I scoff and am about to tell her that opals aren't actually worth very much when she goes on. "I don't remember the last time I got a gift that someone put some thought into. If I get anything, it's usually cash."

"Cash?" I say, trying to keep track of what she's saying while her curves are pressed up against me. We fit together so well. I pull her tighter, nuzzling into her neck, her scent driving arousal into my groin. "Cash is lame, though probably not as lame as the other thing I brought you."

She pulls back. "There's more?"

"Not really. But don't pretend you didn't notice how heavy that gift bag was."

She giggles, which adds to how much I want her, so I move the situation along by reaching over and pulling the gift bag forward on the island. She peeks inside and immediately jerks her eyes up to mine.

"Is that my . . . er, your hoodie?" she asks softly, suddenly on the verge of tears. Not the reaction I was going for.

"Should I have just chucked it in the trash?"

"No! It's the first thing you ever gave me."

"I know. But I wasn't sure what to do with it."

She pushes up on her toes and in my ear, whispers, "Thank you."

Despite their simplicity, her words send an erotic shiver down my spine. Then she's kissing me so sweetly that I can barely stand it. I press my now very hard dick into her belly. My hand roams to her breast, finding the outline of a tightly peaked nipple through her bra and tank top. Groaning, I back her up, getting her moving in the direction of her room and her bed.

Once the condom's on and we're horizontal, all bets are off. Hands, lips, tongues, it's frantic, forceful and so fucking good. With her here sprawled across my chest, both of us completely spent, I'm convinced that I'll never get enough of this woman.

"Best birthday ever," she says languidly. "And . . ." she pushes up on my chest, grinning down at me, "there's cake for dinner."

I grip the bottom of the condom so she can get up, then toss it in the trash, watching her naked ass as she walks out of the room. When she comes back, she's balancing two plates with huge slices of cake in one hand and has the girls' birthday cards in the other.

Handing me one of the plates, she settles back against the headboard and takes her first bite. "Oh, that's good," she moans. "How'd you know to get chocolate?"

"Lucky guess," I say absently, not sure which is more interesting, her lips wrapping around the fork or her breasts, still bare, out in the open like it's no big deal. I could so get used to this.

"You're going to hurt someone with that thing," she says.

"Huh?" I follow her gaze to my lap and smirk. "That's all your doing, *señorita*. I'm permanently hard for you."

She taps her lips with the tines of her fork. "Mmm. Obviously there's something to be said for this cradle robbing thing."

"Definitely. Is that an invitation?"

"No, *señor*, it is not." She sets her cake aside and then waves the cards at me, arching a brow. "I'm busy checking out my presents." Turning her attention to the homemade cards that come complete with awkwardly drawn balloons, cakes with lit candles, flowers, hearts, animals, and rainbows, she beams.

"This one has a bunny!" she exclaims.

"Yeah. They go through phases. Last month it was bear cubs . . . that looked more like cows."

This time she does whack my arm like I deserve. "Don't be mean," she laughs. "This is the sweetest thing. Did you ask them to do this?"

"No. They jumped all over the chance. They're dying to meet you."

"Really? I'm dying to meet them too."

My heart clenches. "You are?"

She nods jerkily.

"I worry about it sometimes," I admit.

"About me meeting them?"

"Yeah." I flinch internally. "My life outside of work mostly revolves around going to the park, or board-game night, or homework issues." Rubbing the back of my neck, I do my best to re-meet her eyes. "I'm worried you'll get bored."

"Bored? Outside of school and work, I stay home, Scott," she says, her voice laced with irony.

"Yeah, me too, but that's actually what I'm worried about. My life isn't . . . changeable. The girls are permanent. I mean, how long will you be okay with a 'boring' life?"

She takes a breath. "I haven't wanted to say anything, because you're so protective of them, but I'm really looking forward to . . . maybe having them in my life . . . if you think that's okay . . . one day. I *want* a boring life with you."

The utter skepticism I'm feeling must show because she adds more.

"Scott, one of the reasons I'm so crazy attracted to you is that you know who you are and what's important to you. I've never been able to answer those questions for myself."

And? I want to press, but I keep my mouth shut to see if she's got more to say.

"I think it would be good for me to surround myself with people whose needs and wants would be above my own . . . because frankly, I'm a bit sick of myself."

I snort.

"I'm serious! I need change, and you can't stop me from looking forward to meeting them."

I smile. This woman. "Okay then." I break off a piece of my cake and hold my fork out to her. "But we don't have to stay home all the time, right? We should do something for your birthday this weekend."

Swallowing the mouthful, she perks up with interest. "Oh, yeah?"

"Yeah. We can do anything you like."

"Anything?"

"Anything," I confirm, though I'm not sure I like the mischievous expression that's appeared on her face.

"A chick flick?"

"Sure."

She seems disappointed that I agreed so readily. "Well, my birthday only comes around once a year. I'll have to think of something better. I don't suppose you can salsa?"

I laugh at that. "Of course I can salsa. If I couldn't dance, I'd *never* get laid."

Oh shit. As soon as the words come out, I wish I could stuff them back in my mouth. But she seems to only be focused on her excitement, thank goodness.

"Will you take me dancing then?"

"Of course I will . . . if you think it's a good idea."

"Oh, I . . ." The delight on her face dims a bit. I'd guess she's contemplating herself being in a club setting. "I think it would be okay. Maybe you'd consider not drinking? I mean, I don't want to tell you what you can or can't do or anything, but maybe, I don't know, since it's a special occasion?"

"El –"

"Yeah, I know," she says nervously. "Just because I have this problem doesn't mean you do. I didn't mean to ask that of you, I –"

"El, stop." I set my cake aside. "Not only will I take you out, but I won't touch a drop of alcohol and I won't be the least bit upset about it."

"You won't?" she whispers.

"I won't." The idea that I'd rather drink than be with her is absurd. "How about *next* weekend though?" I lean in to brush a kiss to those delectable lips which taste of chocolate. "To give me some time to set something up with my friends. Like my kids, they're dying to meet you. The *chismosos* all want to know where I've been hiding."

That gets a smile back on her face. "¿Chismosos? Seriously?"

"Oh, yeah. They're worse than the *señoras* at church, like a bunch of gossipy hens pretending they're all swagger."

She giggles, and . . . not to sound like a total pussy . . . the sweetness of it makes me feel pretty freaking good inside. I lean in again, kissing her thoroughly this time, stopping only to sprinkle in filthy endearments, here and there, as we make love on her twenty-seventh birthday.

Chapter Twenty-Two

Ellie

Another week flies by and I come to the conclusion that when life is coming at you filtered through disgustingly optimistic thoughts, it can barely touch you. Not ornery customers at work or Ramen noodles for dinner or even Mr. Bostwick's creepy gaze can bring me down. For the first time in a long time, I'm feeling nothing but contentment.

So what if he hasn't mentioned meeting his family again? There's no hurry. He certainly hasn't met mine yet. We're taking things logical step by logical step. And that means his friends are up first – tonight. It's Friday and he's taking me out.

Naturally, he hasn't been far from my mind all day, not when I was getting ahead on my school work or when I went for a run or when I went through my entire closet, hunting for the perfect dress for tonight.

When the intercom sounds, I get a nice, swoon-worthy shot of pleasure. "Hi," I breathe after I've yanked open the door.

"Hi."

God, he's delicious. He came straight from work so he's a bit dusty and disheveled in his work clothes. Is it weird that his work boots turn me on? Probably. It must be the extra height they give him.

As soon as the door is closed, I'm on him. I've got his genuine amusement with my zeal converted into hard-core lust in under a minute. In between the frantic kisses and groping hands, I strip myself, then with only his jeans open, I roll a condom down his length and he slides into me from behind, me on my tippy-toes facing the wall, and he gives us both what we want right there in the hall.

"Fuck, El," he grunts on a powerful thrust, and I can tell he's torn between chasing his own climax or mine.

"Come for me," I demand, squeezing my inner muscles around him.

"You first," he pants, wrapping an arm across my chest to hook his hand over my opposite shoulder, giving him more leverage and letting me feel how every muscle in his body strains against me.

"No. I want you to come."

I guess he's not going to argue because my pronouncement is the last intelligible sound out of either of us before he comes hard on a long moan, his dick kicking inside of me. Thrilled, I revel in the hot, panting bursts of his breath against my shoulder. "Woman," he groans when he finally slides himself out of me. "What was that?"

I bite my lip and gather up my scattered clothes along with the duffle bag he dropped when I jumped him. "Oh, just something I've been imagining *all* day," I say innocently, leading him into the bedroom, where I dump our stuff on the floor and flop naked onto the bed. "Sometimes a girl's fantasies need fulfilling, you know?" Stretching languidly, I reach for the drawer in the bedside table and pull out my favorite vibrator.

"Opal," comes out low and threatening from where he's leaning against the door jamb.

I flip the switch, struggling to curb my burgeoning smile. I knew provoking him would be entertaining, I just wasn't sure what exactly his reaction would be. "Yeah?" I ask, feigning indifference as I lower the vibrator to where I want it. It doesn't make contact though, because he's got my wrist trapped in his grip.

"What're you doing?"

"Just having some fun." Except I spoil the effect because I'm unable to hold back my laughter any longer. "Kidding. Come on, you're wearing too many clothes, McCarthy."

We have such a good evening together. We make love, we order in, we watch a movie on Netflix, we shower together, and then we get ready to go out. It's all so domestically blissful.

"So, I need you to help me choose between these two," I say, holding up a silver mock turtleneck sequined mini dress with long sleeves as option A and a black sleeveless number with a flowy skirt that would reach my knees as option B.

He's lounging on my bed in just a pair of jeans, watching me with those dark eyes, like he's about to eat me up. To keep him on the task at hand, I jiggle the hangers. "What do you think?"

"I think you'd look great in either of them." My obvious displeasure compels him to add, "But I think I like the silver one. Try it on."

I'm pulling the dress off the hanger when my cell starts ringing from the bedside table. Scott leans over to check the screen. "It's your dad," he says, throwing me a curious glance.

I scoff good-naturedly. "He couldn't be more transparent if he tried, making sure I'm behaving myself at 10:30 on a Friday night." I answer the call. "Hi, Dad."

"Hi, Ellie. How's my girl?"

"Good. You?"

"I'm good. I was calling because I think I have a good opportunity for you."

"Oh, yeah?" I answer, my guard immediately snapping into place. I'm always wary of my parents and their attempts to help me.

"Yes, I've got two tickets to a charity gala in a couple of weeks that your mother and I can't attend. I thought you'd like to go."

I pull a face. *Why would he think that?* But I try to be diplomatic. "Um, you know that kind of thing isn't my cup of tea, Dad." I'd rather swallow hot coals actually.

"I know, but this would be for business. A friend of a friend is raising funds for a new anti-poverty initiative in the Bay area, and I thought you could get some exposure with potential employers. The mayor of San Francisco will be there, as will the Governor's chief of staff."

My mind races as he speaks. "Wow. That sounds great, Dad." It definitely couldn't hurt to attend.

"I knew you'd see it my way. One thing though . . ."

My shoulders sag. Of course there's a catch. There always is with my parents.

"Your mother's already given the other ticket to Peter."

"Peter? Who's Peter?" I turn to Scott and throw up my free hand to show him how annoyed I am.

"Peter, from your mom's birthday brunch?"

I sigh. "Sorry, but I'm drawing blanks." But then I have an inkling. "Oh, you mean the guy I sat with?"

"Yes, he said you guys hit it off."

I snort in a very unladylike manner. "We didn't hit it off, Dad. He rambled on about himself like a conceited ass."

To my father's credit, he finds that funny. "Yeah, okay, I can see that. So you don't want to go with him?"

"No, I definitely do *not* want to go with him. Plus, I doubt my boyfriend would appreciate me going with some guy that my mother wants me to marry."

There's a pause. "You've got a new boyfriend then?"

"I do," I say, and even I can hear the happiness in my voice. "His name's Scott. He's so great, Dad."

"You sound happy. When do you think we'll get to meet this lucky young man?"

"Uh, I don't know. My graduation ceremony is in a few weeks." And since I can feel a huge inquisition coming on, I try to steer the conversation back on track. "So, if I don't go with this Peter guy, will you still let me have the tickets?"

My father hesitates. "Let me talk to your mother, see what I can do."

Hanging my head, I try not to let him hear the disappointment in my next words. "Okay, thanks for calling Dad."

"I love you, Ellie," he says quickly before I can hang up.

"Yeah, I love you too."

Throwing my phone back down on the bedside table, I groan out an, "Ugh," as I sit on the edge of the mattress.

Scott comes to sit behind me, bracketing me with his body. "Your parents trying to set you up on a date?"

"Yeah."

"Good to know I'm not the only one. My grandmother tried to set me up with Señora Trujillo's granddaughter a few weeks ago."

"She did?"

"Yep. It's a universal thing, I think. Now, weren't you going to show me that dress?"

An hour later, we're on our way to the club, the same club I almost took that drink in three weeks ago. Apparently, it's a favorite with his friends. Am I worried? Yes and no . . . but mostly no. With my almost-defeat still so fresh in my mind, I can't imagine a scenario that would have me considering a repeat. The sting of the experience is still too raw, too new. Even if Scott does something completely out of character, I've mentally prepared myself. I feel strong, stronger than I ever have as an adult. Nothing could stop me from taking care of myself at this point. In fact, tonight, when I peeled back the case on my phone to insert my ID and a few bills, I didn't feel so much as a twinge of trepidation.

Once he's found a parking spot, we start the two-block walk to the front door.

I hold out my phone to him. "You mind keeping this in your pocket for me?" Though he takes it, he's not paying much attention to my words. I repress a smirk. "You said you liked the dress, Scott."

He scoffs. "I love it, but I don't see how I'm going to keep every guy's eyes off of you tonight."

The silver dress is fabulous. Though the top half has me well-covered, it fits like a glove, and while it's not obscenely short, the bottom half leaves most of my legs on display, especially in the three-inch heels I'm wearing that make us almost the same height.

"Eyes don't matter," I tell him. "And yours are the only hands that will even come close. If there's one thing I know how to handle, it's handsy assholes." Flashing him my brightest smile, I hold up our joined hands and duck under his arm to turn a circle. My mood is sky-high at the idea of being on his arm when I walk into a room full of people.

"Let's hope I don't end up being charged with some *handsy* asshole's murder," he mutters, heading for the back of the long line snaking down the block.

"Come on," I say, tugging gently at his hand. "I might be able to get us in."

Leading him toward the entrance, I love the way the muffled thump of the music urges me to start moving already. The few catcalls I get from the guys and grumbles of annoyance from the girls about the fact that we're not waiting like everyone else barely register with how much anticipation is flowing through me right now.

Chico is working the door again and sees me coming. He pushes to his feet from his usual spot on his stool. "Well, well, well, mami," he says, leaning in to receive my quick kiss to his cheek. "*This,*" he indicates the dress, "makes it much easier to recognize you."

My smile falters a fraction as I step back, but Chico doesn't give me a chance to think on it overmuch. "Nice to see you keeping better company these days," he says, giving Scott a nod. "Scotty."

"Chico," Scott replies simply, but there's something to the tone of his voice that I can't identify, a wariness maybe.

I give his hand a reassuring squeeze, hoping to move this along even if I'm dying to ask how they know each other.

In Spanish, Chico says, "I've got something for you."

"For me?"

Reaching behind the security podium, he pulls out one of this place's coveted wrist bands that entitles the bearer to unlimited free drinks. "That's completely wasted on me, Chico. Give it to someone who'll use it."

Chico's not taking no for an answer though as he holds out his hand for mine. "Humor me. Rene will kill me if he sees you and you're not wearing it."

My stomach turns over. "He's here?"

"Not at the moment, but you never know when he'll show up."

Rene, the owner of this and a lot of other nightclubs in the Bay area, is a good friend of Gunnar's, my ex.

Chico continues, "He just wants a couple of tweets, or whatever it is you do that boosts business."

Jesus, I shut down all my social media long ago. I cover my wrist just as he's about to seal it. "Listen. I'm going to pass," I tell him, still in Spanish, my accent getting thicker with my agitation as I grapple with the possibility of unlimited alcohol and thoughts of having to see either Rene or . . .

What if Gunnar himself is here?

But then, a sudden calm comes over me. *So what if he is?* My life doesn't revolve around anyone I don't want it to. With the calm, returns my confidence. "We just came to dance. If Rene shows up, I'll explain."

Chico's surprise takes a moment to ease. I'm sure not many people turn down a band. "All right, if that's how you want it." He jerks his chin at the door. "You two have fun."

"Thanks," I say with relief.

Inside the doors, Scott pulls me aside. The music isn't so loud here that he has to yell, and I can hear the concern in his tone. "I don't know what that was about, but we don't have to stay."

"I . . ." *Do I still want to be here?* Now that we're inside, I think I do. "I'm good. What about you?"

His smile in the dim entry way triggers one of my own. "Come dance with me, Opal."

Taking my hand, he leads me straight out onto the dance floor. Nostalgia tinged with euphoria still hits me, but this time, it has a different feel to it. Now, it's secondary to Scott's grounding presence. Instead of reckless, I feel safe. Instead of brittle, I feel whole. And within minutes, everything is forgotten except him and the beat of the music.

Scott may not be the greatest dance partner I've ever had, but he knows what he's doing. We quickly find our rhythm together and we have so much fun. He's tall enough that we line up perfectly and the strength of his body is obvious as he twirls me. And best of all, I *want* him close to me; the smell of him, the sight of his laughing face, the feel of him pressed up against me is more than welcome.

After a few songs, we're happy and sweaty and ready to take a break. "Let's go see who's here," he says into my ear to be heard over the music. I nod and start to follow him off the dance floor.

"Oh my god! Piper, it *is* you!"

"Oh, hey . . ." my brain spins for this woman's name.

"Kelly," she finishes for me, weaving on her feet, obviously drunk.

"Right, Kelly." She's a friend of Candy's cousin maybe, one who doesn't notice my lack of enthusiasm.

"I heard you were back, but I didn't believe it." Her heavy-lidded eyes roam over Scott. "Who's the hottie?"

Before I have a chance to say anything, more people I know from days gone by come up and join the 'conversation,' and soon I'm introducing Scott to a bunch of people while at the same time trying very politely to extricate us from them.

Scott looks to the balcony where he was standing those weeks ago with his friends and laughs as he flips someone off. "You need me to stay here with you?" he asks, eager to be gone.

"I'm coming," I assure him. There's no way he's leaving me down here by myself. I'm not here to be with any of these people. I'm here to be with him. He starts walking and I pretend like he's dragging me away as I give a little wave goodbye.

He lets me head up the stairs first, but I've barely made any progress when he pulls me back against his body. "You didn't tell me I was dating a celebrity, Opal," he says into my ear, his tone playful.

The sarcasm that sits on my tongue never gets its chance at freedom because his hand snakes up under my short dress from behind and squeezes the inside of my thigh perilously close to its apex.

I jerk around to face the very impish grin of a devil, one who's clearly quite pleased with himself. I don't think I've ever seen Scott so relaxed. Leaning in, he says, "You're beautiful as fuck, you know that?"

"How romantic," I say with as much of a straight face as I can manage.

He jerks his chin at the stairs behind me. "Get moving. I want to see my friends' faces when I introduce you as my girlfriend."

I practically float up the staircase on a cloud of happiness. At the landing, he takes my hand and leads me to the right where his friends have their territory staked out at a few tables along the railing. A guy steps forward immediately, his face beaming. He holds out his arms and says loudly, "How'd you get a woman like that?"

Scott laughs as they do some weird kind of handshake that interlaces their fingers together and then pound on each other's back. "El, this is Mikey," Scott says in Spanish. "Mikey, this is Ellie. And she speaks better Spanish than you and I combined, so watch your mouth."

Mike's eyes jerk from me back to Scott and back again. *"Hola, ¿qué tal?"* I say, giving him the proper kiss on the cheek greeting.

"No shit?!" He looks me up and down, obviously impressed . . . though I'm not sure if it's with my Spanish, my appearance, or my height. In my heels, I'm a good few inches taller than he is. I just smile.

Others come forward and I'm introduced to a very curious group of people, guys and girls alike. They're all welcoming, if a little surprised . . . and I now get why Scott said he feels like he stands out with his blond hair and pale skin. His friends are all Latinos, mostly of Mexican descent as far as I can tell by their turns of phrase and exclamations.

It's obvious that these people mean a lot to Scott and vice versa. I've never been more thankful I don't have problems fitting in anywhere. I love to talk and if I put my mind to it, I could charm a bear away from a bee hive.

For a while, I chat with a girl named Cindy who glowed with pride when Scott introduced her as his best friend Jorgie's girlfriend. They'd shared a meaningful look that seemed like gratitude from her and understanding from him. I'll have to get used to that I suppose. Friends like these, ones he's probably known since he was a young child, have a lot of shared history that can be daunting for an outsider. After an hour, though, I'm grateful for how easy this has turned out to be. I was prepared to face ex-hookups or even the jealousy of unrequited love, but I haven't had a hint of either.

Then my heart kindles with joy when Scott takes my hand and leads me back to the dance floor. "I promised you dancing, not boring conversation with people you don't know."

"They're not boring and they're being very nice to me."

"You don't want to dance then?"

"Very funny. Let's go."

And so we do, and we have such a good time. The music is great and my partner is everything I've ever wanted. I love that Scott gets perturbed the few times guys ask if they can cut in. After he gets rid of the third guy, he mutters something that sounds like, "Am I invisible, or what?"

After another couple songs, we both need a break. "Let's go get some water," he says, a bit out of breath. As we head for the bar, he lifts his hand in greeting. "There's Jorgie."

I know immediately who he means. There's only one guy who's staring directly at us. Strangely, he's got his arms folded over his chest, not giving the impression that he's the slightest bit happy to see us, even from this distance. The closer we get, the colder he becomes, his eyes rebounding back and forth between Scott and me. He seems vaguely familiar, but it's not until we're standing in front of him that it hits me that I know Jorgie . . . and that he knows me.

My heart falls all the way to the sticky floor.

"*¿Qué onda, Jorgie?*" Scott greets, not yet feeling the tension. I'm at a total loss of what to do, of how to diffuse the situation . . . which makes sense because I don't even know what the situation is. But whatever Jorgie's problem with me is, it's not good.

They do the same weird handshake thing Scott did with Mike, but Jorgie's not smiling. "*Necesitamos hablar,*" he says with all seriousness to Scott. *We need to talk.*

Scott makes a face. "Jorgie, I'm not in the mood for –"

"*Ahora, Scotty. Nada más tú y yo.*" *Now. Alone.*

My heart, that's still hovering near the floor, is starting to get roughed up by our shuffling feet. My buoyant mood has now been replaced by a dull sense of horror and resignation. "Pass me my phone," I say half-heartedly to Scott. "I'll get the water while you talk to him."

Scott wavers, but then he digs my phone out of his pocket. "All right. I gotta make a bathroom run anyway. You'll be okay for a minute?"

"Yeah, of course," I say with false cheer. "I'm a big girl."

Still not picking up on the tension, he laughs and leans in to kiss me before he and Jorgie go down the hall towards the restrooms. Alone, I stand there and wonder if Jorgie knows something about me that Scott doesn't? I cringe. Scott only knows about Piper in the general sense, and the quickly growing ball of lead gathering in my stomach tells me that Jorgie knows something specific. Something with details.

I take in the crush around the bar. The wait is at least two people deep.

"Piper! Where have you been hiding yourself?"

The unwanted greeting of yet another person from my past has my feet carrying me toward the freedom on the other side of the main doors.

Outside, I attempt to take deep breaths of the cool, night air, but it feels like there's a noose wrapped around my neck. Leaning against the brick wall, I brace my hands against my knees, barely aware of the line full of people gawping at the girl who's coming close to having a panic attack.

"Hey, hey, hey, *mami. Tranquila. ¿Qué pasa?*"

Chico's grip on my arm gives me enough of a shot of reality that my throat decompresses slightly and I get a decent breath into myself. From there, things improve and then I feel like a fool with Chico hovering over me.

I wave him off. "Sorry," I whisper. "I'm fine. I needed some air, that's all."

"Do I need to go in there and haul Scotty's ass out here?" Chico demands, straightening up and folding his massive arms across his chest.

Glancing up, I give him a shake of my head. "No."

"Someone else then?" That seems to piss him off even more.

My chuckle, feeble and bleak, mirrors my inner turmoil perfectly. "The only ass that needs to be kicked is mine. But it needed to be done around this time last year."

Chico takes hold of my elbow and gently guides me to sit on his stool. "Take a load off, *mami*. You're not making much sense." He pulls a bottle of water from the podium beside us and cracks it open for me. "Drink this."

"Thanks," I say, taking a much appreciated sip.

"You wanna tell me what's going on?"

"Nothing's going on. Just my past catching up with me, that's all."

Chico grunts, which I take to mean something like *I see*. "Scotty doesn't know anything about it?"

I sigh. "He knows some. Enough, I hope."

Looking me over with concern, he says, "You know how I know him? Well, aside from his occasional appearances around here?"

I shake my head as I tug my dress down lower on my thighs.

"Parent/teacher night. Our kids go to the same school. He seems like a stand-up guy."

"He is," I say sadly. "He's way too good for me."

"What? No, *mami!* The opposite. I want you to hold on to him. You were never –"

"Yo, boss! I need you over here."

At the head of the line, one of the other bouncers is getting into it with someone. As he walks away, Chico finishes his sentence, "You were never meant for this life long-term."

I pull in a deep, shaky breath. Chico is right. If Scott is what I want, then I need to fight for him. I wake the screen on my phone and see . . . nothing. No messages, no missed calls. Either he's not looking for me yet or Jorgie has convinced him to throw me over.

With a heavy heart, I text him.

Ellie: I'm outside with Chico if you're looking for me.

Chapter Twenty-Three

Scott

Fucking Jorgie.

The thought makes me laugh and I almost piss on my shoe. I should concentrate on the task at hand, but come on, how many times have I thought the phrase *Fucking Jorgie* in my life. A hundred? A thousand? More likely, tens of thousands. I don't care how much he gets on my nerves, I love my best friend.

I zip up, hit the lever and then move to the sinks to wash my hands, trying not to grin at myself in the mirror like an asshole. I don't remember the last time I had such a good night. Ellie is just . . . everything. I'd be lying if I said that her 'popularity' hadn't taken me by surprise in the beginning. It's a heady experience to realize that almost every eye in the building is on your girl, that she's one of those charismatic people that others are naturally drawn to. The bizarreness of it all didn't get my panties in a twist though because even if everyone was looking at her, she was only looking at me. Like I said, heady.

So why, exactly, did I leave her to fend for herself in this wolves' den?

Fucking Jorgie.

I exit the washroom and find the man I've been cursing waiting for me, still looking like someone pissed in his Cornflakes. Jesus, if I have to listen to him go on about another squabble he's having with Cindy, I'll be forced to strangle him.

"Listen," I say, already heading in the direction from which we came. "Can this wait? I need to get back to Opal."

"*That's* Opal?"

I stop, looking down at the hand he's got wrapped around my arm to prevent me from leaving. I don't like his tone.

"You *do* know that's not her name, right?" he says like I'm an idiot.

I shake him off. "What's it to you what I call my girlfriend?"

His eyes almost bug out of his head. "Your girlfriend? That girl is the last woman on the planet you should be taking up with."

"Excuse me?"

"I *know* her."

A wave of nausea hits me. "What do you mean, you *know* her?" I bite out as my brain flounders with something along the lines of *Jorgie's slept with Ellie?*

"Well, I don't know her like *that*," he says, backtracking. *Thank. Fucking. God.* But he's still talking. "But I *do* know *of* her. The whole club scene on the peninsula knows of her. She's a professional party girl and her *boyfriend* is loaded. I've dealt to them too many times to count."

Every undesirable emotion conceivable thrashes within me. *Is he implying my Ellie is a cheater? A whore? An addict?* "What's your fucking point?"

"What's my fucking point?" he repeats derisively. "Since when do you run around with trash like that? She and her boyfriend are into some seriously douchey stuff. Word is he'll loan her out."

Fury sweeps everything else away and leaves me seething. I jam my finger into his chest and he's lucky it's not my fist. "Why are you talking about this like it happened yesterday?"

He wasn't expecting that and stays silent for way longer than my patience will allow. "When was the last time you saw her?" I demand, and I watch him as he tries to remember. "Yeah, that's what I thought." My fist curls into the material of his shirt and I push him back into the wall. "This is the first and last time we will *ever* discuss this, Jorgie. Ellie is –"

"That's not her name either," he protests.

I thump him back into the wall to emphasize my point. "*Piper* is not a name she uses anymore, and it will never cross your lips. Do you hear me? Not with me, not with our friends, not with your 'contacts'. Ellie is *my* girl now. Period. If I hear that you've been talking shit about her, I will make you regret it."

For once in his life, my best friend is speechless.

"Are we clear?"

Silence, except for the dull thud of the bass. A group of girls circles around us, giggling, drawing his attention.

"Are we clear, Jorgie?"

He scowls. "Yeah, I guess. It's your life."

"That's right. Don't forget it." I drop my hand from his chest and he smooths his shirt front.

"Goddamn bully," he mutters irritably, but then can't resist giving me one of his trademark smirks. "You've got a girlfriend? Have you lost your mind?" We start back down the long hallway. "Either we're in an alternate dimension or hell has frozen over."

I'm still not quite over the little show he put on back there, so I can't muster up any amusement, but when has that ever stopped Jorgie? "Though either of those scenarios is more likely than you having a *girlfriend*." There's a quick pause in the narrative before he goes on in a much more animated voice. "Hold up, hold up. Exactly how old is this chick?"

My glower fades and damn it if my lip doesn't twitch. He's like a dog with a bone.

"No way! How far into cougar territory are we talking?"

I huff out a short laugh. "Don't push your luck."

"No, come on, me and Mikey have a *long*-standing bet on this."

I'm sure that would piss me off if it weren't for the fact that Ellie isn't where I left her. Scanning the bar, I don't see her and my heart rate ticks up a half a notch. The thought of her dancing with one of the many guys who've been watching her all night makes my stomach turn. Ugh. I need to shut that down. It's doubtful Ellie would appreciate the sentiment, I think wryly as I search for her tall figure on the dance floor. Nothing. Since she didn't pass us on the way to the restrooms, maybe she went upstairs to hang out with my friends.

Taking the stairs two at a time, I'm met with Cindy's eager face on the landing. "Where's Ellie?" she chirps. "She's so nice, Scotty!"

"She's not up here?"

"No, I've been waiting for you guys to come back." Her face pinches when she spots Jorgie coming up behind me. I have no desire to get in the middle of their tempestuous, on again/off again relationship, so I turn to go.

"Lost her already?" Jorgie says smugly.

Ignoring him and the tiny niggle of worry that's starting to grow in my chest, I head back down. I shouldn't have left her alone. Logically, I know she can handle guys on her own, but what if she's tempted to take a drink? At the bottom of the stairs, I feel myself at a bit of a loss. Then I recall there's this newfangled machine called a cellphone that can put you in touch with people.

Opal: I'm outside with Chico if you're looking for me.

Relief, pure and simple, hits me. After that brief spark of fear, seeing her safe and sound at the security podium triggers some kind of proprietary instinct inside of me. As I approach her, the feeling only builds on itself until a visceral possessiveness is being pumped through my veins with every beat of my heart. She is mine. I'll do whatever it takes to make this thing between us work. I don't care how unfamiliar the sentiment is, it's the only outcome I can live with.

But my own needs get knocked back when I'm standing in front of her and see her face. *Shit, she knew what Jorgie was about.*

"Hey," she says tentatively, not quite meeting my gaze.

Fuck that. I lift her chin so she's forced to look at me. "I misread the situation," I tell her straight up. "If I'd known what he was going to say, I would have told him off from the start."

She bites her bottom lip, still unsure. "So, he, uh . . ."

I don't leave her hanging. "He thought what he'd say would change how I feel about you. He was wrong. Nothing could do that."

The soft brown of her eyes flashes with emotion. "I was a little worried," she says in a small voice.

"And for that, I'm sorry."

She begins to shake her head, but I stop her by leaning in to cover her mouth with my own. It begins innocently enough, but we're both needy, emotionally after the drama and physically after all the foreplay on the dance floor, so it quickly morphs into something that gets us whistles and catcalls from our audience.

"Should we get out of here?" I murmur into her lips.

Under mine, her mouth pulls into a smile. "Finally," she sasses me, drawing the word out. And I have to laugh, a full-out, tilt-your-head-back kind of laugh as I pull her off the stool and we start walking, hand in hand.

"It wasn't that funny," she says, waving goodbye to Chico.

"Maybe not, my sweet Opal, but it reminded me of all the reasons I like hanging out with you."

"There's more than just the one then?" she teases.

"Oh yeah, there's a bunch. But we can definitely go over the one you're thinking of when we get back to your place."

We quicken our pace.

The ride back to her place is as charged as it always is; all the tension and electricity gets trapped in the cab, and with nowhere to go, it becomes a simmering morass of lust and anticipation.

Before we get out of the truck, I stop her. "Remember that time you said you'd let me know if I came on too strong, the caveman thing or whatever?"

Her eyebrows shift upwards. "Yeah."

"I need to hold you to that tonight."

It takes a moment before understanding sluices over her features, parting her lips, hitching her breath. I all but watch her pupils dilate in the overhead light of my truck.

"Don't let me push you too far, okay?"

She licks those delectable lips as she nods. "Okay."

The short walk is made in silence, every step ratcheting up my need for her.

At the building's entrance, she goes ahead of me to unlock the door. God, those long legs in those heels? All that smooth skin stretched over lean muscle that flexes as she walks? The sight twists me up further, making the want stretch and claw inside of me.

As if she can sense my eyes all over her, she winks at me over her shoulder. The notion that she thinks she has some control over this mounting tension between us is intolerable. Tonight, I need things my way. She'll be the one yielding.

Once we're inside her apartment, she moves closer, but I stop her. "In the bedroom." The harsh tone of my voice has her steady gaze clashing with mine, holding it until the connection between us is strung as taut as a piano wire. Without a word, she finally turns on her heel and strolls that incredibly sweet ass across the living area and into her bedroom.

She bends over to switch on the bedside lamp and I almost groan. When she faces me, I lean back against the wall. "Strip," I order.

I should have known it would take more than a simple command to fluster her. As she slowly opens the side zipper on her dress, her lips still have that haughty tilt to them, like she knows exactly how desperate I am for her no matter my attempts to play it cool. The irritation I'm feeling ebbs though as soon as the dress comes over her head and she's left in the most incredible lingerie I've ever seen. Holy shit, she didn't give me a preview of that earlier. The bra is all black. The barely there cups are edged with lace, and show off the creamy flesh they're holding, serving her up like an ice cream sundae. The matching bottoms are also lacy but in a much more wholesome way with a lot more material to them than the usual thongs she wears – boy shorts, my brain comes up with. The contrast created between the two pieces, one sinful, one sensible, sends another shot of lust through me.

I tell her to spin with a twirl of my index finger and my jaw drops. If the panties are innocent in the front, from the back, they're anything but. The lace that edges the front makes up the entire backside, leaving nothing to the imagination.

Facing forward again, she strikes a pose, her hands landing on her hips. "You like?"

"I do," I tell her honestly, though the idea that she *still* has the upper hand re-frays my nerves a bit. "Come here," I demand. She swings her hips of course, then stands in front of me still in her heels, leaving us almost eye to eye. God, she's my every wet dream.

She reaches for me, but I give her a shake of my head . . . and finally, I get a flicker of uncertainty. It's not quite as satisfying as I thought it would be, so I lean into her and run my nose from her shoulder to her ear, breathing her in. "You're the most gorgeous thing I've ever seen," I say, undoing the clasp on her bra and letting it fall to the floor. "Don't ever doubt that."

She hums softly as the tip of my index finger slides down from her collar bone, circling first one tightly beaded nipple and then the other before continuing down over the slight swell of her belly to trace her navel. Hooking her underwear, I slip them down her thighs, then her calves until I have her step out of them. Her heels are the next to go and when I'm back on my feet, an irrational sense of triumph floods my system at being able to loom over her again. In fact . . .

"On your knees."

She responds with an eagerness that has my dick jerking in my pants. I step back and look my fill of her sitting on her heels, clad in nothing but the opal necklace. The incredible picture she makes only gets better when she waits for my eyes to meet hers and then primly lays her hands on her knees and spreads her thighs wide to show me how slick and swollen she is. *Damn.*

My clothes come off, piece by piece and then she watches my very hard, very heavy dick sway slightly as my arousal fights with gravity. I step closer and she pushes up on her toes to get some height and parts her lips, so very keen to get her first taste. Before she can make contact, I push my fingers into the hair at the top of her head, stopping her forward momentum. Guiding my dick to her mouth, I paint it with the precome that's beaded at the tip.

I hiss, jerking back when her tongue ventures out to dip into the delicate slit on the head. "Put your tongue all the way out," I order. She obeys and I slide the sensitive underside along its scorching heat. Soon temptation grows too great to resist and I push past her lips and into her mouth, forcing her jaw wider.

"Look at you," I rasp. Sitting at my feet with a big mouthful of my cock, she about does me in. Her stretched lips are obscene, yet beautiful, as I slowly slide myself deeper. Caressing her jaw with one hand, the other stays rooted in her hair to hold her steady as I slowly work myself in and out of her mouth, wallowing in the incredible sensation. This is heaven.

It's the feel of her pushing herself forward on me that brings me out of my fog. *Is she trying to choke herself?* Quite possibly if I go by the glint in her eye.

I pull out and grip her jaw with both hands. "You want more?"

"God, yes," she whispers and then opens her mouth again.

Who *is* this girl?

"Is that right?" I taunt, pushing back in, further this time, coming to rest at the back of her throat. "That's an awful lot of dick in your mouth, Opal," I say softly, loving the way her gag reflex twitches faintly in warning. Pulling back slightly, I let her swallow and take a breath. "Let's see how much of it you can take."

I sink deeper this time. My first instinct is to retreat when she gags, but it's completely obliterated by the incredible feeling of her throat compressing around the head of my dick. *Fuuuuuck.* After a moment, her throat settles and seemingly out of nowhere space opens up and I sink in another inch. I stay there, stunned until I spot her hand moving toward her center to work her own clit. I think my head is going to explode – both of them.

"Don't you dare."

Lodged down her throat like I am, the vibration of her hum – of either protest or pleasure – travels up my length and settles in my balls. It's so good that my knees go weak. *How is this even happening?* A tear runs from the corner of one of her watering eyes, yanking me back into reality.

Oh, shit, what am I doing?

Pulling out, I crouch down and hold her as she sputters and chokes. "You okay?" I whisper worriedly as she calms.

"So okay. But," she gives me an accusing look, "I need to come."

In my relief, I almost laugh at her petulance. "Oh, yeah? You let me do that again and I'll consider it."

I'm expecting some kind of protest, I really am, but when her response involves the re-parting of her lips, I get to my feet again, ignoring my astonishment. If she's all in, so am I. "I want your hands behind your back this time."

She licks her lips and then does what she's told. My dick absolutely throbs.

Once I'm back inside her hot mouth, her tongue laps and strokes at me while I let my hands explore her face, tracing her eyebrows, sweeping my thumb along her cheekbones, outlining her stretched lips. The filthy picture she makes burns itself into my memory as I finally push myself deep, gagging her, letting her settle, pushing deeper – and by the sounds she's making, it's possible she loves it more than I do.

After multiple rounds of this, I can't take much more.

"Enough playing around. Get on the bed," I tell her, helping her to her feet.

She gets her knees on the edge of the mattress. "That's far enough. Spread your knees and put your head down." I get the condom on as I watch her follow my commands. By the time I'm wrapped up, I'm so ready to come. "Keep your hands where I can see them, Opal."

That gets me a thin noise of discontent, but I couldn't care less as I very slowly push my way into the dripping wet heat of her tight pussy inch by inch by inch.

"Scott," she groans, pushing back, trying to hurry me along. "Get on with it."

I sink my thumbs into her ass cheeks, pulling her further open to get a better look at my dick disappearing inside of her. "You'll get what I give you."

Ignoring her mewls and whimpers of frustrated pleasure, I finally start to glide gently in and out on short strokes, exulting in the feel of her. I don't even try to stop my orgasm from barreling down on me, hard, strong, and full of ecstasy. "Fuuuuccckk, yeah."

Shaking my head to chase the momentary stupefaction away, I lean over her. "Do. Not. Move."

I get rid of the used condom and get another. Since she's had me wound tight all night, shooting that first load has only warmed me up.

"Where you got those hands, Opal?"

"Here," she says sourly, stretching her fingers wide against the sheets on either side of her head.

I run a hand up the inside of her thigh until I'm skating through her soaked pussy lips. "Oh, I'm sorry," I say unable to repress the sarcasm, "did you not come yet?"

I'm sure she'd be giving me a verbal smack-down if I hadn't finally 'found' her clit and rubbed it in a few tight circles. Instead of complaints, the only things falling from her lips are moans that arrive on panted breaths. She's close, my girl.

Removing my hand, I quickly line myself up and shove in deep. She still hasn't come yet and I bet she has no idea if she's pissed or in rapture. The one thing I do know is that she has a thing for the long, deep strokes I'm giving her now.

"This what you wanted?"

"Yeaaaaaah," she moans. Definitely rapture then. I give it to her how she likes it, tip to base to tip, again and again, not harshly, but with enough force that she's gripping the bedsheets. I swear I could go forever like this, listening to the sweet noises she makes, watching her . . . that's what's missing. Watching her.

I pull out and flip her over. She blinks up at me with surprise, her eyes glazed with desire. Yes, that's definitely what was missing. That glassy look of oblivion. I'm back inside of her without missing a beat, encouraging her to press her bent knees high on the sides of my chest as I clamp my fingers over the tops of her shoulders and let my thumbs caress her throat and collar bone. Then I fuck her. Really fuck her. Hard, rough, using her shoulders as leverage, the way we've both been craving all night. Soon she she's squirming under me, filling my ears with what I know are the precursors to an epic orgasm.

I bend my legs a bit, adjusting the angle, give her a few more strokes, and then bear down hard on her clit. As I swivel my hips, she goes off, back arched, chin up, mouth open in a silent scream. "That's my girl," I groan, stalling out and letting myself glory in the feel of her contracting around me, loving the reminder of how her throat did the same earlier.

As always, watching her come, hearing her, feeling her, jacks up my own arousal, fills me with a renewed sense of urgency and has my dick back to throbbing for this now loopy and loose-limbed creature who has so completely taken me over. Except the urgency is accompanied with the need to be closer to her, and I can't do that with my feet still planted on the floor.

I get an arm under her back and neck and haul her further up onto the mattress. It allows me to settle into the cradle of her hips and rest some of my weight on her, to put my lips on her, to feel her skin.

"That was . . . Scott, that was . . . so beyond good."

I smile against her neck in response to that.

"Good thing we're just getting started then."

The warm sound of her giggle permeates everything around us until it dissolves into a wanton moan when I start moving inside of her again.

We rebuild the fire between us, together this time, stroke after stroke, touch after touch, with our mouths and tongues fused in an erotic dance. It's intimate and close and drawn out. And when we finally come in each other's arms, it's everything I never knew I needed.

Chapter Twenty-Four

Ellie

This man. This kind, generous man has completely turned my life upside down. He makes me laugh, he makes me think – *gah!* – he makes me come.

"Scott?"

"Hhhmmm?"

I gasp as he flexes his hips.

This man who's still lodged inside of me, his weight keeping me grounded, his face buried in my neck as his hand skims the side of my breast with so much tenderness that I feel my chest swell with heavy emotion.

As he nibbles at the sensitive flesh of my throat, I whisper, "Thank you for standing by me tonight."

He freezes.

"I thought maybe you would . . . that I would . . . lose you."

He lifts his head, giving me a chance to see the concern on his face.

"Friends are important," I continue, cupping his cheek. "I know you could easily have sided with him." The feel of unexpected tears sends my heartrate into an erratic trot. *Why am I crying?*

"Hey," he says gently, wiping away a renegade tear I can't hold back. "I made a commitment to you. And I mean to keep it."

Oh my god. This man. I'm overwhelmed by him. I have to fight to take my next breath, but then like a stopper being pulled from a bottle, my emotions pour out with my next exhale.

"Oh, Scott, I love you so much."

Something sparks in his eyes, but it's hard to say if it's surprise or panic or reciprocal feeling. Strangely enough, I feel no regret or panic at my admission . . . only a mild sense of amusement at the timing. Then the amusement becomes an all-out smile that has his eyebrows lifting in question.

"I'm sorry," I half giggle. "Maybe this wasn't the best time to say those words, what with you balls deep inside of me." I squeeze my inner muscles, forcing a soft grunt from him.

Leaning his weight to one side, he takes hold of my hand and gently kisses the tips of my fingers before clutching it to his chest. "It was the perfect time," he says earnestly, his seriousness cutting off my silliness.

Instead of saying more though, he lets go of my hand and grips the condom to slide himself out of me. If I wasn't so addled by his words, I'd protest him leaving the bed to dispose of the condom.

The perfect time?

"It was?" I ask quietly, expectantly, needing him to clarify.

He turns to grin down at me ruefully. "I've never felt the way I do about you . . ."

He reaches his arms above his head to stretch out his muscles, but the view doesn't distract me. Actually, as the seconds tick by, a bit of panic starts to squeeze me in its grip. "But . . ?" I croak.

He seems surprised. "Oh, no. No buts. Just . . ."

Just what? Except he remains silent. *Just don't rush me?* That would be fair. *I just don't love you back?* That would wreck me.

He clears his throat a bit nervously. "Just, I've never been in love before."

And?

Yet again, he remains mum as he searches for his underwear among our discarded clothes. Finally, a withered chuckle seeps from me into the air around us. Admittedly, Scott's honesty, no matter how cryptic, is better than Gunnar's indifference or Nathan's crushing deceit. He said he's committed to me. That's real. That's more than I've ever had before. I should be grateful . . . but when Scott finally starts talking again, I'm a bit lost in my disappointment.

"I mean, what is the criteria for love anyway?" he says absently, pacing the room now.

I kind of wish he would stop.

"Obsession?" he muses. "Because I've definitely got that checked off the list. I haven't been able to stop thinking about you since the day I jumped over that counter."

He keeps on, oblivious to my growing dejection.

"Possessiveness? Check. I wanted to throat punch every guy who even glanced in your direction tonight."

I snort, calling his full attention back to me.

"And that, right there," he says, pointing at me. "Your attitude, or maybe your confidence, is a total turn-on." His face takes on some kind of confused, WTF expression.

"Look," I say, very much wanting to change the course of the conversation.

"*And* we have the same sense of humor. You're *crazy* smart, and *insanely* beautiful. You're perfect in every way."

Silence. I feel a sickening slither of unease shift under my skin. "Except one?"

"Huh?"

I shouldn't be annoyed with him, I know I shouldn't. *But perfect yet unlovable? Come on.* The helplessness that's creeping up on me now feels eerily similar to earlier when I thought I might lose him.

I haul myself off the bed and scan the room for my robe, thinking maybe it would have been better if he'd let his best friend warn him away from me. At least that wouldn't be on me. Because being unlovable would definitely be on me. Isn't it funny how you can dodge one bullet, only to put yourself into the path of another? One you didn't see coming?

Great, I've been shot, metaphorically speaking. I plop back down on the edge of the bed and rub my temples. *Why didn't I keep my mouth shut?*

The bed shifts beside me and like a fool, I don't pull away when his arms gather me to his chest. Because who am I kidding? He's the hurt *and* the comfort all rolled into one.

"What do you mean by that? That you're perfect in every way except one?"

I take a deep, steadying breath. Anything I say at this point is going to make it worse. "I didn't mean anything. I'm going to take a quick shower."

When I try to pull away, his arms tighten around me. "What's wrong?"

Okay, I'm getting angry. Men can be clueless, but not that clueless. And damn it, my next breath is accompanied by a sniffle.

"You're *crying*?" he asks, appalled, gripping my biceps to hold me at arm's length. "Oh, shit, you *are* crying. Did I hurt you?"

Full of despondency, I huff out, "I'm fine. Last time I checked, embarrassment never killed anyone."

"Embarrassment?" His gaze roves over me as if it's something visible to the naked eye. "I embarrassed you?"

I shake my head. "Nope, I managed it all on my own."

"I'm, um, not sure what's going on here, Opal."

Brushing my tears away impatiently, I sigh. "Don't worry. It's not you. It's me. Putting the cart before the horse. Again."

His brows pinch together. "Tell me."

If he wasn't looking at me with such sincerity, I'd probably get angry. But he actually does seem dumfounded. But what can I say? *I told you I loved you and you didn't say it back.* It may be the truth, but that's *not* coming out of my mouth.

"I'm serious, sweetness. Tell me, so we can deal with it."

And what if dealing with this mess I've created doesn't end the way I need it to?

"Please," he says, his voice softening. "It's better to get it out in the open."

I smile feebly. "How are you more mature than I am?"

"It's one of the reasons you love m–. Oh."

I block out the sight of *his* embarrassment only to feel more tears track down my cheeks. "Yeah. Oh," I whisper, gently slipping from his grip. "But I get it." Though the emotional side of my brain has no idea what I *get. That I'm not the type of person that others love?* Luckily, the logical side of my brain still works. "I get that I backed you into a corner by saying it too soon. I'm sorry for making it weird." I head for the bathroom, wanting to escape the awkwardness and to avoid further humiliating myself with all these unwelcome emotions that are leaking out of me like I'm a sieve.

In the bathroom, I slump back against the closed door. *I hate it when I get like this.* Wrenching back the shower curtain, I start the water and try to rationalize that he can't be expected to express feelings he doesn't have. And just because he doesn't have those feelings now doesn't mean that he'll *never* have them. Right?

The idea just unleashes another round of tears. *Fuck rationalization.* I can't do it, at least not right now while everything is so close to the surface. I get in, hoping the heat of the water will soothe me before I have to go back and face him.

I hear the door open.

"Hey," he murmurs, pushing back the curtain a bit. "Listen, sweetness, I –"

I don't want to hear his platitudes. With my emotions attempting to drown me like they are, nothing in the world could make this better. But I have to stop him with something, and that something turns out to be a quest for an explanation. "Was I too forward with you?"

"Huh?"

"Was I too forward?" I insist on a shaky breath. "Was I too aggressive?"

"What? When?"

"I tend to run my mouth," I explain. "My mother says that's not an attractive quality in a woman. And I don't have the whole innocent vibe going on, do I? I saw your face when I brought out that box of condoms. That was stupid of me, to let you see the whole box."

"Opal, you're not making any sense. Why don't you get out now?"

I shake my head and wipe at my tears. "Tell me. Please. Could I have done something differently?"

"El," he says with exasperation, shutting off the water and pulling me from the tub. "Come on."

He wraps a towel around me and I feel my shoulders slump. "Sorry," I whisper. "I'm being irrational, too emotional, aren't I? It seems like I'm always *too* something. Too opinionated, too eager, too full of myself, too drunk. Every guy I've ever been with has had one for me. Nathan's was pretty good. He said I was *too stupid* to see what was right in front of my face." Scott stops trying to wring the water from my hair with a hand towel and frowns at me. "That's not what it is for you, is it?" I ask, breathing through the stab of pain just under my ribs. "Because some of them hurt more than others."

Even if I know I'm rambling, I can't stop the words from spilling out of me. I've never told this to anyone, and now that I've started, I don't have the strength to patch up the holes and dam it all up again.

"If I had to pick one for you," I continue, "it would be something like *too tall*. Because I can't do anything about how tall I am." Sniffling, I pull back to look up at him.

"You're not too tall, Ellie," he says, his eyes pleading, his voice stern. "You're perfect."

Resentment surges. "Don't say that!" I push away from him, letting the towel fall to the floor as I march back to the bedroom. Grabbing a tank top and pair of underwear from my dresser, I yank them on and then face him.

My indignation dissolves almost instantly when I turn. With his arms folded over his bare chest, still in just his underwear, his posture is stiff and unsure – and I hate that I've done that to him. I take a deep breath, trying to compose myself.

"El," he starts, "you're not *too* anything, okay?"

I hold up my hand, wincing slightly. "Don't. It's okay. I know I'm messing this up."

LL MEYER

"You're not messing anything up, sweetness," he says, his voice laced with caution. "Just tell me where this is coming from."

My heart thumps in my chest – one beat, two, three – and I rub at it to try to ease the throb. Maybe being honest will repair some of the damage I've inflicted on us. "I . . . well, when you say you've never been in love, I can say the same, only in reverse."

His brows hitch down, and a trickle of optimism begins to seep into my gloom because I know him well enough to know that look. It means he's thinking. But I've tortured him enough tonight so I quickly add to my admission.

"And by that, I mean no one's ever been in love with me."

Imagine a scoop of ice cream melting on the pavement. It perfectly encapsulates both the way his expression softens into understanding and then pity, and the way mine turns to dismay.

He comes toward me, his hand outstretched, but I dodge him. Clearly I didn't quite think this through to its logical conclusion. I'd rather stab myself than be on the receiving end of his pity.

"El," he warns as I scoot past him again. We end up squared off on either side of the bed, but he's closer to the door so I can't get out of the room.

He props his hands on his hips, considering the situation. Then he has the nerve to grin at me as he crooks his finger. "Come here."

I purse my lips. "Bossy time is over."

"Bossy time?" He bites his lip to stop himself from laughing, and can't help but wonder how the mood changed so quickly. "You like bossy time. And you heard me. Come here."

His voice drops low on the command, making my stomach squirm, but it's not enough to divert my attention from his steps as he comes around the bed and makes a grab for me.

I go over the mattress and make a break for the door, but he catches me around my waist. "Scott!" He throws me down on the bed, jumping on top of me to straddle my thighs, holding me down by my wrists. I buck up against him, trying to dislodge his weight, but he's too heavy.

"You can wipe that smug look off your face," I grouse, trying to buck him off again. I feel a traitorous smile start to spread across my lips though because he does seem to have accepted my explanation of what was eating at me without judgment.

He leans down to kiss each corner of my mouth. "You caught me off guard tonight, that's all. No girl has ever said she loved me. I didn't know how to handle it, and obviously *I* messed up." He grimaces. "But I don't want you thinking that *you* and *love* haven't been floating around in my head for weeks. When I said you were perfect, I meant it."

My protests get shut down.

"Let me finish. This stuff scares me, but I want *you and me* almost more than anything else I've ever wanted in my life, El."

He stares down at me with an intense sincerity as if willing me to believe him.

"Now," he says gruffly. "You realize I'm screwed, right? No matter when I say those three words to you, you're going to think I'm full of shit." His lips tilt sheepishly.

"I wouldn't think that," I object. "And I'm a horrible ass for making you feel like you had to say them back."

He chuckles mirthlessly. "At least I didn't say *thanks,* right?"

"At least," I echo witheringly.

"See?" His whole face lights up. "There it is again!"

"There what is?"

"That attitude. It makes me hard."

I look down and sure enough, his dick is trying to make a jail break from behind his boxer briefs. "Is there anything that doesn't make you hard though?"

"True. But he's got a particular fetish for your legs in heels, and of course, your lips."

I nod with mock wisdom. "Of course, what self-respecting dick would say no to lips – of any kind?"

We'll be fine, he and I. This is a marathon, not a sprint, and the sooner I realize that, the better.

In the ensuing days, Scott seems inclined to let my meltdown go. He doesn't give me sidelong looks, and he doesn't tease me about it, and he doesn't hint that my behaviour has freaked him out. In fact, he goes out of his way to shower me with affection. I'm both grateful and relieved. I'm not going to lie and say that I don't worry myself sometimes, but I'm hoping now that I've voiced my insecurities, I've exorcised them and we can move forward.

It's almost a week later that my Dad texts me, taking my mind off the incident almost altogether.

Dad: Hi Ellie. You at work?

Ellie: Yeah, why?

But that's all I get until a local courier walks into the café an hour and a half later with a delivery for Ellie Summers. In a lull between customers, I rip open the envelope tab and pull out a parking pass and two gold-embossed tickets to *The First Annual Action against Poverty Gala.*

Huh. Seems my dad somehow wrestled the extra ticket away from my mother. Considering how much he dislikes going up against her, to stick his neck out like that for me is a big deal.

Ellie: Thanks, Dad! You're the best! I'll be sure to put them to good use.

I get a thumbs up emoji in response.

That night, despite having had class in the morning and then working a full shift, finding Scott waiting for me outside my building wipes away any trace of tiredness I was feeling and replaces it with joy.

"Hey," I say, bouncing up to him. "You're early."

He grins down at me. "Yeah, I know. I'm pretty much a keener when it comes to you."

Since we're still caught up in the mother of all honeymoon phases, that's about as far as the conversation gets until much later when we're nested down in my sheets, both of us drowsy and sated. With my head on his shoulder, we talk about our days.

"Oh, so hey," I say, sometime later. "Remember my dad wanted to set me up on that date last week?"

"Mmmm," he acknowledges absently.

"Well, he got the other ticket back so we can both go."

"Go where, sweetness?" He nuzzles at my temple.

"My dad has tickets to a charity gala that he can't use. He thinks it might be a good opportunity for me to schmooze with potential employers."

The nuzzling stops, but I go on.

"You'll have to rent a tux because it's black tie and it'll probably be deathly boring, but I think it might be worth it for me to go. I need to get a real job as soon as possible."

"And you want me to go with you?" He sounds skeptical.

"Of course I do. Unless you *want* me to go with Peter?"

His growl of protest wanes toward the end. "But black tie, El? What are we talking here? Standing around with rich people, making small talk?"

"That's actually a pretty good description. But don't worry. You won't have to make small talk if you don't want to. You can just stand there and look smoking hot in your tux."

"Is that all you want me for?" he deadpans. "Arm candy?"

I giggle with delight. "You found me out. I'm using you to further my career in the cutthroat world of non-profit charitable foundations."

He laughs, but it's a weak one. "I don't know. I don't want to embarrass you."

Scoffing, I lift my head so I can see him. "Like that's even possible. It'll be easy. We'll go, eat a very expensive meal, listen to some speeches, then I'll do my best to charm a few people." He doesn't look very convinced, so I'm forced to beg. "Please, Scott. Don't make me go alone. If nothing else, your presence will keep the creepy, older guys from hitting on me."

His answering expression is an encouraging mixture of disgust and *over my dead body*. "So, you'll take me?" I press.

"When is it?"

"Not this Saturday, but the next. Downtown San Francisco. We can park at my dad's office building that's down the block from the hotel."

"And where am I going to get a tux?" he whines.

"I'll find out and text you the details." I sit up, smiling gleefully, knowing I've got him. "Thanks, sweetness," I mimic his nickname for me as I lean down to kiss him.

Chapter Twenty-Five

Scott

My life is markedly better with Ellie in it. She makes all the usual stressors seem less dire, or maybe less important. I've become a regular optimist.

Lolita hasn't contacted me since the girls' choir performance? Instead of dreading the inevitable call, I'm thankful for the delay. *My mother's work calls me looking for her on a Monday?* Instead of worrying myself sick that she hasn't been home in a few days, I revel in the peace and quiet around the house. *Jorgie shows up for work so hungover that I have to send him home?* Instead of being royally pissed, I tell myself I'll have legitimate cause to fire him sooner.

Because at the end of even the shittiest day, I get to see her. I get to talk to her, laugh with her, hold her, and make love to her. I'm not going to get all cliché about it and say she makes life worth living, but . . . damn.

If only there was no flip side to this idyllic coin.

Because the flip side involves some very unsteady ground for me. I don't like uncertainty or indecision or doubt, and this thing with Ellie, well let's just say that I'm worried that I'm completely out of my depth. That *I love you* fiasco? I didn't handle it well and she'd rightfully gotten more than upset over it. I hate that I'd caused her pain again after I promised I wouldn't.

What if I mess up so badly one day that she can't forgive me and I lose her? Or worse, what if the girls come to adore her like I do, and *we* lose her? The idea turns my stomach. Which is probably why Ellie hasn't met them yet. Even if the girls ask about her daily, and Ellie does the same. Even if the birthday cards they made for her still hang on her fridge and I catch her peeking at them all the time, I still haven't pulled the trigger. I'm undecided if I'm being protective or cowardly.

God, I hate uncertainty.

Plus, I'm still scratching my head as to why Ellie's under the impression that I'm some kind of catch. Because the gaps between us are real. Not only is she years older than I am, she's a college girl. An Ivy League college girl. What would a woman like that want with a guy like me? A guy who got his GED last year, works construction, and has limited prospects?

And then there's this charity thing.

Fuck me.

Over the last few days, I've questioned myself countless times. But I haven't once seriously considered backing out on her. Not even when I went for the tux fitting. I'm not interested in disappointing Ellie, not for anything in the world.

Hopefully, I *don't* ruin anything because this girl sitting beside me is something special. We're in my truck on our way to the gala and she's rapping along in Spanish to classic *Molotov*, looking incredible in a pale pink sleeveless dress with her hair up, and it takes everything in me to keep my attention on the traffic.

She directs me through downtown to her dad's office building where we scan the pass he gave her to get into the underground parking. The pass has a specific stall number on it, a prime location right near the elevators. *Reserved 24 hours, Summers & Fieldstone, LLP*, the plaque reads.

We get out and as I wait for her to come around the back of the truck, I notice a brand new, very shiny, Audi Q8 in Metallic Samurai Gray a few spots down. I'm thinking that some lucky bastard gets to drive around in the equivalent of a small fortune when I see the plaque attached to the spot. *Reserved 24 hours, Jonathan Summers.*

A choked laugh crawls its way out of my throat. "That's your dad's car?"

Taking the hand I hold out for her, Ellie shrugs, neither impressed nor seeing the irony of my little truck being parked anywhere near a Q8. She does frown though. "It's not like him to work so late on a Saturday."

Her heeled steps echo against the concrete walls of the parkade. "You cold, Opal? You want my jacket?"

She shakes her head. "I'm fine. And you look way too good to start messing with that tux."

Hitting the elevator call button, I give her a pointed once over. "No one will even notice me standing next to you. You look . . . amazing." The V neck of the dress leaves her collar bone exposed and gives just a hint of cleavage. She's sexy, yet classy, and I'm irrationally pleased that she's proudly displaying the pendant I got for her.

"Thanks, honey," she sasses playfully, but then turns serious. "Thanks for doing this. I know it's not your first choice when it comes to Saturday night entertainment."

"Or fiftieth."

The guilt on her face immediately makes me feel bad.

"Sorry," I tell her. "Ignore me. I'm being an ass. If this is where you need to be tonight, then I'm with you. I kind of like us being a team."

Her expression softens and then she says, ever so earnestly, ever so softly, "You are so getting laid tonight."

I laugh as I lean in for a kiss, but she turns away. "Ah, ah, ah, not on the lips."

"Fine," I grumble and instead place a line of open-mouthed kissed along the column of her neck.

"Oh," she breathes, her whole body shivering. "If I didn't think security would lodge a complaint with my dad's office, I'd say we should fuck, right here, right now."

"Opal," I whisper hoarsely. "You can't be saying shit like that." I pull her close so she can feel me. "A hard-on will seriously ruin the lines of this monkey suit."

Thankfully the loud ding signalling the elevator's arrival is enough to pry us away from each other. The ride up to street level and then the short walk to the hotel is made in silence while I do my best to picture images of the least sexy things possible to beat my dick back into submission. I'm only partially successful until we hit the lobby of this fancy-ass hotel and then my nerves work wonders to solve the problem. I don't know if she feels my trepidation or what, but I appreciate the way her hand tightens around mine as we follow the signs to the ballroom.

There's a short line outside the room where two employees are checking tickets and gesturing to the seating chart behind them. When it's our turn, Ellie hands over the tickets and the woman checks her list. "Thank you so much for joining us this evening, Ms. Summers, Sir. You'll be seated at table 14, which is here." She points to the chart, and then hands back the tickets. "I hope you enjoy yourselves."

Inside the doors, there's a big sign that reads *The Elizabeth McCarthy Foundation proudly welcomes you to The First Annual Action against Poverty Gala*, but I barely scan it because the room takes up most of my attention. It's huge and filled with glittering people, standing around in fancy clothes, holding champagne glasses.

"Let's do this," Ellie mutters beside me. I turn in time to watch her square her shoulders and paste a smile on her lips. Despite my nerves, I have to grin. *That's my girl.*

She takes my elbow and we venture in. "We should find our table first. I'll ditch my clutch, and then we can scope out the people on my list." Before we left her apartment, Ellie showed me pictures of all the important people she wanted to meet tonight. She's done her homework; I have to respect that.

We're approaching our table when I hear a frosty, "Piper." We both turn, and Ellie stiffens. "For fuck's sake," she hisses under her breath. "I'm so sorry, Scott."

I don't even get a second to consider what she means before a woman with long, honey-blonde hair is on us. She's tall and slender, dipped in diamonds, and wearing a floor-length, shimmering black cocktail dress. She'd be beautiful if she weren't scowling.

"You're late," she scolds and my eyebrows rise.

"I'm fine, Mom, thanks for asking. How are you?"

What? This is her mother? I look a little closer. Yeah, I guess I can see a resemblance in the cheekbones, the shape of the face maybe, and the mouth.

"Don't be rude to me, Piper."

And now my eyebrows are mashing together in a frown. *What's with the attitude and the name?* Except Ellie pays no attention to the comment.

"This is my boyfriend, Scott. Scott, this is my mother, Janine."

"Nice to meet you," I say after a beat of silence.

Janine throws me a scathing glance that's somehow muffled by her face's weirdly stiff features.

"Your father went to a lot of trouble to get these tickets," her mother goes on, ignoring me. "The least you could have done is show up on time."

Ellie finally relents under the criticism. "We're not late," she says through clenched teeth. "What are you doing here anyway? Dad said you guys couldn't make it."

"Well," she scoffs haughtily. "I had to see why you were passing on a date with richer-than-Croesus Peter Denton." She deigns to set her eyes on me again. "When are you going to grow up, Piper? These flights of fancy of yours have gone on for far too long."

"Janine?"

"Dad." Ellie sounds both accusatory and relieved as her father puts an arm around his wife's waist. "You said you guys couldn't be here." Okay, now, it's all accusation.

Ellie's dad is as tall as I am, with graying hair at his temples. Behind his glasses, his expression is much more welcoming than his wife's. He steps forward and brushes a kiss to his daughter's cheek.

"Yes, well, plans changed," he says with a trace of discomfort. "Are you going to introduce me to your young man?"

Ellie's posture relaxes. "Dad, this is Scott. Scott this is my father, Jonathan."

I smile when he puts out his hand for me to shake. "Nice to meet you, sir." The man's got a firm handshake, and I immediately get the impression that Ellie's personality has a lot to do with his influence.

"Good to meet you, Scott."

Ellie's mother harrumphs. I shit you not; she actually, in real life, harrumphs.

Just then, the lights dim for a moment.

"Saved by the dinner bell," Ellie says, her voice shaded with sarcasm which quickly becomes horror when she goes on, "We're not at the same table, are we?"

She and her father share some kind of look. "No, the original table was already sold out. We're over there," he says, pointing to the other side of the room. "You kids have fun."

Ellie and I both stare after them as they leave. "I am so sorry," she whispers, leaning in to rest our temples side by side.

I reach my hand to her hip, pulling her closer. "Did we just get ambushed?" I ask on a laugh.

She turns to me with surprise. "You're not upset?"

"Why would I be upset?" I manage to say with a straight face. "I'm sure your mom just wanted to make sure you weren't dating a thug."

Her mood visibly brightens at my reaction.

"Think the tux fooled her?" I add.

"Doesn't matter. I couldn't care less what she thinks. She'll never be happy with anything less than a billionaire."

"Well, yeah," I say with mock seriousness, "millionaires are so passé nowadays."

Her smile makes all this worthwhile. "Thanks for being so understanding."

"You do remember meeting *my* mom, don't you?"

She slips her hand back into the crook of my elbow and we make our way to our seats.

"*Your* mom was actually very polite."

"Just wait till you meet her when she's sober."

I pull out the chair for her before taking my own seat. For the next few minutes we ignore the world around us as we re-group with our heads together, joking, teasing, laughing . . . pretending. Because her mother didn't just ambush Ellie, she assaulted her. And I don't like it, even if Ellie did hold her own.

A waiter comes around, asking if we'd like red or white wine with dinner. When Ellie waves an uninterested hand and accompanies it with a weary, "Red, thank you," I give her a questioning look. "It's just easier this way," she says in a low voice. "Wine is the last thing I'd ever drink. You don't have to worry."

I nod, and then follow her lead, all the while wondering what would happen if I asked the guy to scrounge me up a Coke from somewhere.

"What brings you here this evening, dear?"

Turning to the voice beside me, I find an older lady with snow-white hair, wearing enormous dangling sapphire earrings that pull heavily at her lobes. Her question leaves me a bit stumped.

"What brings me here?" I stall, adding what I hope is a distracting grin.

"Yes, Elizabeth was one of my closest friends. Honoring her memory is the least I could do."

Uh oh. "Elizabeth?" I ask carefully.

"The Elizabeth McCarthy foundation is hosting tonight's gathering." She seems affronted that I don't know this.

"Right. Sorry. It's actually my girlfriend," I sit back in my chair and gesture to Ellie, who's talking to the man on her other side, "who has the passion for helping people. I'm just here to make sure another man doesn't steal her away."

The lady's hostility dissolves. "Oh, my. How gallant."

I decide if I have to chat, I may as well sound her out for a job for Ellie. It can't hurt, right? "Ellie is going to graduate from Stanford soon and she'll be in the market for a job where she can really make a difference." My ears ring with how corny that sounds even if it is the truth. The old lady eats it up though.

"Really?" she says with enthusiasm as we both sit back in our chairs so the first course can be put in front of us. "Perhaps I could introduce her to Richard, he's Elizabeth's husband. Or was. I tell you, her passing last year was such a shock to us all."

From there, I only listen politely as she goes on and on about people I don't know. But I'm happy because an introduction to the guy in charge of this whole thing can only be a good thing for Ellie.

When dinner is done – I won't complain about that, because it was pretty good – the speeches start, which turn out to be a total snooze fest. Ellie barely keeps a straight face when I give her my best long-suffering look.

"Oh, that's him," the old lady whispers, calling my attention to the stage. "That's Richard."

Again, I nod politely and hope that *Dick* will be able to do something for Ellie.

Finally, we're able to get up and stretch our legs and 'mingle'. After I introduce Ellie to my dinner mate, they chat for a bit. Ellie charms her with such casual ease that I can't help but be impressed. By the end of the short talk, they're all smiles and agree conspiratorially to wait for a time to catch Richard, or Mr. McCarthy, as Ellie calls him, when he's not surrounded by so many people. Then Ellie and I spend a good hour working the room. Well, Ellie works the room and I watch in awe as she wheedles her way into conversation after conversation without seeming to intrude. She's a natural; articulate, knowledgeable and charismatic.

We manage to hit up most of her targets, including some woman who invites her to send her CV. She squeezes my arm. "I would love to work for her," she gushes. "I'm so glad this hasn't turned out to be a waste of time. Thanks so much for coming with me."

"I'm not really doing anything," I protest.

"You are," she assures me. "It's pretty hard to loiter, waiting for a chance to jump into a conversation when you're standing alone. Plus, if you weren't here, guys would be hitting on me and I wouldn't be taken as seriously."

I tsk. "What?"

"I'm serious. So I appreciate you doing this for me. I know how bored you are." Before I have a chance to answer, something past my shoulder catches her eye. "Shit," she murmurs. "We have incoming."

I start to turn but she takes hold of my arm to stop me. "It's my mom again. Why don't you run to the bathroom or something? I'll handle this."

"El, I don't want —"

"Please? For me?"

"Are you sure?" I hate the idea of her facing so much hostility alone.

"Yeah, I'm sure. If she's rude to you again, I'm going to lose it."

I repress a grin. "We wouldn't want to cause a scene."

"Exactly. It would defeat the whole purpose of tonight. Find me in ten minutes or so?"

"All right." I kiss the corner of her mouth. "Text me if you need me."

The men's bathroom is a huge, over the top marble affair with recessed lighting and a sitting area. All I'm thinking as I empty my bladder into the urinal is that I'm glad the furniture is far enough away that it's not in the splash zone.

Ellie probably needs a few more minutes so I kill some time with my phone in a hopefully sanitary arm chair. I answer Jorgie's demands to know how the 'monkey suit affair' is going and he texts back telling me that he spotted Richie Vasquez at a house party with his arm around a girl who is *not* Lolita. Gotta say, that eases my mind. Soon, almost twenty minutes have passed, so I quickly head back out to make sure my girl is still in one piece.

It takes a bit of circling the room, but I finally spot the pink of Ellie's dress in a group of black suits near the stage. She has her back to me, but I smile when I see who she's talking to. It's the old guy, Richard McCarthy. She must have introduced herself. Not wanting to interrupt, I come up beside her and gently lay my hand at the small of her back to let her know I'm there. She stiffens.

"Just me," I murmur. When she turns to me, immediately, my instincts come to life. She's pale, shaken. Her arms are crossed over her middle, almost in a defensive posture. "What's wrong?" I ask, my eyes jerking up to scan the men she's standing with as my fingers curl around her hip to pull her closer.

If anyone touched her . . .

At first glance, not a one of them seems concerned that I'm about to commit murder, but their attention *is* all on me. They're staring. They're silent. A second sweep of the group shows me a guy whose mouth is hanging open.

"El?"

She blinks at me.

"I need you to tell me what's going on."

"We should go," she says, making to move away. My grip on her tightens and I hold her in place.

"Not till I know what happened."

Again, suspicion has my eyes crawling over the men who are present. There are four of them. Two younger, two older.

"Scott, I think it'd be better if –"

There's an audible gasp and I angle her away slightly, the urge to protect her overwhelming me. *What the fuck?*

"Let's go," Ellie insists.

"Please don't," the old guy, Richard says, sounding worried or panicked or something. "Let me . . . let me introduce myself. I'm Richard McCarthy." He holds out his hand to me and I glare at it for a moment. I look to Ellie one more time and when she nods at me, I shake the man's hand.

Richard blows out a breath before continuing. "And these are my grandsons, Eric and Shane." Okay, so I still have no idea what's going on when one of them nods in greeting and the other gives me a "hey," that sounds like it's being squeezed out of a clogged ketchup bottle. "And this," Richard says hesitantly, gesturing to his other side, "is my son . . . Prescott McCarthy."

I frown, finally focusing on the last guy. One who shares my name? *How unlikely is that?* He's . . . it takes a couple of heart beats – just a couple – for my existence to slowly begin to twist on its axis. In a landslide, realization hits me. Because it's like looking into a mirror.

Something approximating a scoff leaves my mouth. "Are you kidding me right now?" In the back of my mind, I'm so pleased that my voice is rock steady, because inside, I'm fucking rattled. My father. This man is my father. Holy shit. *This man is my father.*

In an instant, shock becomes anger.

"Let's go," I say darkly.

Ellie reads my body language like we've been together for years, not weeks, and easily falls into step beside me, our hands finding each other's as we make our way between the tables. "You've got your purse?" I say, trying to keep the sharpness out of my tone.

"Yes," she holds it up, "we can go."

It's not until we're crossing the hotel lobby that I hear my god forsaken name – again.

"Scott! Scott, wait!"

Ellie hesitates, but I keep right on walking, towing her along with me.

The time it takes to get through the revolving door at the entrance allows whoever it is that's chasing after us to catch up outside.

"Please, Scott, wait!"

One of the grandsons gets in front of us, forcing us to stop. "I'm sorry," he pants. "I know it's a shock. For all of us. Here, just take my grandfather's . . . *our* grandfather's card and when you're ready . . ." His voice abruptly drops. "You're my brother," he whispers in wonder.

Disgust churns in my gut. "No. I'm not."

The wonder falls from his face, replaced by hurt. He must be younger than . . . *forget that! I won't feel sorry for him.* I've never needed anything from that side of my family, the side I've never known. I'm not about to start now.

"Get out of the way." It's a warning that this kid needs to heed. The rage swirling inside of me is beginning to eat away at my self-control. After a few beats, he reluctantly steps aside and I tug Ellie around him without another word.

I almost make it a full block before I lose it.

Stopping dead on the sidewalk, I haul in a breath as I jam my fingers into my hair, tugging fiercely. "Fuck!" I yell, the single word echoing through the mostly empty street.

"Scott?" Ellie says tentatively.

I wheel on her. "Did you know?"

Her head jerks back like I've slapped her. "What?"

"Did. You. Know?"

She glares, shattering my now obviously bullshit accusation with the dirtiest look I've ever received. "I'm going to let that go because you've just been dealt some serious shit. But I am *not* the enemy here."

Along with her words, the outrage in her eyes gives me a much-needed dose of reality. I press my palms to my face to give myself a second. When I finally look at her, she's got her arms folded across her chest, still glaring daggers at me, standing tall and proud and confident.

"I love you, Ellie," drops from my lips, completely unbidden.

Her expression morphs slightly with confusion.

"I mean it," I tell her. "I love you so much. You were incredible tonight." I inspect my shoes for a second. "And I'm sorry." I reach for her. "I didn't mean to say that."

"I know," she whispers as she lets me fold her into my arms where she belongs.

I breathe her in, marveling at how right we feel together, at how the night's events begin to dim with her so close. "Come on, Opal. Let's go home."

Later that night, after we're both sated, I watch her sleep, focusing on the details of her beautiful features in an attempt to keep the nervous shock in my gut at bay.

My father.

Holy fucking shit.

My father.

It means nothing, I chide myself. He's never been anything to me . . . except I have brothers, two at least, and a grandfather. And next, I realize Elizabeth McCarthy would have been my grandmother. That surreal world of buffed perfection and casual arrogance that I experienced for the first time tonight is their natural habitat. Rolex watches and diamond necklaces are the norm for them. Figures. My father went slumming twenty three years ago for shits and giggles and never looked back. Fuck him. Fuck them all.

I think back to how hard my family struggled to keep our heads above water after my uncle was killed, how tight money was, how hard it was to come by. And all the while, my father was sitting on piles of cash.

The rage starts up again, so I turn my attention back to Ellie.

Two simple truths become clear in that moment. One, I want nothing to do with my sperm donor. And two, I want everything to do with the woman lying beside me.

She's the only future I want.

Other Books

Not So Far Away (A Worlds Collide Duet, #1)
The Here and Now (A Worlds Collide Duet, #2)

His Lucky Penny (The Penny Books, #1)
Pennies for Wishes (The Penny Books, #2)
Find a Penny (The Penny Books, #3)
Pennies from Heaven (The Penny Books, #4)

Written as Lisa Lynn Meyer
A Touch of Silence